Beach Days

Rehoboth Beach Reads

Short Stories by Local Writers

Edited by Nancy Sakaduski

Cat & Mouse Press
Lewes, DE 19958
www.catandmousepress.com

PERMISSIONS AND ACKNOWLEDGEMENTS

Cover illustration/book design by Emory Au. © 2015 Emory Au.

"Beach Daze," Margaret Farrell Kirby. © 2015 Margaret Kirby. Reprinted with permission.

"Beached," Jean Youkers. © 2015 Jean F. Youkers. Reprinted with permission.

"Chance Meeting," Thomas F. Linehan, Jr. © 2015 Thomas F. Linehan, Jr. Reprinted with permission.

"Dead Man's Sendoff," J.L. Epler. © 2015 Jennifer Epler. Reprinted with permission.

"Face-to-Face(book)," Judy Shandler. © 2015 Judy Shandler. Reprinted with permission.

"Family Beach Week A to Z," Renay Regardie. © 2015 Renay Regardie. Reprinted with permission.

"Haiku Kites," Robert Hambling Davis. © 2015 Robert Hambling Davis. Reprinted with permission.

"I Do," Glory Aiken. © 2015 Glory Moyna Aiken. Reprinted with permission.

"Molting," Kathleen L. Martens. © 2015 Kathleen Langmaack Martens. Reprinted with permission.

"New Beginnings at the Beach," Barbara Nuzzo. © 2015 Barbara Nuzzo. Reprinted with permission.

"Oksana and Carly," Fran Hasson. © 2015 Frances Hasson. Reprinted with permission.

"Salting the Beach," MaryAlice Meli. © 2015 MaryAlice Meli. Reprinted with permission.

"Second Wind," Lisa M. Coruzzi. © 2015 Lisa M. Coruzzi. Reprinted with permission.

"Seven Scenes," Hyl Norman. © 2015 Dawn Norman. Reprinted with permission.

"Somewhere Between Crab Cakes and Cocktails," Jeanie P. Blair. © 2015 Jean Pitrizzi Blair. Reprinted with permission.

"Synchronicity," Gail Sobotkin. © 2015 Gail Sobotkin. Reprinted with permission.

"Telltale Coin," Wayne Hughes. © 2015 Wayne A. Hughes. Reprinted with permission.

"The Break Out," Katherine Melvin. © 2015 Katherine Melvin. Reprinted with permission.

"The Debutante Learns to Drive," Matthew Hastings. © 2015 Matthew T. Hastings. Reprinted with permission.

"The Magical Suit," Lynnette Adair. © 2015 Lynnette Rittenhouse. Reprinted with permission.

"The Wineglass Clue," Nancy H. Linton. © 2015 Nancy H. Linton. Reprinted with permission.

"Time in the Sun," Terri Clifton. © 2015 Terri Clifton. Reprinted with permission.

"Waiting for Summer," V.K. Dorner. © 2015 Vonda K. Dorner. Reprinted with permission.

"Witchy Women," Connie L. McDowell. © 2015 Connie L. McDowell. Reprinted with permission.

Table of Contents

PREFACE

These are the winning stories from the 2015 Rehoboth Beach Reads Short Story Contest, sponsored by Browseabout Books. Writers were asked to create a story—fiction or nonfiction—that fit the theme "Beach Days" and had a connection to Rehoboth Beach. A panel of judges selected the best stories, and those selections have been printed here for your enjoyment. Like *The Beach House* and *The Boardwalk* (other books in this series), this book contains more than just "they went down to the beach and had a picnic" stories. The quality and diversity of the stories is simply amazing.

For information on the contest, go to: www.catandmousepress.com.

ACKNOWLEDGEMENTS

Thanks to Browseabout Books for their continued outstanding support. We are so lucky to have this great store in the heart of our community. They have supported the Rehoboth Beach Reads Short Story Contest from day one and continue to be the go-to place for books, gifts, and other fun stuff.

I thank both the Rehoboth Beach Writers' Guild and the Eastern Shore Writers Association for their support and service to the writing community. These two organizations provide an amazing array of educational programming, and many of the writers whose stories appear in this book benefitted from their classes, meetings, and events.

I thank this year's judges, Austin S. Camacho, Alex Colevas, Dennis Lawson, Laurel Marshfield, Mary-Margaret Pauer, and Judith Reveal, who gave generously of their time. They asked me to express how difficult their job was and how hard it was to choose from the many great stories that were submitted.

Special thanks to Emory Au, who so beautifully captured a day on Rehoboth Beach for the cover illustration and who designed this book, cover to cover.

I also thank Cindy Myers, Amanda Libby, and Carolyn Colwell for providing valuable production assistance.

An extra-special thank-you to my husband Joe, whose support and encouragement sustains me.

I would also like to thank the writers—those whose work is in this book and those whose work was not chosen. Putting a piece of writing up for judging takes courage. Thank you for being brave. Keep writing and submitting your work!

—*Nancy Sakaduski*

Chance Meeting

by Thomas F. Linehan, Jr.

The boardwalk sprawls south like an abandoned railroad line. Maybe a long weekend at Rehoboth Beach in early November wasn't such a great idea, but hey, got to keep trying. I'll find *her* again. Well, eventually. I see the beach tourists are long gone, beach fries and hot dog stands boarded up. A "See You Next Summer" sign stapled to a weathered, plywood wall catches my eye. Just ahead is Grotto Pizza. I pat my stomach and move on by.

The ocean breeze makes it all the colder. I pull down my gray cap and zip up my fleece pullover for protection. I won't last much longer out here. Keep up the pace, keep off the weight. Paunches turn into fat tires with little effort.

A head snap-back confirms I have company on the boards behind me. An older guy, sporting straggly locks, passes the big Dolle's sign. Not the thirtysomething brunette I dreamed up. Two years since Bonnie died. Sick of loser dates. Why did I come back here now? To *our* boardwalk? Maybe I thought I'd meet someone here again. I increase my Skecher-pace.

White enameled benches line the split-board runway, the quickest path home to my cheaper-in-the-off-season cottage rental. Trying to forget King of Prussia and the rest of my pharma world is high on my priority list. Find someone. The right woman. Make it a project, like at work. The project plan in my head doesn't feel quite right, but I've tried everything else.

My weekend research project. Objective: to discover a woman with that sublime mixture of looks, brains, and personality. And one who is totally devoid of serious baggage. Alas, none have caught my eye for the last three days. Well, we're talking Monday morning now, complete with dim, overcast sky. What are the odds of making "project goal"? Negligible at best. I detour off the boardwalk and proceed down the sloped plank exit ramp toward the private cottages and ocean-view mansions. Maintaining pace, I head up New Castle Street. The Realtor's sign on the lawn of the house just ahead is my landmark to turn toward my little cottage, sandwiched behind and between the big boys on the beachfront.

"Hi," I hear, as I pass by a massive beach house, or rather, a starter castle. I turn and crane skyward, hoping my eyes will cast upon a vision, worthy of the sexy, sincere voice that calls to me from the castle parapet one story above. In a split second I concoct a brilliant response, careful not to come across as a jerk. I say, "Hi."

Part of me thinks I should stop and say something more, but my inertia carries me forward. Sensing opportunity in a flash, I halt forward progress and back into view. I know in that instant, the "laboratory experiment" is a go. She occupies one of four rattan lounge chairs precisely set across the deck as if arranged for winter storage. The woman is about my age, maybe a little younger, although I'm poor at guessing ages. She's bundled up, her hair wafting in the on-shore breeze.

Now, I just have to convert her "Hi" into a date. Step one in the lab procedure. I feel my heart thump. Is it the challenge or desperation? Upon initial inspection, the vision is "exceeding target," even "outstanding." So much for statistics.

"Not a great day for a walk, I suppose?" I say, looking up at the deck with my best smile. "How is the lounging?" Oh, that's brilliant! Couldn't a pharmacokinetics PhD come out with something a bit more sophisticated? Find your game, dude, and quick. You can do this.

"Well, I thought I'd read out here and get some air, but just sitting is too cold. I need to move around," she says, placing her book down. I nod. She stands and stretches, arms reaching up. Her fingers comb through blond curls that flow past shoulders and down her back. I swallow hard.

"Are you with your family, or friends? It looks like that place has plenty of room. It's impressive."

"My family's getaway. One of them, anyway."

"I'm Kevin. Would you like to take a walk? Might warm you up." I figured, what the hell. I'm freezing, but hey, I've got to follow through on this.

"I need to ask the obvious. I don't see a ring."

"Oh, me? No, no. Not married."

She hesitates, then says, "I'm Cindy. Maybe we could go into town and have a drink or something?" Leaning against the white metal railing toward me, she says, "But you seem to be in a hurry. Do you have somewhere to go?"

"Ah, no," I say. "Just trying to keep in shape, you know. And yes, I would like to go into town." I silently praise my propensity for lightning-fast thinking on my feet. Yeah, sure.

"I'll be right down," she says. A coy smile and eye shot boost my confidence considerably. "Meet me around front."

I have to say, her smile surprises me. Never expected to get this far. She is really nice. And sexy too, even in her bulky hoody with "Rehoboth Beach" across the front. Definitely a local. I guess I'm the beach tourist here.

I watch her behind as she disappears from the deck. "Oh, yes," I hear myself say. The lab stats are definitely on the rise. Project on.

* * * * * *

The right side of the solid oak, double front door swings open and out steps Cindy. She's about five-three, maybe a hundred and ten pounds. Not a bad match for six feet, but I could lose a pound or two. The stats are aligning for a Phase 1 trials winner. Well, so far. But science can be tricky, particularly when females are concerned. I should know.

"Any place in mind?" I say, my right hand pointing toward King Charles Avenue. It's only about a five-minute walk to First Street, right? Lots of places still open.

"Not the boardwalk?"

"Too windy off the ocean. Let's take the streets, okay?" I say, pulling up my collar.

"Okay. Coffee?"

The street is empty. We head north toward the action. A heavy guy in a blousy Adidas parka and black gym shorts hustles down the sidewalk past us. No eye contact. Drives me nuts when they dress like July in November. Definitely not a local.

"Yeah, all right," I say, probably lacking enthusiasm.

"Or would you rather go for something stronger?"

"I wouldn't mind a pinot, how about you?" I figure I'll skip the beer, and not sound like a Neanderthal. I'll be pissed if she orders a hoppy brew.

"The Pond? It's not fancy, but it's close," she says, dark brown eyes looking up at me.

"Um, I've heard things, but, okay."

"Everyone goes there now."

"Hey, I'm with you," I say, catching her eye. "That's all I need to know."

We cross Wilmington, ignoring the light. She jumps the curb just ahead of me. I feel the air hit us from behind, as a UPS truck, a thin blonde at the wheel, blows through the intersection. Cindy takes risks. Interesting.

I grab the door handle of the bar and my hand overlaps hers. We hadn't touched before. Her nails look a bit worn, but I guess even women with money don't worry about fancy manicures when they're at the beach.

The waitress glances up from a table of setups as she sorts silverware. A woman, late thirties maybe, sits at the end of the bar, nursing a bottle of Bud. Lots of piercings and an almost-shaved head. Local hangout, but the place is practically deserted. That works.

"Cindy, how about that booth in the corner?"

She scans the room, catches the bartender's eye, and says, "Yep."

The waitress comes over and drops napkins on our table. "Hi, I'm Katie, what can I get you?" she says, looking at Cindy.

"I'll have a glass of chardonnay," Cindy says. I can't help noticing the exchange of glances between them. They seem to know each other. Cindy gives me a smile.

"Pinot grigio. And could you bring some bread?" I ask, not sure Cindy would go for fries. Not with her figure.

"How about flat bread and hummus?" Katie replies, checking in with Cindy.

Cindy smiles and nods.

"Yes, that would be…" I start, and give up midsentence. Katie has already turned to leave. The guy never gets any respect once they spot a sharp woman at the table. The server is all about knowing who is in control.

In the middle of small talk, I am surprised to see the bartender delivering the wine and bread. He's friendly enough, but something about him bothers me. Oh, yes. Pinky rings. Never liked them. As I turn from him back to Cindy, I see her finger lightly tap the table. She folds her hands, eyes snapping back from him to me. I sense something in her gaze. Checking back toward the bar, I see the guy disappear into the kitchen. Maybe she's been here a lot. Knows the guy? Don't know.

"How's the wine?" I ask, sort of glad she didn't go for a beer.

"It's pretty good."

"So, what do you do when you're not hanging out at the beach in November?" I ask, wishing it was about ninety-five in July, imagining her in a string bikini. There we would be, basking on side-by-side lounge chairs, overlooking the ocean from her shore palace. And then...

"Oh, well, I manage people's money. Stocks and bonds, that sort of thing. Kinda boring, don't you think?"

"You mean at one of the big firms?" I ask, ripping off a chunk of flatbread and spreading on some hummus.

"Ah, no. Not exactly. My father's business. Wealthy clients. Like in New York and Chicago," Cindy says, sipping her wine. "I do what I'm told, mostly. Dad, you know."

We talk about the upcoming holidays for a while. She isn't looking forward to her family get-togethers. I can relate. Things don't seem to be great between her and old Dad.

"What about you?"

"Me, yeah. Well, I'm a pharma research guy. Making new drugs, stuff like that."

"Do you like it?"

"Sure, it has its moments, I guess."

"Must pay well. You high up on the ladder?"

Hmm, do I say I'm loaded or a poor struggling lab guy?

"I'm well-paid. Done fairly well for myself, so far. Not trying to brag, though," I say, searching her eyes for a reading.

"Oh. Okay," Cindy says, voice dropping. With her glass almost empty, she glances toward the bar.

Oh no, don't let this fall apart now. Say something!

"You want another wine?"

"Oh, no, I think I should get back. This has been nice."

Think. Think. "I'll walk you back?" I ask, thinking the worst. But she did say meeting me was nice, whatever that meant. She nods.

I pay the waitress. Then Cindy and I stroll back the way we came. I can't tell for sure where I stand with her. At her door I think, what do I have to lose? Go for it.

"So, will I see you again?" I blurt out. Probably uncool.

"Hmm, I'd like to, but I'm only here 'til tomorrow morning. Off to BWI for an early flight to Chicago."

"So dinner tonight? Somewhere upscale?" I ask, grinning nervously.

"I don't know. I'm worried about catching my flight in the morning."

"It would mean a lot to me," I say, not able to resist. She frowns, then smiles.

"Well, okay. Can you stop by at seven? I'll be ready, Kevin," she says, and turns to face the door. I hear her keys jingle and she presses her thumb on the door handle lever. Peering over her head, I notice some of the hair roots in her part are dark, not blond. I think maybe she cheats a little on the pure blond thing. The door swings into the foyer. The house is dark.

"I'll see you later, then," Cindy says, flipping on the foyer light. I study her face through the gap in the closing door. "Later."

I can't believe I pulled off a date. I figured she was done with me. Something about my being paid well or well-off. Don't think she liked that. But, yeah, my "project" is still on track.

* * * * * *

Going on seven, I walk over to Cindy's with high hopes. As I approach the beach palace, I notice most of the windows in the house are dark. Shrugging my shoulders, I knock on the oak door. No answer. Then it hits me. What if she changed her mind? Didn't tell me. Wait, I didn't give her my cell number. I knock again. Nothing. I guess its game over. Crap. Well, maybe she went out and is late coming back. I grab the brass door handle and press down on the thumb latch. No resistance and the door just opens. Whoa. That's not good. A young woman alone, not…

A light comes on, which stops me cold. The ocean breeze creeps up my back, with the door half-open.

"Do you usually just walk into people's homes?" Cindy asks, smiling and holding a bottle of white wine and a corkscrew.

"Ah, well, no, I mean I knocked. Twice," I say, feeling completely off my game. "It looked like no one was home, no lights, so I tried the door. In case you didn't hear me knock, I mean."

"I said seven, so why wouldn't I be here?"

"Yeah, you're right. I just didn't expect the door to be unlocked." I stole a glance around the room. A staircase with a mahogany banister leads to the second floor. At least six or eight bedrooms, I think. Cindy stands in the foyer that leads into a large room with a cathedral ceiling. A sitting area enhances the foyer. She's wearing about the sexiest low-cut top and tight jeans I've ever seen. I wonder if I'm a little out of my league.

"I trust you. I unlocked it for you."

"Oh. I was worried you were alone and… Never mind."

Cindy holds out the wine bottle and raises her eyebrows at me for help. "I thought we could have a little vino before heading out."

"Sure, got it." I grab the bottle neck and corkscrew from her and go to work.

"Let's sit here," she says, pointing to a sandalwood love seat and coffee table with two wine glasses on it.

I pour, and then we touch goblets with the ring of fine crystal. Nice to be rich, I think.

"I'm going to put it in the fridge. I like my wine really cold," Cindy says, picking up the bottle. As she bends forward, her neckline drops, exposing a dragon tattoo on her left breast.

"I know. Not a connoisseur like Dad, but I don't care."

"Well, I like it any way I can get it." Oops, that didn't come out right. I glimpse a wisp of smile before her hair swings back, masking her reaction. She heads for the kitchen and I take a big swallow of pinot.

The tattoo surprises me a little, but I decide to ignore it. And isn't white wine supposed to be cold and red is room temp? Well, okay. What's the difference?

We talk about my career a bit, part of the routine, I suppose. I'm dancing around that topic until our glasses are empty.

"I'll get us a refill," she says, standing with a wine glass in each hand.

"I'll help," I say, starting to get up.

"Oh no. You just sit. I like playing hostess. Besides, Mom never lets me be the adult in her house. Frustrating."

"I can relate." I can't, really. Been on my own since twenty-three, but whatever it takes. Cindy comes back with a country club pour—half-full glasses—and hands me one. I wonder if we are actually going to eat. I planned on Blue Moon, but things might get much more exciting right here.

The wine seems bitter. Not what I expected.

* * * * * *

A noise startles me. The modern grandfather clock in the foyer chimes me into morning. I seem to be lying on my back on the love seat. I hoist myself up. My head is splitting. My watch reads 9:01. Looking around, I don't see anything disturbed. It looks like a house left clean while the owners are away.

"Cindy? Are you here?" I call out, pressing my palms into my temples. The house is deathly silent. I check each floor, calling her name. The place is empty.

I feel my jacket pockets for my phone. Not there. I feel a burning stone in my belly as I pat my back pocket. No wallet. I'm screwed.

I get myself together, flip the lock, step outside, and close the door. A quick check, the thumb latch bottoms out. Lock broken.

"Shit," I say, staring at the grain in the oak door. The apartment. Go. Hurry.

I get back to my rental. Where is my BMW? Damn. She must have followed me home. I am so screwed.

The cops. This is going to be embarrassing. Kevin, you jerk. If this gets back to the senior VP, more than this little project will be a train wreck. "Project" aborted. Shit.

I start toward the police station. I remember it's next to City Hall. As I approach First Street, I see The Pond and I can't help but wonder. I go in. Nobody is behind the bar. Katie, the waitress, walks out of the kitchen.

"We're not open. Thought I locked the door, sorry."

"Ah, could you help me? I was in here yesterday and…"

"I remember. With the blond girl, right?"

"Yeah. The bartender. Is he around?" I ask, scanning the place.

"Yesterday was his last day. Short-timer. Didn't like the guy."

"Does he live around here?" I ask, trying not to sound too desperate or stupid. I glance over at the corner booth where Cindy, or whatever her name is, and I were sitting yesterday. I half expect her to be waiting for me, revealing the big joke, all in fun.

"He said he was off to the West Coast. But I never believed much of what came out of his mouth. Always vague."

"Vague? You mean he said he was going to somewhere like San Francisco or L.A.? Something like that?"

"No, like who knows where he was really going? You know, vague like people that don't ever give you a straight story."

"Yeah, I think I do know. Thanks," I say, as I push open the unlocked door and step out into the cold.

Thomas F. (Tim) Linehan, Jr., began creative writing in 1985. He holds BS and MS degrees in engineering and had a forty-year career with major corporations. Tim is a graduate of the Institute of Children's Literature, a member of the Coastal Writers (at Rehoboth Art League), and a past president of the Bucks County (PA) Civil War Round Table. He teaches English as a second language and religious studies, and instructs at the Osher Lifelong Learning Institute at the University of Delaware. Tim's poetry has been published in *The Broadkill Review*. His young adult Civil War historical novel, *Drums of Courage*, was originally published in 2005 and republished in 2010.

Judge's Comments

The first sentence is full of promise and uses setting well. The boardwalk stretches south...as train tracks do; the reader is in for a ride. This weekend goes "south" in an unexpected twist. Characters are developed through action and inner monologue, offering sufficient wry humor to satisfy. The use of the November chill is a nice departure from the sun and fun. "Chance Meeting" keeps reader interest throughout. Good use of the structure of short fiction.

The Magical Suit

by Lynnette Adair

It would have taken a category five hurricane to make this much of a mess. At least, that's what Callie thought as she looked around her room. *What have I done?* She had managed to pull every stitch of clothing she owned out of each overstuffed drawer. It was her fault; it always was. Hurricane Callie had struck again. She had let things go too far. The tears fell. *Fat and slow, just like me,* she thought. She yanked her old black one-piece from under a stack of shorts strewn over her bed. Just as she was about to thrust it into her weekend bag, she noticed them—mocking her from their silent little flexible world. About a million tiny little white strands of broken overstretched elastic that were poking out from every seam of her decades-old "slimsuit." The suit which, by the way, had never touched water.

"Shit!" she yelled, dramatically throwing the suit onto the dusty floor in the corner of her room. She plopped onto the bed and the tears poured out. Moments later, the slime started. God, she hated that part of a good cry.

It had been a month, but still his words echoed in her head, over and over. Word for word, just as if he had said them yesterday. "Cal," he had started tentatively, "are you happy with me? Really happy?"

Alarms had screamed in her head as she tried to answer enthusiastically. "Of *course* I am. I love you." She had inched closer to him and tried to nuzzle into his neck to get one last whiff of his intoxicating man-scent, when he brutally cut to the chase: "It's not working. We have different lifestyles."

Mr. Muscles, gym rat and neat freak, was finally tired of her (originally appealing) voluptuous curves, lack of interest in housekeeping, and passion for reading. Sometimes—let's be honest, most times—books took the place of chores. She tried to be a gym girl, but even with the treadmill set at only 1.5 mph, she sweat profusely, and the books she tried to read while working out kept falling off the machine with a loud and humiliating clunk. Callie knew from that reading that this kind of story never had a happy ending. Eventually, she would have to come clean and be herself. And Mr. Muscles (Mark, for real) wasn't really going to like what she had to show him.

Her sniffles were intensifying when her cell rang. She held her breath, trying not to whimper into the phone.

"Callie, it's Mel. Are you there?"

Nothing.

"Callie, I'm downstairs and I'm coming up. Answer me! It's time to go—I'm not letting you break our tradition. That's it, I'm using my key." The phone clicked off in Callie's hand.

She heard the squeaky door complaining as it opened downstairs. Mel took the stairs two at a time—she really was a gym girl. They were best friends, even though their lifestyles were different. Mel blew into the room and rushed the bed. She grabbed Callie's arms and forced her abruptly to her feet.

"Okay, you. It's been a month since you've had any fun. Our Rehoboth weekend starts tonight. We aren't leaving without you, so don't even try to get out of it."

"I can't go, Mel. Look around. I can't find anything to take and I just…well…I can't." She slumped back onto the bed. Her shiny black hair flipped forward over her face, giving her startling blue eyes a place to hide. Mel noted that no matter how Callie landed, it always looked as though she was posed, like a curvy 1940s pinup girl waiting for the photographer.

"I call 'bullshit,' Callie. Rita is in the car waiting. It's time to go."

Mel managed an analytical scan around the room and mentally threw together four outfits, one maxi dress, a pair of sandals, and flip-flops. Within five minutes, Callie's weekend bag was packed and she was being led, clutching a handful of Kleenex, to Mel's purple Trans Am, which she had left running with Rita inside and music blaring. Mrs. Murphy, next door, looked none too pleased with the assault.

"We've got a full-blown number 8 on our hands this time," Mel informed Rita, as she pulled the Trans Am away from the curb with a squeal and headed toward Route 1. Mel and Rita tried to get Callie started on some karaoke therapy, but she withdrew, deep in thought.

Just what I need, Callie thought, *a weekend at the beach with Mel—tall, blond, curves in all the right places, and a laugh that brings even the worst critic along for the ride. Then we throw in Rita, the "girl next door" brunette with white teeth, shoulder-length curls, and a butt that has made men cry out in joy as she walked by. I fit right in... Not.* Callie recognized Katy Perry on the radio and couldn't resist smiling when the girls started belting out the lyrics to "Roar," in an attempt to wake Callie up from her negative self-talk and victim-mentality coma.

I can do this, Callie thought. *They're right, it's time. It's the annual girls' weekend with my besties and I'm not going to ruin it.* The song changed and Callie's sniffling stopped when Mel turned toward her, car dancing and singing at the top of her lungs, "I'm all about that bass..."

Mel yelled to Rita, "I couldn't find her bathing suit, so we've gotta stop on the Avenue."

"Guurrrl, I know just the place, but first, give me a swig of that green smoothie."

Mel reached down and picked up the beverage container. When she straightened up in her seat, the wind caught her golden hair and swirled it around her head like a halo. *No, not* like *a halo, it* was *a halo,* Callie thought. *Both of my friends are bona fide angels.*

Rita grabbed the container from Mel and, without question, gulped some down, smacked her lips, and passed it back to Callie. "Callie, don't even try to get out of it. Drink some green and do it now," she commanded with a hearty giggle.

The ninety-minute drive passed quickly, with smoothies and music flowing. The trio of friends were smiling when they hit the bridge and got their first hint of sea air. They could feel the stress releasing from their shoulders and the toxins draining from their souls.

They always honked the horn when passing through Five Points; it was tradition. The only thing that was particularly interesting about the corner was the very important fact that they were now only five miles and a few moments (depending on traffic, of course) from their Rehoboth destination. They were officially in beach territory.

They turned off Route 1 and started getting giddy when the Rehoboth Beach shops came into view. Mel expertly wheeled around and pulled in front of the Pineapple Princess swimwear boutique.

"Pineapple Princess?" Now Callie broke into a full laugh. "Really? Now I'm a Pineapple Princess?"

"Not yet," Mel retorted. "You have to earn that title. When these ladies are finished with you, you'll regret mocking my choice." Her grin convinced Callie to drop the drama and head into the shop.

As they stepped over the threshold, Rita took charge and engaged the owner in a quick conversation about how Callie needed a swimsuit that would show her how beautiful she was.

Callie groaned at Rita's descriptive words and was embarrassed by how desperate they made her seem. *Here comes the painful part,* Callie thought.

"Honey," said the owner, "you're beautiful. We just need to find the suit that feels gorgeous on you, and I think I have just the one.

I'm guessing you're a size 14 with an F-cup bra, is that about right?"

"Wow, I'm impressed," Callie reluctantly admitted.

The shop owner returned with an ordinary-looking black suit on a hanger. "Let me tell you about this one. I've had dozens of ladies report that amazing things have happened while wearing this suit. I can't keep them in stock. Word on the street is that they are magical. One of my customers even bought a winning Powerball ticket while wearing one."

Moments later, Callie found herself behind a green curtain, feeling like the man in *The Wizard of Oz*. The black suit hung on a hook, as if waiting for Callie to make the first move. Callie looked in the mirror and rolled her eyes. *Okay*, she thought, *let's get this over with.* She groaned while recalling the owner trying to convince her that the suit was "magical." Callie slipped off her flip-flops and shorts, pulled her shirt over her head, and unfastened her bra. Standing naked in front of the mirror, she looked at herself objectively and ran her hands slowly down her sides, appraising her form. *This is going to take some serious magic.* She reached for the suit and stepped into it. As she eased it up over her thighs and waist, it felt as if it had been made just for her. She pulled it over her breasts and poked her arms through the straps. She made a quick boob adjustment in the front and then turned to look in the mirror.

Callie instantly knew she looked fabulous, and it showed. When she opened the dressing-room door for the reveal, her fans didn't disappoint. They whooped and hollered their approval. Before she could blink, Callie was standing at the counter with a big-print sarong, glam sunglasses, and a wide-brim hat to complete the ensemble. As she pulled out her card to pay, the owner leaned over the counter toward Callie and whispered, "I know you don't believe me, but that suit really *is* magical. Just wait and see."

* * * * * *

Settling into the sand, Callie pulled Jennifer Weiner's book, *Then Came You*, out of her overstuffed bag and settled back to get comfy and anonymous. Her friends bellowed to some volleyball players and then bounded away to join the game. Remembering the importance of sunscreen, she dug around in the bag, feeling for the greasy bottle. As she pulled it out, it slipped and landed right in the sand. She brushed it off the best she could before opening the cap and beginning her ministrations. Tiny grains of sand mixed with the lotion and made her application something akin to a bad exfoliation job. *So much for the magical suit*, she thought. *If it really were magic, it would've saved me from this coating of sand.* She silently chided herself for hoping that maybe there was some scintilla of magic strengthening its elastic threads. She felt beads of sweat forming on her upper lip and between her big awkward boobs. The droplets trailed down her chest and gathered at her belly, making her itch under her "magical" bathing suit.

Callie slid her glam glasses down on her nose and leaned back against the fluffy red beach towels she had rolled up like pillows. She bent one shiny leg at the knee, with her foot off the towel so it could touch the life-affirming sand, and relaxed the other leg, her red-tipped toes pointing toward the water.

That was when she noticed him, sitting in the sand, alone with his camera. He was focused on the water and likely didn't notice the beautiful picture he made all on his own. The wind had tousled his deep brown hair. His shoulders were broad and tan, and he had some sort of tattoo on his left arm that she couldn't quite make out. His trunks were coral. *Coral, for God's sake.* What confidence it takes to wear coral and know it's exactly the right color to set off his bronze skin.

Callie chortled to herself, thinking maybe that was *his* "magic" suit. When he stood to walk closer to the water, her eye was drawn to where his trunks began. The muscular "v" pointing from his hips and leading her eyes along his happy trail made her gasp quietly; it was her favorite part of the male anatomy (almost). She didn't know what that spot was called, but she knew it made her stupid.

She spotted him again in Dolle's, when the girls were each buying containers of their favorite saltwater taffy. As usual, Callie didn't settle for just the taffy, so it was taking longer to wait for her caramel corn and mint sticks. She marveled at the fact that Dolle's had been open for over one hundred years. Her eyes were absorbing the piles of candy, eager clerks, and brightly colored displays when her eyes landed on him. He instantly looked away, as if she had caught him in the middle of something he was ashamed of. His camera strap and bag hung casually from his shoulder, and as he glanced back at Callie with eyes that were the sky blue match to hers, he smiled broadly with perfect white teeth and waved. She swore she felt her ovaries drop onto the floor and melt in a puddle.

Callie turned around and was disappointed to see the cute little clerk who was waiting on her wave back at him. Callie's cheeks went pink with embarrassment. She paid for her haul and joined her friends on the boardwalk. She didn't mention her mystery man, but out of the corner of her eye, she watched him saunter down the boardwalk steps and head toward the water. "I think I'd like to get a little more sun," she said, as casually as she could manage.

Back on the beach, she lined him up with her red toes, allowing her to secretly watch him and fantasize. She propped open her book but kept her eyes focused above it. After several minutes of secretly stalking her stranger, she reminded herself that he likely was waiting for the pretty young clerk to end her shift. On that dismal note, she lay back and directed her attention to the book. She had to admit it was a beautiful beach day; the breeze was perfect and she tried to put herself in relaxation mode. She became intoxicatingly drowsy and allowed her eyes to close for just a few moments.

She became aware that the handsome stranger had stood and was looking toward her. As she watched through half-closed eyes, he sat back down in the sand facing her and hoisted the camera to his eye. She couldn't believe it. Without being obvious, she tried to shift herself into a more appealing pose, sucking in her stomach and straightening her shoulders, but it was as if she couldn't move a muscle. She was glued to the spot, frozen with dread thinking he was snapping pictures of her. And without asking first.

He stood up and started sauntering toward her. *Oh, God.* The next moments were excruciating, as conflicting thoughts flew through her brain. "Monkey Brain," was what Rita called it. It had Callie in a death grip.

"Hey," he started tentatively. "I wanted to say hello earlier, but I needed to get down here to take a few shots of the water while the lighting was good. May I join you?"

"Of course," she replied. "I would say, 'Why don't you take a picture, it lasts longer,' but it appears you already have."

"Yes," he stated clearly, looking directly into her eyes. "Yes, I've taken several. I hope that doesn't offend you."

"I'm not easily offended, but I'm wondering why, in such a target-rich environment, you're taking pictures of me?"

He swung the camera off his shoulder and turned it on. After a few beeps and dings, he turned the camera toward her. "I'll delete every picture you ask me to." He smiled and added, "Against my will."

The image on the camera screen stunned Callie. The photo showed her reclined, with her book resting on her hip. She had one arm curled over her head, and her large breasts, instead of looking awkward, sloped gracefully, creating a curve that went to her waist and then to gorgeous round hips. The line then tapered into firm thighs, muscular calves, and dainty, gorgeously pedicured feet.

"You're beautiful," he said.

She felt tears building but didn't want to embarrass herself. She was grateful to this man she didn't even know. She was trying hard to form a sentence of thanks in her mind.

Suddenly, a sharp smack on her arm roused her. "Hey there, lazybones, how long have you been asleep? You better roll over, or you're going to regret it later." Mel smirked apologetically for startling her and ran back to her volleyball game with the bottle of water she grabbed from the cooler, along with a handful of taffy. She called back over her shoulder, "Get ready—in ten minutes we're gonna hit Thrasher's for vinegar fries and Grotto's for pizza!"

Of course it had been a dream.

Her eyes floated over the ocean of beachgoers to rest on him again. He was still there, with his camera. This time, he really was facing her. She ignored him and began packing up her bag with the sandy bottle of sunscreen. She stood up and knotted her boldly printed sarong low on her hips, sliding her feet into her flip-flops. She grabbed her bag and started walking. Her head bent, hiding beneath her hair, she took slow, deliberate steps toward the recently ended volleyball game. She heard his rapid breathing and his running footsteps right before he touched her arm.

"Excuse me," he started. "Sorry if I'm bothering you, but I can't let you get away this time without saying something. I saw you earlier when I popped my head into Dolle's to wave at my sister, but you were busy with your friends and I didn't want to interrupt. I'm Michael. Look, I know this seems a little forward, but any chance you would join me for some fries?" As he turned, a James Patterson novel dropped out of his camera bag. He smiled, bent down, and scooped it up. "I noticed that you like to read and I thought maybe we could talk books?"

She made her decision before she reached her friends. She called out to them, "Hey, guys, we're heading to Thrasher's. Meet you there."

His blue eyes sparkled and his smile mirrored hers. Their discussion about literary genres over vinegar fries was intoxicating. After a few minutes Mel and Rita had seen enough to know it was time for them to move on. Mel said to Callie, "Give me a call," as she and Rita headed toward Grotto's.

Michael and Callie continued to talk, gleefully discussing the character Lisbeth from *The Girl with the Dragon Tattoo*. Michael readily admitted that he could easily identify with her. Hours later, as the sun set, they were still chatting away happily. Callie suddenly remembered something.

"Hey, what kinds of pictures do you take?" she asked, pointing to his camera.

Michael grinned, obviously pleased by her interest. "Take a look." He turned his camera over and clicked through spectacular photographs of sunrises, sunsets, ocean waves, and seashells. No shots of Callie, of course.

That was a dream, you idiot. She tried to hide her disappointment. "Gorgeous," she said, admiring the images as they flipped by.

"*You* are gorgeous. I'd love to take photographs of you sometime. You have such a natural way about you. It's as if you don't even know how great you look."

Callie flushed.

Michael gently brushed some sand from her shoulder and leaned in. As his lips touched hers, Callie had to wonder if her suit…really was *magical*.

Ever since she picked up her first pencil, everyone said Lynnette Adair should be a writer. Finally having the ability to carve out some personal time and gain the hard-earned confidence to take the first step, she began to write. Having seemingly lived over a thousand lives all rolled into one, she will never run out of material. "The Magical Suit" was her first official submission. She is currently writing her first novel, *Diamonds in the Rough*, a suspenseful thriller, and a series of short stories called "Tales from an Innkeeper." She lives with her husband in Wilmington, Delaware.

Salting the Beach

by MaryAlice Meli

Never made time for a wife and never had kids, so I'm not sure about the ages of the two who come to the beach each morning. School age for sure, but young, maybe primary grades. Their slender, sun-browned legs and arms pump across the sand, before the heat and burn of the sun grip the shore.

I come to the beach every morning, too. Usually just after dawn. The ocean breeze leaves a salty tang in my mouth, a pleasant reminder that I'm alive. I often need that. My routine used to be quite different before I awoke in a hospital. Music was meditation for me. When possible, I'd play my keyboard every morning to focus my mind and imagination for whatever job assignments would come up that day. That's not possible anymore.

I don't claim a specific patch of beach as my territory, so at first I settle at a spot farther down the beach from the kids. Then they move closer, but maintain the same distance away as they are when their mother is with them. No matter where I shift, they follow. Makes me feel like a planet with accompanying moons. Maybe not. It's more like being adopted by two goslings. Maybe my aqua chair, wide straw hat with the frayed brim, and flapping Hawaiian shirt form a reliable part of their external world. Their recent chatter reveals their world may be about to change.

The kids carry buckets with tools and other supplies. The boy lays out a series of roads with his shovel. The girl watches and sometimes directs. "Put our car on the road to Aunt Elaine's house in Milton. She always gives us chocolate chip cookies," she says. It's quiet enough to hear seagulls arguing overhead. The girl levels lumps in the sand away from the roads to form her part of the project, which is always the airfield. "Danny, do you think Grandma will move to our house in Rehoboth after we go?"

"It's still not definite we're going." The boy sets a Lego house from his bucket at the end of one of the roads. "Why would Grandma move from her house in Dewey?" He pulls Matchbox cars and trucks from his bucket, sets one at the Lego house and another on the road heading for Aunt Elaine's. The little girl sets her Matchbox Cinderella carriage and horse on the sand she had smoothed to serve as the airport. The only disagreement I witnessed between the two kids was over whether his limo or her carriage would pick up their father at the airport. To my surprise, I find myself smiling at this daily soap opera in the sand.

When their interest lags, they turn to an equal love—digging for treasure. They dig and scrape and chatter about what to do when they find real treasure. *When*. Not *if*. Optimism like that is hard to kill, but die it does after a while. For some of us, anyway.

I have to admire these two. They're aware of me. Probably see me as a sleepy, one-armed old guy sipping from the cup of a dented Thermos, but they never acknowledge me. Never make eye contact. I appreciate that. Peace and quiet are treasures that take a different kind of digging.

I'm always sitting in my beach chair before they get here. Usually, their mother is with them, but not this week so far. The boy carries a cell phone in his bucket when they come without her.

I don't mind listening to them. Listening and watching made up much of my career. What I don't do with the kids is ask questions to elicit more information, confirmation, or verification, and then write down what I've learned. Just as I don't need to talk to them, I don't think they want to talk to me. We're from different worlds, old versus young, damaged and worn versus fresh and hopeful.

The little girl runs to the lazy surf and rinses something, then skips back, spraying tiny fans of sand. Even her bare feet are brown.

"Look, Danny, all the pretty colors." She shoves it in front of him. "Maybe we can sell it to that lady who makes jewelry at the market."

The boy rubs the shell, then turns it this way and that with the focus of a surgeon. "Maybe. Save it in your bucket, Emmy."

The little girl sets the shell in her bucket as though it were a precious gem. She accepts her brother's authority in their partnership without question. She holds up an earring she had found the previous day.

"Do you think this is a real ruby?"

"Could be. Keep it," he says. "You may find the other one. Then we can ask the jewelry shop man over there." He points to a building along the boardwalk.

"We have to find a treasure this summer, Danny." A note of desperation coats her words. "What if we never come back to Rehoboth?"

"That's only if Daddy takes the job in Chicago," the boy says. "Then we'd be too far away to come here every day. Unless we visit Grandma. But we can't walk here from her house."

"Do they have beaches in Chicago?"

"I don't know. Daddy said there's a big lake, but it's cold." A cell phone melody echoes in his bucket. He picks it up and says, "Hi, Mom." He listens and says, "Yeah. Why?" Another pause, this one longer, "But why do we have to come now?" Another pause. "Oh, okay. We'll leave right now."

He had been digging while he was on the phone and unearthed a plastic card.

"Emmy, look, here's a card like the one that opened our hotel door at Disney World."

"What good is that?"

"This one is from a hotel on the boardwalk. If we turn it in, there might be a reward."

"Let's go there first," Emmy says, sliding her shovel in her bucket beside the Cinderella carriage and picking up her flip-flops. "If we get a reward, we can buy some candy for Mommy."

"We'll stop there tomorrow," he said. "We have to go home now. Mom wants to take the baby to the doctor's for medicine and we have to go with her."

He shoves his tools into his bucket with the card and heads for the boardwalk. I overhear Danny say, "You mean candy for you, not Mommy."

Emmy gets the last word, "She likes the same kind I do."

I eye the sand where they'd been digging. Danny had marked the spot with a line of shells. The afternoon crowds may disperse them, so I estimate their location in line with the tall grasses along the boardwalk. I consider how easy it would be to slip a few items under the sand. I think about what I have on hand that would fit the criteria of treasure. Nothing really valuable. Nothing to point attention toward a barefoot, gray-haired guy, dry as driftwood and missing half an arm. I'll just bury a few coins picked up in my travels to make tomorrow's search more exciting than plastic hotel key cards and costume jewelry.

* * * * * *

I get there early. I have to admit, I feel amused at what I'm going to do. Not excited, exactly. Well, maybe excited, yes. Makes me realize I haven't looked to the promise of a day in so long that I've forgotten the surge of anticipation and pleasure it brings. I kneel and shove a handful of coins from my pocket into the area the kids will explore, then set my chair the requisite distance away. As I settle myself, I realize I forgot my Thermos. That's never happened before. Wouldn't that make my therapist and that nag of a doctor happy?

I could probably fast-walk to my cottage before Emmy and Danny show up, but I see them already ambling down the boardwalk at a pace slower than usual and, as usual, talking nonstop.

They continue talking as they set down their buckets. "But what if we don't want to go to Chicago, Danny?"

"It's not up to us. We're still kids."

"We could run away," says Emmy, plunking down in the sand. Her tank top's rhinestones read, "I'm the big sister."

"We can't run away. We have to call Mom when the phone alarm goes off. When it goes off the second time, we have to go home. If we don't show up, she'll call the police like that time we were late." He sits near his sister and lightly scratches the sand with his rake. "I don't want to go, either," he says, gouging the sand harder. "Leave Cub Scouts, my friends." His voice thickens. "My piano." He bows his head and pushes the sand back into the furrows he's made between his feet.

"Don't cry, Danny. Maybe they'll get a new piano in Chicago."

He sniffs his tears. "Mommy says the apartment is too small for a piano."

They sit silently, the boy rhythmically pounds the beach with the rake, the girl uses her hands to pull up fists of sand to dribble over her legs.

My hat shades my eyes from the encroaching sun, but allows full view of the scene. I realize as I anticipate their discovery of the coins that I'm rubbing the end of my stump where my elbow used to be. I watch the sand mound higher on Emmy's legs. Finally, one of her knees seems to blaze with light as the sun reflects off a coin.

"Danny, Danny," she whispers as though sound would make the shiny, wobbling silver disk disappear. "What is that? A game token? Real money?"

Her brother scoots closer and bends over her knee to examine the coin, still not touching it. "No. Not a game token."

"It says half dollar."

"It's a Kennedy, like Mom has," he says, on his knees now.

Emmy sloughs off the sand and rolls onto her hands and knees. Her sense of mission brightens the glow on her cheeks.

"Help me search. There may be more," her voice higher. I feel a growing sense of excitement as theirs builds. I don't dare move or smile.

Since her hands found the last treasure, Emmy digs with them as though swimming her way through the sand. I know there's much more to find. I want to turn them and set them on the right patches, but Emmy doesn't need my help. With a screech, she holds up another treasure.

"One dollar," she reads. "Aww. This can't be real. There's a lady on it. Ladies aren't on money, are they?"

"Yeah. Susan B. Anthony," Danny reads. "Mommy has this one, too." He flips it up and down in his hand. "Feels like a quarter. Big as a quarter, too." He gives it back to Emmy. "Should be bigger or heavier if it's a dollar."

Now Danny rakes with the fervor, if not the care, of an archaeologist at a royal Egyptian tomb. Deeper ridges in the damp sand reveal more coins. "Emmy, fill my bucket with water so we can rinse them. I think some of these are from other countries."

Emmy takes off for the surf, her feet barely touching sand. Together, they scavenge for coins and toss them into the bucket. I forget how many coins I buried—not many, but they should have found them all now. Emmy's momentum keeps her plowing and, with another screech, her face beams with the glory of a real treasure find.

"Danny, here's the other ruby earring! Now we can show them to the jewelry store man."

Danny dunks the earring up and down in the water and gives it back to Emmy.

"Put it with the other one. Let's spread out the coins," he says, patting the former airport until it's smooth and even. He sets down four coins in each of two rows.

"Danny, there's another coin with a lady on it. She's wearing a crown."

Danny reads both sides of the coin. "It says Queen Elizabeth. Wow. It's from Hong Kong. This one coin is worth two dollars."

Emmy takes the coin. "That's Queen Elizabeth? She looks like that high school girl who works at Dolle's. Mommy says Queen Elizabeth's an old lady. Maybe it's a fake."

"Maybe. But the Susan dollar and Kennedy half are real. Maybe the Queen's real, too."

"What about these other coins?" Emmy asks. "The words aren't in English."

They can't see my eyes, but I close them anyway when they glance over at me. Will they finally cross our silent boundary and ask me about the coins? They bend away, shaking their heads, and I hear fragments: "no," "don't ask," "won't know." I dig the metal edge of my chair into my left palm to keep from laughing. The coins are worth more than their face value now, but only a few bucks. I'd saved them and quite a few others over the years as novelties. It doesn't matter to me if the kids keep them, spend them, or give them away. The morning's diversion will stay with me regardless.

The kids' phone chirps. Danny answers and says, "Okay, we're coming." I guess they've been told to go home for lunch. The familiar spicy fragrance of hot dogs creeping through the air awakens my appetite. I usually leave now anyway, as the beach gets crowded.

I feel shaky as I sling the strap of my chair over my chest. I thought all I had wanted was nothingness, away from battlefields, deadlines, and headlines—away from life with half an arm, alcohol for a buddy, and a dead journalism career. But seeing Emmy and Danny transported by the thrill of a find reawakens that childhood rush of coming to the beach with my family. How we roamed in capes of independence, feeling joy in discovery!

* * * * * *

I get to the beach later the next morning with my chair, Thermos, and a scratched black case holding something that was once important to me. The brother and sister aren't digging for treasure and they aren't alone. To my surprise, they're bobbing up and down in the surf, calling and waving to a tall, slender woman in denim shorts and an oversize Maroon 5 T-shirt, who is positioning an umbrella over the baby carrier.

They must have arrived early. I see a partially constructed castle with battlements decorated with silver coins that look familiar.

I set my Thermos in the sand, having decided I'm not ready to give it up. Not yet. I set the black case beside my chair and walk to the woman with long blond hair loosely gathered in a ponytail. She waves to Emmy and Danny, who yell, "Mom, look!" about every ten seconds.

I hold out my left hand. "Hi. I'm Harry Doyle." I keep it simple.

"I remember seeing you last week." She smiles and uses her left to shake my hand, as if it's normal. "I'm Kelly."

"How's the baby?"

"The kids told you?"

"Actually, they didn't say a word, but they talk a lot and it's hard not to overhear."

"They definitely can talk. Gracie's doing better, thanks. Just picked up a nasty cold that moved into an ear infection. The doctor gave her an antibiotic. I hope sunshine helps her, too." Shadows under Kelly's eyes reveal exhaustion. She waves again at the two bobbers, and then asks, "Are you vacationing?"

"I'm recently retired—non-voluntarily," I say, gesturing to my absent arm. "I was a newsman in the wrong spot at the wrong time."

She nods and says a quiet, "I'm sorry."

"Me, too," I say, and lower my voice. "I hope you won't be offended—I also overheard the kids talk about your move west."

"Oh, no," she says, and kneels on a towel spread next to the carrier. I hunker down near her. She says, "They've been so upset. We feel bad."

"Sounds like the typical trauma. Losing friends, familiar places, school."

"It's not just the kids who feel that. My husband and I grew up here, our families are here. They're all upset. We're upset, too, but the job offer is too good to pass up."

"I understand you won't be able to have a piano in your new apartment."

She laughs a loud, clear peal and the baby begins to rustle. "They've talked about everything, haven't they?" She gently rocks the carrier.

"I have a reason for asking." I straighten, knees protesting, and walk back to get the scuffed black case. I carry it over, set it on the towel in front of her, and open it to reveal a dusty, but still shiny, electronic keyboard with headphones. "He can shove this under his bed. If you accept it, I'll be happy to know it's getting good use."

Her eyes are wide. "But why? Are you sure you want to give it up?"

I gestured toward my stump. "I could probably experiment, but there aren't too many concertos for the left hand." I smile, hoping she'll get my flimsy attempt at humor. "I need to move on. Keeping this is a waste of opportunity for someone else—someone like Danny."

She looks up from the keyboard and stares at me. "I don't know what to say."

The baby's fussing turns serious, possibly revving up to a howl. Kelly picks up the carrier, then stops and looks at me, pushing her sunglasses up to hold back strands of hair the breeze has pulled loose. The kids are running from the water. Time to go home. She looks at me with steady gray eyes.

"The coins?" she asks, and then smiles. It's more statement than question. She knows.

I answer her smile, latch the keyboard case, and give it to Danny as he runs up.

"Carry this for your mom, okay?"

MARYALICE MELI IS A WRITER LIVING IN STEELERS COUNTRY, AKA PITTSBURGH, PENNSYLVANIA. SHE IS A RETIRED READING TEACHER AND NEWSPAPER REPORTER. SHE EARNED A MASTER'S DEGREE IN WRITING POPULAR FICTION AT SETON HILL UNIVERSITY, GREENSBURG, PENNSYLVANIA, AND IS WRITING A MIDDLE-GRADE MYSTERY SERIES. HER FLASH FICTION HAS APPEARED ONLINE AT *EVERYDAYFICTION*, *INFECTIVEINK*, AND *UNTIED SHOELACES OF THE MIND*. SHE IS THRILLED TO BE INCLUDED IN THIS WONDERFUL BOOK IN THE REHOBOTH BEACH READS SERIES.

Beached

by Jean Youkers

Her beloved Atlantic Ocean was crazed that day, water rolling, roiling, smacking her in the face. Julie didn't mind, having just arrived for a week's hiatus at Rehoboth Beach between graduation and her first real job. But suddenly, she found herself being pulled farther from shore, felt the urging of the undertow, beckoning her out to sea, and flailing to right her course, she began to feel fear. As the bandstand and the boardwalk scene receded from view, wave after wave pushed her under and she couldn't breathe. Fear turned to panic.... She was sucked downward toward what must be the ocean floor, the end of the universe, darkness. Her lungs burned and she didn't know if she was upside down, inside out, or sideways. As she felt herself slipping away, Julie felt regret about the life she would now surely miss.

* * * * * *

Her family paced the shore, having sped down Route 1 from Wilmington immediately after Julie's friends had called. Coast Guard patrols searched the waters; EMTs and volunteers were at the ready. Onlookers moved up and down the beach, kicking helplessly at sand dunes, convening on the boardwalk, speaking in whispers. Julie's mother, Michelle, almost her double though she was twenty-three years older, was distraught, bright blue eyes brimming with tears, hands shaking, afraid to hope yet afraid to give up. How could her beautiful daughter be gone? She'd brought her to Rehoboth almost every year since she was a young child, and Julie knew how to keep herself safe in the water. Michelle's husband, Doug, kept his own shaking arm tight around her as friends, volunteers, and firefighters continued the vigil. Julie's younger brother Daniel raced back and forth as if possessed, and finally shrieked when his flashlight, playing upon a pile of seaweed, illuminated the ring: University of Delaware, 2015.

* * * * * *

A crashing wave slammed onto the beach, spitting the body out and onto the sand. Saltwater in her eyes, sand in her nose, one arm surely broken, Julie groaned and realized she was actually *alive*. She rolled over and spit out water, tried to bring her breathing back to normal, and grasped the sand for dear life lest the ocean reclaim her. Her long blond hair was entangled about her face; she felt brush burns on each leg from being tossed with such force onto the damp, hard sand. Her left ankle throbbed as if from a jellyfish sting. Gulls soaring above seemed to be laughing.

Oddly, nobody came to her aid. She realized it was early evening. Dusk was settling and the sunbathing crowds must have scurried back to hotel rooms and beach houses, or gone off to the outlets. Maybe Madison and Taylor, her roommates at the Atlantic Sands, thought she had gone off for a walk, as was her habit. The familiar bandstand looked strange and dark in the distance. Just a few cars were parked along Rehoboth Avenue *There must be some kind of antique car show,* she thought, as she noticed a two-toned dark blue and light blue boxy Oldsmobile just like the one in her grandparents' photo album. A long white Chevrolet convertible with black fins and red interior zoomed by and the sounds of "Mrs. Brown You've Got a Lovely Daughter" drifted through the air. Julie lay on the beach and listened. *Someone must be playing the '60s channel, Grandmum's favorite.*

What on earth happened to the Atlantic Sands? Obviously, repairs were underway, some parts boarded up, though it had been fine before she'd been sucked into the maelstrom. The outdoor pool was conspicuously absent. And the Boardwalk Plaza wasn't there at all. Instead there was some type of old-fashioned motel. Julie strained to read the sign but gave up as the pain in her arm clamored for attention. Julie felt panicky again and then nauseated. Her eyes began to close.

* * * * * *

Two days later, Julie woke up in a dimly lit hospital room, thin curtains drawn, antiseptic smells surrounding her. She saw a cast on her arm and an IV pumping its mysterious juice into the other arm. *This must be Beebe Hospital.* Gripping the bed rails and trying to grasp the situation, she searched unsuccessfully for the controls to elevate her head for a better look around.

Just then, the door inched open as a friendly voice called, "Knock, knock."

"Hi," Julie managed to squeak, though her voice felt unfamiliar. She felt dopey, drugged.

The friendly voice belonged to a beaming nurse with a name tag that read "Miss Nelson." She was dressed in an old-fashioned white nurse's uniform, with white shoes and stockings. A crisply starched cap with multiple points and some sort of a logo was affixed, atop a mass of excruciatingly permed brown hair. She checked Julie's IV, then positioned the blood pressure cuff on her arm.

"So you're finally awake, Sleeping Beauty! Do you know where you are?"

"Of course. I'm in the hospital."

"Do you know today's date?"

"Not sure. But I know it's June."

"What year?"

"Do you think I lost my brain in the surf?" Julie's forehead wrinkled as she frowned.

"No insult meant, sweetie. I ask all my patients the date and year. I have to document that I'm doing my job, right?"

Julie smiled. "Okay then. It's 2015."

Now it was Nurse Nelson who frowned. "Think again."

"It's 2015!"

"Okay, dear. What is your date of birth?"

"April 22, 1993."

The nurse made a note, then elevated Julie's head by operating a creaking hand crank at the foot of the bed.

"Now, tell me the name of the president of the United States."

"Obama."

"Oh, dear."

"What?" Julie scowled.

As Nurse Nelson rushed out the door, Julie noticed that someone had left a copy of the *News Journal* folded on top of her over-the-bed table. She saw a headline about President Johnson and glanced at the date. Surely a perceptual anomaly from head trauma, she thought, because it looked like it said 1965. Grabbing the paper in consternation, Julie strained to hear a hushed conversation going on just outside the door to her room.

"She's definitely not oriented to time. But of course, she just woke up. She's been delirious, muttering something about a sale phone or a self phone," Nurse Nelson was telling one of the doctors. "When I gave her the phone, she didn't even remember how to dial. And then she kept dialing ten-digit numbers and getting disconnected. She must've really hit her head hard when she crashed onto the beach. Better get a neurology consult."

"I'll order a psych consult as well."

* * * * * *

Two weeks passed, during which time social services had no

luck in locating Julie's next of kin. They even began to question her identity, as there was no listing for the address she had given for her parents in Wilmington. Finally, Nurse Nelson came to her room accompanied by a tall man with kind eyes who was wearing a black suit with a clerical collar.

"This is Chaplain Brown. He's a visiting chaplain and he's worked with a lot of other amnesia victims. I'll leave the two of you to get acquainted."

Chaplain Brown sat on the edge of the visitor's chair that he'd pulled up close to Julie's bed and the warmth of his smile made her sense she could trust him. After an intense hour-long interview, he stood up and took a deep breath.

"I've known two other young people like you. They had no funds and no identification, so my wife and I took them in as boarders and helped them find jobs. One of them still lives in our house. I think that would be a good starting point for you as well."

"What do you mean they're like me?" Julie asked.

"Time travelers."

Julie gasped.

* * * * * *

The next day, the hospital allowed Julie to go home—that is, to the home of Chaplain Arthur Brown and his wife, Emma. That first night, Julie was so scared by her new situation that she barely spoke to anyone. After dinner, she sat in the living room of the comfortable home and looked around. Soothing music was coming from a large cabinet in which a vintage vinyl record was spinning. Intrigued, Julie watched the arm rotating through the grooves.

"Oh, that's the new Dean Martin record." Julie jumped because she had not heard the young woman walk into the room. "I heard we had a new boarder in the house. I'm Ruby. I work up on the boardwalk. Maybe I can help you find a job."

Julie just stared at Ruby, who appeared to be about eighteen years old. She wore a waitress uniform and had long red hair pulled back in a ponytail with a red, silky scarf. In fast order, Ruby explained that she had lived with the Browns for the past several months and worked at Dolle's, making taffy and fudge. Within minutes Ruby revealed that she, too, had been transported to 1965, but from 2106.

"Just a word of advice," she offered. "Don't let people on the boardwalk or at work or church hear you claim that it's 2015. They can put you in a mental hospital for years if they think you're psychotic. There aren't that many time travelers around, so we meet in secret at the library, disguised as a book club. We're supposedly reading *Atlas Shrugged* for this month's selection, if anyone asks."

"Thanks for the tip, but what I really need to know is how to get back home," Julie said, tears welling up in her bright blue eyes. "My family must be frantic! Where is the portal to get back?"

"Julie, I hate to tell you this, but you can't go back. There is no portal."

"But, but...every book I've ever read about time travelers, *The Time Traveler's Wife* and others...Well, Stephen King...every single time, the characters believe they've been gone for days or years, then they go back and learn they've only been gone for minutes or hours!"

"Those books are all fiction. This is real life." Ruby took Julie's hand. "I'm so sorry, but the time tunnel is one-way only."

"So how can I see my mother?" Julie started to sob. Julie's mother was the one person Julie could turn to in a crisis, the one person who loved every moment of her childhood, who cheered her on in every endeavor, and who was truly her best friend. Many people thought the two were sisters.

"Well," Ruby explained. "The only way to get back to 2015 is to live another fifty years. Then you can see your mother."

"But, fifty years from now I'll be seventy-two. What if my mother doesn't even recognize me?"

"A mother always recognizes her daughter."

Julie took off running and headed toward the beach. She ran until she was out of breath and sank onto the sand, pounding it with her fists and screaming, cursing the Atlantic.

"Mom, where are you?"

* * * * * *

Without her birth certificate, driver's license, or college transcript, Julie's first challenge was finding a job. Chaplain Brown came through with his promise of help in that regard, first by having her type up the church bulletins on a manual typewriter, using a white liquid to paint over mistakes. *Where on earth is the delete button?* she had screamed to herself throughout that first day. Next, she'd had a summer job selling T-shirts and postcards at one of the boardwalk shops. But the best opportunity came when Emma Brown, who worked at the local library, needed assistance there. Julie loved books and, as an English major, had written a lot of research papers about authors of earlier times, so this seemed to be her obvious calling.

Her first day of work, she almost blew her cover when she asked where the computers were. A coworker just laughed nervously while staring at Julie. "I saw a computer once where my husband works," she'd explained. "There's no way we'd have room for one here—it was the size of a small car."

Without Internet access, her work of sorting, shelving, and reviewing books became a lot more laborious. But Julie learned how to assist students in using the card catalog to locate the books they needed. She was amazed that they all carried stacks of little index cards on which they made meticulous notes to be transcribed by hand later, then typed on their typewriters, with smeary carbon paper between the pages.

When she complained to Ruby, she learned that things could have been worse. Ruby, who had had GPS and Internet devices implanted in the spaces where wisdom teeth no longer grew in her generation, could not get any reception at all in the '60s. She had been born with a retractable propeller-like device in her back for auto-flying short distances, but dared not make use of it for fear of being thought a witch or a crazed inventor. She let her hair grow down almost to her waist to cover the equipment when she wore backless sundresses. Julie found Ruby not only exotic but also admirable in the way she always made the best of her situation. It turned out she was twice as old as she appeared due to the new innovations in youth preservation that were available in the twenty-second century.

"If they have so many innovations," said Julie, "don't you think someone in your time could develop a way to reverse the time tunnel? That way, someone might come to get you."

"That's not going to happen," Ruby said with a sigh. "But since our average life span is so much longer, I'll probably still be going strong when I do get back there in another century or so."

* * * * * *

Over the next several years, Julie gradually managed to come to terms with her predicament—not that she had a choice. She had resisted at first, but then slowly began to appreciate simple things, such as the solitude that prevailed in the absence of cell phones, and the camaraderie in the Brown household when the women chatted while washing and drying dishes by hand. She enjoyed listening to all the new songs that were coming out: "A Whiter Shade of Pale," "Hey Jude," and "Aquarius," which became her favorite. She felt she had one foot in the '60s and the other in 2015, as the Vietnam War raged on and protesters marched on the campuses. Richard Nixon was elected, a man walked on the moon, and Ruby put flowers in her hair and ran off to San Francisco with a bearded hippie. The rest of the world seemed far from the quiet beach town Julie now called home, where she used up most of her energy trying to keep her identity secret and maintain some sort of equilibrium, while saving money so that she could move out on her own very soon.

In 1970, the inevitable happened. Julie met a wonderful young man named George. She was sitting on the porch of the Browns' house, listening to a small radio as strains of "Let It Be" lulled her into a relaxed state. She barely noticed the tanned man in Bermuda shorts and a white golf shirt vaulting down the street in the direction of the ocean. When he passed the porch, he suddenly backed up with exaggerated waves of his arms and stopped by the porch steps. Julie laughed.

"I love that song," he explained, and began to sing along. Julie joined in. He introduced himself and explained that he had a week's vacation from his job at DuPont in Wilmington. Under his arm he had a book he was planning to read on the beach. The book led to a conversation, which led to Julie's offering him a seat on the porch and a glass of iced tea, which led to his asking her out to the movies that night.

They laughed through *MASH,* stopped for burgers and fries afterwards, and made another date for the following evening. When George left town, he promised to drive down the following month and to keep in touch in the interim. A long-distance romance ensued, during which they drove around in George's gray VW bug, visiting lighthouses and listening to the Carpenters on the car radio. When they weren't together, they exchanged letters.

On a drive up to Wilmington, Julie held her breath when they passed the wooded farmland that would one day become the development where she had grown up. No signs of her family, of course.

It was with these mystifying issues still rattling around in her head that Julie sat at the Dinner Bell Inn the following week, enjoying a lovely dinner, then hearing the words of George's marriage proposal. Her tears were not just from happiness but from the realization that she and her mother would not plan the wedding together and her father would not give her away. Who would be there for her? But then she remembered how Chaplain Brown and Emma had helped her adapt to her new life, and she knew they would come through for her.

It's time I really live in the times that I'm living in, she told herself. To George, she just said, "Yes. Oh, definitely yes!"

It was in this happy spirit that Julie walked down to the beach to commune with the ocean the next day. Large waves were splashing onto the shore but in a friendly, not a menacing, way. All was forgiven. The seagulls were soaring above, but they weren't laughing at her this time. They must have known something was up. Something good.

As she strode back up the staircase to the boardwalk, Julie saw a young woman wearing blue-and-white-striped bell-bottoms, a shell top, and a bright pink headband around her long, flowing hair. *Looks just like the pictures of Grandmum in her post-hippie days.*

And then Julie saw the baby stroller, in which an adorable blond baby girl was sitting and holding onto a little white stuffed bunny rabbit. She walked up closer, stooped down to see the baby, and their matching blue eyes locked. The baby reached out her chubby hand, pointed toward Julie, and with certain recognition, nodded.

Jean Youkers writes humor, poetry, and fiction. In her unpublished novel, "Full Moon over Estrogen Island," she gives a light touch to the experiences of four women who find new directions in midlife, just as she herself returned to school at fifty-one to earn an MBA. "Beached" is her first published short story, inspired by her fascination with time travel and love of Rehoboth Beach that developed after attending two conferences held there by the Rehoboth Beach Writers' Guild. Jean appreciates attending programs sponsored by the Written Remains Writers Guild and is a member of the Wright Touch Writing Group in Wilmington. She is also a regular reader at open-mic nights at the Newark Arts Alliance and read at the first (and only) performance of the Red Dragonfly Haiku Poets.

The Break Out

by Katherine Melvin

CJ Swift pulled into the parking spot wondering what her grandmother was dragging her into and what her father would say when he found out. Gramma had cooked up a plan to break out of the nursing home and talked CJ into helping.

CJ parked the silver Mini Cooper, raised the soft-top, hopped out, and stood in front of Potomac Twilight Center, which wasn't in Potomac at all, but in Gaithersburg, Maryland. As she approached the doors and pulled off her sunglasses, it occurred to her that she'd never meet anyone special hanging out with her grandmother.

She strode down the wide corridors.

"Excuse me," demanded the imperious-looking woman sitting at the information desk.

CJ barged on by.

"Ma'am," the admin barked.

Damn. So much for her plan to scoot down the hallway without being noticed.

"All visitors *must* sign in," the admin continued. This included an unspoken "tsk, tsk."

"Sure." CJ flashed the woman a brilliant smile, the one that had landed her a leading role in *Baltimore Streets*. All the schooling to become a bioengineer at Hopkins, and she had ended up working in television, making a lot more money. Due to the show's success, it was getting difficult for her to go out in public unrecognized. Today, she'd tucked her long dark hair under a red National's cap and applied no makeup. The woman hadn't recognized her. *Good.*

This was a covert operation.

The previous night's text exchange with her grandmother had set the scheme into motion.

U free 2moro, her grandmother had asked.

AFAIK

Rehoboth

Beach?

Yes, beach. Get us 2moro. ♥ Gma

Us?

Me & Mildred. Time2 break out.

RU ok?

Not in jail. Tell no one

OK

CJ signed the nursing home register "Dixie Dortmunder," in honor of her grandfather, who gave "John Dortmunder" as his name for all restaurant waiting lists. He was certain it got them seated faster than using actual names. Turned out Dortmunder was a German beer. A tasty one, too.

"There's my girl." Her grandmother grabbed her in the hall and hugged her all the way into the room. "You're taller."

"Gramma, I think you're shrinking."

"Nah! Can't be."

The pants she wore dusted the floor, but CJ didn't argue.

She studied her grandmother Louise. It was the final week of summer and she hadn't seen her since May. She looked fragile. As CJ took her hand, she noticed the skin, while soft, was paper-thin.

Louise wiggled her eyebrows. "Did you bring the stuff?" she

imitated Cheech and Chong.

Rascal. CJ held up the Target bag. She stage-whispered, "I've got the stuff." Then, in a normal voice, asked, "Why is your hair blue?"

"You like?" Louise touched her chin-length bob. "Tired of gray. Bor-ing. Mildred's is orange." She sat in the chair next to the bed and wiggled her slippered feet at her granddaughter. "We've been friends since your father was in kindergarten."

CJ pulled off the slippers. "That's a long time."

"We've gotten into a lot of trouble over the years."

She helped her grandmother undress. At the shirt, Louise said, "Turn your head. You're too young to see what happens to the boobies. All the trouble they caused with your grandfather—that's how your father got here—and this is what you get in the end. Tube socks."

"TMI, Gramma."

She helped her grandmother put on hot-pink capris and a matching shirt.

"There," she tied her grandmother's sneakers. "You look cute."

"Cute? I don't want cute. I want hot mama." She stood up and looked at herself in the mirror. "Well, I guess those days are behind me." Louise wiggled her rear end for emphasis. "Now for the bangles. Help me out, kiddo." She pointed to the dresser and jiggled her wrists. "I love sea glass, don't you?"

"Yes."

"You want them when I die?"

"Would you stop?"

"What? It's gonna happen sooner rather than later."

"Ready?" Mildred popped her curly orange head in the room. She was a perfect picture in purple: cropped pants, checked top, high-topped sneakers, even ruffled anklets—all purple. She hadn't wizened down as much as Louise.

"Why isn't your cane purple?" CJ asked.

Mildred looked down at herself. "Couldn't find one."

"I'm teasing." CJ gave her a peck on the cheek.

"But I do have these." Mildred donned a pair of sparkling purple sunglasses.

"Anyone have to use the bathroom?" CJ asked. "It's a long way to Rehoboth."

Mildred and Louise shook their colorful heads no.

"Let's blow this joint," Mildred said.

* * * * * *

It took longer than expected to get out the door and into the car. CJ sighed. Maybe she shouldn't have agreed to take two eighty-year-olds to the beach. What if something happened to them? She'd never live it down. The beach meant so much to her grandmother; she couldn't say no.

Once they were situated, Louise buckled into the back and Mildred up front, CJ started the car. They had only gone a couple of miles when the "girls" started whining like children: "Turn on the radio." "Put the top down." "I'm hungry." And the classic, "Are we there yet?" That got them hooting.

"You're not going to ask me that for the next three hours? Gramma? Miss Mildred?"

"I'm offended." Louise paused. "Maybe just a few more times."

"We're stopping to get hats," CJ said. "I'm not returning you with burnt heads."

"Who said we're coming back?" Louise groused.

CJ searched for the oldies station, staying on one station long enough to hear "Josh Brady was seen with starlet Penelope Pope outside..." Why did her costar persist with the playboy antics when he could be such a nice guy? Like today. He agreed to meet her at the beach to help with the grandmothers.

Louise ordered, "Blast the radio!"

When they realized what song was playing, Mildred and Louise exclaimed, "Maggie!"

Together they sang, "Wake up, Maggie, I think I got something to say to you."

They were to the ICC, the shortcut to I-95 for upper Montgomery County, when Louise asked, "Did you get the money?"

"Of course."

"What?" Mildred said.

"I asked her if she got the money," Louise yelled.

"What for?"

"To see if she did or not."

"What? That's not what I meant."

Louise yelled again, "Talk up. I can't hear you with all this wind."

"Why do we need money?"

"For the food, of course—French fries, hot dogs, cotton candy, ice cream—you name it, Millie, we're gonna eat it."

CJ felt ill just thinking about all that junk.

"I'll need my teeth," Mildred said.

"Your what?"

"My teeth," she yelled. "I'll need my teeth if we're going to eat."

Louise flared up. "Now why wouldn't you have your teeth in, for goodness' sakes?"

"Gramma," CJ tried to keep them calm. They weren't even out of Gaithersburg and the two were already bickering. "It's OK. We didn't get far."

"I don't like 'em. They clack."

"You like to eat, don't you?"

"All they serve is mush. Mush for breakfast. Mush for lunch."

"Last night they served chicken, Mildred."

"I don't like chicken."

"Yes, you do."

"How do you know what I like and don't like?"

"What? Speak up. I think my ear thingy blew out."

"I said," Mildred yelled, "you hardly need your teeth at all for those meals."

CJ returned to the nursing home's parking lot and pulled into the same spot she'd just vacated. "Okay, ladies, stay put. I'll be right out."

Within minutes, they were on the road again, singing with the radio. But before long, the car was silent, except for the old ladies' snores whistling away with the wind.

CJ's phone rang.

"Hello."

Her father said, "The nursing home called."

"Really?"

"I also got a call from Mildred's daughter. Everyone's upset. Return them."

"I can't. Gramma wants to put her feet in the ocean."

"Are you kidding me?"

She heard a lecture coming. "Traffic. Gotta go." He'd call again. She was certain.

＊ ＊ ＊ ＊ ＊ ＊

In Rehoboth, CJ pulled around the bandstand and parked near Dolle's. "We're here."

With CJ's help, Mildred and Louise hauled themselves out of the car and stood on the mosaic cobblestone. They looked small, lost, and a little wobbly.

"You ladies okay?" CJ asked. "Let's get you to one of the benches."

"Give us a minute," Mildred said. "Have to get the body moving again."

Louise straightened herself to her full height of five one. "I've got to pee."

"Me too," Mildred said. "And I'm thirsty."

"There's a public bathroom right over there by the dolphin statue."

Louise looked at all the different shops and squealed, "Thrasher's! Love their fries. Let's eat!"

Bathroom and food stand visits out of the way, the three women sat on a bench looking at the ocean, enjoying the beautiful late-summer day.

"This is what I dreamed of," Louise sighed. "Now I need to put my tootsies in the water and I can die in peace."

"Is that what this trip is about, Gramma?"

"Me and Mildred made our bucket list. We can check this off, now."

"What else is on the list?"

The friends deadpanned, "Line dance."

"We did something like this once before," Louise explained, "when our kids were in school. Took off for a day at the beach."

"We have the pictures to prove it." Mildred popped the last bite of a Nathan's hot dog into her mouth and licked mustard off her fingers. "Yum."

Louise finished the fries. "They don't let us eat like this in the home."

"Nope."

"Oh, poop."

"What now?" Mildred asked.

"I spilt catsup on my new shirt." She nudged her granddaughter, who was finishing a salad. "How about an ice-cream cone?"

"Don't you want to put your feet in the water?"

"I do," Louise said. "I can do it better with ice cream."

"Okay. I'll get you ice cream."

"I'm coming."

"It'll be quicker without you."

"You're not the boss of me, young lady."

CJ prayed for patience. She had turned thirty-two on her last birthday, but her grandmother still called her "young lady."

Mildred said, "We don't want to sit around all day. What if one of those old geezers in the plaid pants hits on us?"

CJ noticed that there did seem to be a lot of elderly folks around. "Look, this is how it's going to be. I'm getting you ice cream. You save your energy for walking down to the water, okay?"

"Fine. I want chocolate." Louise pouted.

"Miss Mildred?"

"Strawberry."

Louise whispered, "I don't know when *she* got to be so bossy."

Mildred said, "She got that from you."

"What are you talking about? I'm not bossy."

"Are too."

"Am not."

"You told me we were breaking out today. You didn't ask me."

"I was merely conveying information."

"Not that place," Louise yelled to her granddaughter. She pointed to the other side of the street. "The Ice Cream Store. It's homemade."

"And tastes so good." Mildred added.

While they waited, the two women enjoyed the warm sun.

"Isn't this wonderful, Millie?"

"Heavenly."

"Do you smell it?"

"The saltwater?"

"That, but something else too. Inhale again." Louise waited. "Well?"

"I give up," Mildred said. "What?"

Louise smacked her lips. "Cotton candy. I'm getting some." She started to stand up.

"How exactly are you going to pay for it? With your good looks?"

"You're a spoilsport, Mildred O'Svenson," said Louise as she sat back down.

They closed their eyes, listening to the sounds: people chatting, children laughing, and seagulls squealing over the hypnotizing swells of waves rolling to shore. Just as they started to nod off, they heard a commotion.

"What on earth?" Mildred said.

"Let's go see."

"CJ told us to wait here."

Louise rolled her eyes. "When did you become such an old stick-in-the-mud?"

"I'm not. CJ was nice enough to drive us here. I don't want to be any trouble."

A siren sounded. Mildred turned to sit on the end of the bench. "An ambulance," she said. "Let's go."

As the pair approached the crowd of spectators, a policeman stopped them.

"I need to get over there." Louise tried her best to push past him.

"Stay on this side of the street, ma'am, while the paramedics sort things out."

"What happened? Did some old geezer fall?" Louise elbowed Mildred.

"No, ma'am."

Louise tutted to Mildred. "Probably some old fart walking too fast to get his ice cream." To the policeman she said, "Is there some kind of elderly convention going on? I haven't seen so many old people in one place in all my life. Not even at the home."

"Not likely," he said.

"There was quite a crowd at George's funeral. You know, George, from down the hall?" Mildred said to Louise.

"Not this many. You think they loaded them up from all the homes in the area and dumped them out here?"

"Look, young man," Mildred said, playing the grandmother card. "We need to get to the ice-cream shop where her granddaughter is. We can't be left alone too long. Someone might take us."

"Doubt it," the policeman muttered.

Mildred gestured with her cane like she might hit him. "Now, Millie, you're going to get us arrested waving that thing."

Just then, the crowd parted.

"That's no old geezer," Mildred yelled as Louise gasped. "That's your granddaughter."

They held out their elbows to the policeman, who sighed and escorted them across the street.

Three ice-cream cones and wrappers littered the sidewalk where CJ had fallen. Tears welled in her beautiful deep blue eyes.

"You really should go to the ER, Miss Swift," said the paramedic wrapping her foot.

CJ's cell phone played *Born to Be Wild*. She knew from the song it was her dad. "Yes?"

"You're on TV."

"What?" *Not good.* She looked around until she spotted the cameraman and the local reporter. *Crud.* Here she was, splayed out on the ground, chocolate ice cream dripping down her shirt, a bloody knee, bruised elbow, and a throbbing big toe, all without a single drop of makeup. Now she really was going to cry.

"That's the least of your worries," her father said. "I just saw your grandmother on TV, and it looks like she is in the custody of the Rehoboth police. The nursing home wants to know when you're returning them. Do I need to come help you?"

"No!" Her frustrated yell silenced the crowd. The paramedics froze.

Just then, Josh Brady, CJ's costar, stepped into the clearing. "Perhaps," he said, as he flashed the crowd an Emmy-winning smile, "I can be of assistance."

The onlookers oohed as they recognized the handsome star of *Baltimore Streets*. At six-foot-two, he was hard to miss. He had the rugged look of a young Tom Selleck, enhanced further by three days' growth of beard and a tan.

"Hello, Josh." CJ stared at her reflection in his sunglasses.

"Perfect timing. Put your arm around me," he whispered, as he helped her stand. "This will be great publicity."

CJ thought about ignoring him. However, his instincts were usually right on target; by leaning into him, she could hide most of her face. Win-win.

"Is this your young man?" Louise asked.

The crowd chuckled.

"This is Josh, Gramma. We work together."

"I see." Louise looked him up and down. "You might want to hang onto this one, honey."

"Gramma!"

The onlookers roared.

"Ladies," Josh said, "this is my buddy Douglas from my old neighborhood. Mind if he helps?"

The crowd parted to let them pass.

The women sat down in front of the bandstand while Josh and Douglas got more ice cream and drinks.

Louise hummed.

"What's that song?" Mildred asked.

"'Achy Breaky Heart.'"

"Catchy." She joined in.

They tapped their feet.

CJ fussed with her phone, searching for the song. When Mildred and Louise heard it, they whooped.

"Come on, Millie." Louise tugged her friend's arm. "Hop up here. Let's dance."

"You know I don't hop anywhere. And there you go bossing me around…"

"Turn it up loud, granddaughter. Isn't technology grand?"

CJ helped them climb the bandstand steps, favoring her good foot. *Quite a sight, what with their colored hair and hot pink and purple outfits.* She restarted the song and watched them shuffle: side step, two to the right, two to the left, step front, step back, clap-clap to the beat of the music. *Almost.* They did it again. And again.

"You can tell my heart, my achy breaky heart…"

"Come up here," Louise pointed at the old folks watching them. "Don't stand there gawking."

"I just don't think I'd understand," the ladies sang.

It wasn't long before a group of seniors gathered on the Rehoboth Beach bandstand singing, while line dancing to "Achy Breaky Heart." They came in all sizes—tall, short, fat, skinny, white hair, died hair, no hair—dressed in a colorful menagerie of Hawaiian shirts, plaid pants, khaki shorts, muumuus, black socks with sandals, and sneakers. They wore an assortment of sun hats, straw hats, and baseball caps, equally split between the Orioles and the Nats.

"Play it again!" Mildred ordered. "We're just getting started."

Louise blew on her fingers and touched her rump, making a sizzling noise.

CJ heard the reporter's voice before she saw the woman.

"This is Eugenia Eubanks with *What's Happening Rehoboth.* And what's happening is a dance-in for people of ages. We've never seen anything like it."

"Tell your Aunt Louise, tell us pretty please."

CJ groaned as her grandmother mangled the lyrics and then

wiggled her rear end at the camera.

The crowd ended the song like Billy Ray Cyrus—with a loud whoop.

"Phew!" Mildred pressed her shirt to her forehead, then collapsed on the bench next to CJ. "We can cross line dance off the old bucket list."

Josh arrived with lemonade, cotton candy, ice cream, and roasted pecans.

"Bless you," Louise said. "Aren't you handsome?" She winked at CJ, who ignored her.

The reporter walked up. "We're standing on the boardwalk with Josh Brady and CJ Swift. Welcome to Rehoboth." She shoved the microphone into Josh's face. "What brings the stars of *Baltimore Streets* here today?"

"Well," Josh retreated from the mike. "You should talk to these lovely ladies. They're the special ones here."

Louise leaned across Mildred and nudged CJ on the knee. "He's a keeper."

Josh had the decency to blush, and CJ continued to groan, mainly due to the pain in her toe. But also because of the pain in her side called Gramma.

"What's your name, honey?" Eugenia asked.

"Well, sweetie," Louise snapped, "no one calls me 'honey' except my husband, and he's dead."

The reporter looked surprised to be reprimanded by a little old lady. "I'm sorry."

"I'm Louise and this is Mildred."

"Are you enjoying the beach?"

"We sure are," Mildred said. "We're going to go in the water." Mildred grinned at the reporter.

CJ was thankful Mildred had her teeth.

"Let's go, ladies." Josh helped each woman stand up and placed his arms around them. "You going to be all right?" he asked CJ.

She looked at him, seeing him for the first time, and realized *here was a good man.* Everyone on the set loved Josh Brady, but she had managed to keep her distance. She had no patience for Hollywood glitter.

Josh whispered, "I have grandparents too. And I was schooled to honor them. Maybe one day you could come to my house to meet my Nana. We live near Reisterstown. I avoid L.A."

"She lives with you?"

"Yes." He winked at her. "My parents too."

"What?" CJ couldn't believe it. "What about the starlets and the rumors?"

"Image, CJ. Part of the image."

"Here"—Douglas took Mildred's hand—"let me help."

CJ touched Josh's shoulder for balance.

"My father told me to never believe the press reports. Stay true to myself. I've tried to do that."

At the water's edge, Josh and Douglas stood with the women where the water rushed over their feet without knocking them over.

"Wonderful." Louise sniffed. "Kleenex?"

"Don't cry." CJ wrapped her arms around her grandmother.

"Can't help it. I do love the ocean. Have all my life. Makes me sad thinking I might not ever see it again." She patted CJ's arm. "Promise me you'll sprinkle me at the beach." She smiled wickedly. "In case your father gets other ideas."

"Of course."

CJ's phone rang.

"Your father?" Louise arched an eyebrow.

"Yep." She answered. "Hello."

"Trizzle trazzle..."

"Trozzle trome…," CJ replied.

"Time for this one to come home," her father finished. "Now."

"Will do." She ended the call.

"How about I drive you back?" Josh suggested.

CJ hesitated.

"How will you manage?" He pointed at her bandaged right foot.

"Oh," CJ said. "I forgot."

Louise maneuvered between them. "Can Douglas take us old ladies home and you two follow?"

"Is it a Rolls?" Mildred asked.

"Lincoln Navigator," Douglas said.

"Sweet!"

"How about it?" Josh reached for CJ's hand. "May I drive you home?"

She dazzled him with her smile. "Sure."

While the sun set on the beautiful day and the two stars talked, Louise, Mildred, and Douglas continued up the beach. At the SUV, Millie gave Louise one thumb up.

Louise echoed the gesture. "We did it."

As the car pulled away, she texted her granddaughter.

PDH kiddo. Pretty darn happy.

KATHERINE MELVIN IS A WRITER LIVING IN THE DC METROPOLITAN AREA. HER SHORT STORY *THE BLACK IMPALA* WON THIRD PLACE IN THE MARYLAND WRITERS' ASSOCIATION 2014 SHORT STORY CONTEST. HER ARTICLES HAVE APPEARED IN *TODAY'S CHRISTIAN WOMAN, CHRISTIANITY TODAY,* AND *CATHOLIC DIGEST.* SHE IS CURRENTLY AT WORK ON HER SECOND NOVEL, *THE MASTER SERGEANT'S DAUGHTER.*

JUDGES' COMMENTS

This story is nothing short of hysterical. And it's nice to see a story about seniors having a fun fling at the beach. This appealing tale of two feisty and unpredictable eighty-year-olds who escape their stifling nursing home (helped by a famous-from-TV granddaughter) so they can spend a day at the beach hits all the right notes. There's the gleeful, thrilling escape from ordinary life. The sensual enjoyment of boardwalk treats. Several unexpected but felicitous accidents. And, topping it all off, a group of seniors gather from thin air and, like the two escapees, feel no embarrassment about line dancing to "Achy Breaky Heart" in the bandstand overlooking the ocean. They're all old enough to know that joie de vivre is far more important than saving face. Besides, what else is a beach day for?

Family Beach Week A to Z

by Renay Regardie

All Together It happens once a year, the family gathering, the time we long for, the time we fear, the five days we convene at our Rehoboth beach house. It's late July. Here they come, four from California, feeling a bit jet-lagged. Two days later, the five from DC burst in, dropping their shoes in the foyer. Everyone's together, two sons, two daughters-in-law, five cousins, ages four, six, eight, ten, and twelve. Bringing up the rear, we have the matriarch and patriarch. Oh, let's not forget the two cats that the parents fear will bite the youngest kids. A valid concern, I admit, but hey, how would you feel if your tail was pulled? The cousins scream and hug and kiss. The adults peck each other on the cheek and mumble "How's it going?" Finally, we're all assembled for sun and fun and the ritual of family bonding.

Brothers My sons are very different. I remember those younger years. The teenager walked tentatively down the street, his long ponytail and nine earrings, six in one ear, three in the other, camouflaging feelings of inadequacy and insecurity. His twelve-year-old sibling, reveling in his red-and-blue-striped Ralph Lauren polo and Waspy khakis, armed me in the side: "I don't want to walk next to him. He looks so strange," he pleaded, claiming his own space apart from his brother's. Now, thirty years later, two mature men, still dissimilar as to careers, hobbies, and pastimes, unite on one front. They are amazing family men, luxuriating in fatherhood.

This, and maybe the Redskins, gives them common ground.

Cousins and Children Six decades ago, when I grew up, family was always around. I can't remember a time when I was not in a howling, screaming melee of cousins, uncles, aunts, parents, and grandparents. My kids live three thousand miles apart. And this family tree has few cousins on its branches. Aside from these five, there's one a decade older, and two who are virtually invisible for reasons I don't know. My husband and I and our sons and daughters-in-law have plied the kids with the importance of family. End result, these kids yearn for time together. They Skype, they send videos, they ask, "When will we see our cousins?" They demanded to sleep together, so I disassembled my beautiful guest room for two and reinvented it as a dormitory for five with a bunk bed, two singles, and a youth bed created from a crib. It's wall-to-wall beds, but the whispers, the laughs, and yes, the fights, fill the night.

Daughters-in-Law I wished for boys and got them. Now I watch as females commandeer their broods. One sneers at gaily colored plastic toys, so I have become a major buyer of Melissa and Doug wooden ones. The other wants everything organic; how many loaves of Wonder Bread I've trashed because I forgot, I hate to tell you. Each has wailed to me about the other, yet they share recipes, exchange outgrown kids' clothes, and hunt in unison for the best deals at the outlets. Different they are, but a desire to instill family unites them during family week.

Effort Perfect, always loving families are fiction. Now that we've been together for over a decade, things improve each year. Little headway was made until both couples had children. Every year I endure the squabbles as the moms seek a uniform date for the family pilgrimage. One mom thinks the other mom scheduled day camp to start on a particular date to get her goat; the other mom thinks the West Coast school system starts early just to spoil her summer. But, all agree that the kids can't wait to see each other. We will be a family united for these few days.

Floor Plan I made a major mistake when I designed my house twenty-five years ago. My kids were teenagers. I created a large suite with an ocean view and oversized bath for guests and two equal-sized rooms for the boys. Adulthood, marriage, and kids came, and arguments erupted. "I deserve the big room; I'm not here very often," one said. "I need the room with the big bathtub for the baby," another cried. Everyone was livid and conversation was either heated or nonexistent. I timidly suggested they should rotate each year and made an emergency appointment with my therapist. Time and age have healed this catastrophe. But be forewarned. If you are building or buying a beach house, make sure the guest bedrooms are as equal in size as possible.

Grands That's what the grandkids are, whether they're playing nicely, fighting nastily, or arguing with me that it's not time to go to bed (and no, one brother did not hit a cousin with the shovel—he'd never do that—and yes, I do sneak them an extra cookie or a couple of pieces of chocolate, and I don't care if the parents read about it here).

Happiness I am happiest when everyone—all the family—comes. I am just as happy when everyone leaves.

Ice Cream I associate ice cream with the beach every bit as much as sand and surf. When we're walking downtown, we stop at Royal Treat. One gets chocolate ripple, another one gets strawberry, the adventurer gets something that looks gross, and the four-year-old dribbles all over her Gap T-shirt, but what the hell. What I like best is letting the kids make sundaes at home. Take a big scoop of chocolate, a medium one of vanilla, pour Hershey's syrup over generously (being sure to lick the spoon), spray a gob of whipped cream in your mouth and then spritz heavily on the ice cream, and top with three maraschino cherries. Now eat.

Jellyfish They arrive just as my family comes. I've watched their slimy innards spill out as the boys puncture them with a stick. I've seen one cousin pitch one at another, laughing gleefully as the younger burst into tears. I've heard the wails of the poor kid with the angry red bite. There's nothing to do but take him in your arms, and when all else fails, slip him some candy.

Kites Along with sand toys, boogie boards, bikes, trikes, Monopoly, sidewalk chalk, and bubbles, kites are things that grandparents must have at the beach house. I have selected kites carefully for each grandchild. Here's how it turned out: My older granddaughter couldn't care less that she had the princess model; she wanted her cousin's airplane kite, which he wasn't about to relinquish. My youngest grandson, who loved monkeys at the zoo, cried hysterically when he saw the monkey kite. Brothers fought over who got the red kite. And the kites in action? The dads run around vigorously, getting those kites in the air; the kids half-watch. One takes the spool and drops it, laughing as the kite plummets. The dad re-sails it, beaming with pride. Five minutes have passed, and the kids are bored. Bottom line: I'm saving my money; no more kites for me.

Lobsters and Crabs The signature event of Family Beach Week is the Lobster and Crab Extravaganza. This starts with my husband and me calculating how many crabs we need (we always overdo it), how many will actually eat lobster (I push for extra, because that's my favorite), whether we need a green vegetable (no—cole slaw and corn rule), and how many buckets of Thrasher's we need (two extra-large, and don't forget the vinegar). My oldest grandson is in charge of the claws, which he cracks, allowing the younger siblings to have a go under his professional eye. Each year I post on my refrigerator a picture of a mound of crab claws and five beaming pseudo-chefs. Of course, there's a snafu here, wouldn't you know. One grandkid only eats peanut butter and jelly, another wants cheese and avocado, and a third develops a stomachache. The adults, meanwhile, have consumed a growler of beer, a bottle of red wine, a bit of white, and all are ready for a round of Beer Pong.

Milestones My closet is the keeper of the family's growth records. The day before everyone leaves, the kids line up for height measurements and weigh-ins. The rear wall of my closet boasts lines of red, blue, green, and black. I can see when a newborn entered the family, when one boy's height shot past another, and when one broke fifty pounds. The boys stretch to be taller; the girls are young enough that they don't worry about weight. I look at the markers on the wall with joy and wonderment at my family's evolution.

Nesting Place We started coming to the shore when our kids were tykes. First, we rented at Sea Colony, delighted that they had day camp. Then, we rented a Rehoboth beachfront condo when the boys were old enough to walk the boards alone and we could gravitate to the restaurants. Finally, we built our Rehoboth house and it nurtured us. This is home.

Once a Year This small family gets together once a year, only for a few days, and it's here, at this beach house, that we nest. For my sons and my husband and me, the beach house provides familiarity, safety, a place filled with happy memories. For my grandkids, it's a place of magical experiences, a time when most everything is smiles, when every wave, every French fry, enchants. With the kids here, I taste the waves, the fries, the fudge, and I am a child again.

Photos Every two years we gear up for those whimsical, romanticized portraits of a family enjoying a perfect beach vacation. We're usually sitting in the sand, white-capped waves breaking in the background, blue skies overhead. At our last shoot we complained. "Why do we have to have a photograph at the beach again?" someone asked. "The baby needs her nap," said one parent. So we have to work around that. "We should do it at sundown," said the photographer. "But that's dinnertime," said the mothers. "So let's do it an hour before—it can't make a difference" (but it did). We primped for the occasion. I considered professional makeup to eradicate wrinkles, but relied on my own hand and Lancôme cosmetics. "Wear light blue" was the edict, but of course the brothers did not want to look alike. Faded clothes, bright pink on the baby, and wrinkled pants made statements of individuality. So there we were at the beach, sun blinding us, the kids squinting, the photographer frowning. When we got the proofs, the analyses were harsh. Critiques included: "My daughter's underpants are showing; I can't have that," "My husband looks sick," and "My head is cut off by my son's body and the shadow makes it look like I have a beard." We unhappily chose pictures. The magic of Photoshop covered the underpants, replaced a sick head with a smiley one, removed the beard and reinserted a full face. Still we said, "Oh, we look better than that." Today I have a silver-framed eight-by-twelve; there's an azure sky, and if someone is squinting it doesn't matter because everyone is smiling, and the grandkids are holding hands and beaming. Together, we are a loving and beautiful family.

Quiet Time There is none when you are at the beach with five grandkids.

Rain I pray for blue skies and hot days, but invariably sprinkles disrupt my illusions. So we have creative fun indoors. *On to the games!* Puzzles work for three or four people, backgammon for a couple. Bingo seemed like a natural winner until a young loser had a hissy fit. Favorite pastimes are: tease the cats; fight with Funland stuffed animals; and spread out all Legos, Mr. Potato Head components, and assorted other games with myriad pieces, for grandparents to clean up. Grandparents' remedy: overdose the kids on chocolate and other no-no snacks while the parents head off to

Dogfish for beers saying, "Have fun with the kids."

Sand, Sun, Surf The sun beats down, the kids are appropriately coated with ten layers of sunscreen, the sand is hot to the foot, the waves crash on the shore inviting everyone to dive in. Sure, I'm not going to be able to read that book, but who was I kidding by bringing it, anyway. I'm busy jumping waves with the four-year-old, making a sandcastle with the six-year-old, tossing the ball with the eight-year-old, gathering shells with the ten-year-old, and digging to China with the twelve-year-old.

Toys My family room has changed dramatically over the years. Our books are now crammed onto the top shelves, while the lower shelves brim with puzzles from ten to five hundred pieces, blocks, Legos of varied versions, Play-Doh, and games like Candyland, checkers, bingo, and Clue. Around the perimeter of the room, milk crates filled with stacking toys, musical toys, miniature cars, crayons, sidewalk chalk, and card games like Old Maid and Go Fish burst from their containers, covering my oriental rug. Cast-off toys spill from a chest in a corner. Creative artwork by young geniuses lies on the coffee table. My house is no longer *Architectural Digest* ready, but it's a paradise for any grandchild.

Umbrella Sitting under the beach umbrella, pushing toes into the sand—heaven. *Doesn't happen.* We load up the red wagon with two buckets, three large shovels, and sand toys, including a large castle, an octopus, a small house, two tortoises, a large orange beach ball, two tennis balls, and three kites. We plunk the youngest kid in the wagon and head to the beach. Then we unload it all and trek to that big blue umbrella with the beckoning lounge chairs. But before we sit down, one kid has to go to the bathroom, another is throwing sand at his sibling, there are shells to collect, there are waves to ride, and then guess who gets to wait for the Grotto pizza delivery.

Visit They've been here three days. I'm exhausted. My stomach's bloated from saltwater taffy and fudge. I'm not used to being woken by some little person jumping on me at 6:30 A.M. *When will this visit end?*

Waves When I lie in bed at night, the doors open, I hear the waves pounding on the shore. The grandkids love the waves, and they each handle them differently. The oldest jumps on his skimboard, undaunted by repeated spills; the next coasts in on his boogie board cautiously; the six-year-old darts tentatively in and out of the water, letting his dad's steady hand calm him; the two girls grab my hand, and we jump endlessly, laughing, until a big wave brings us down and we hug and kiss and I feel loved and loving.

Xanax Grandma's little helper.

Yard When I say, "Go out and play," there's plenty of room in a safe location. The basketball net has a hole in it after years of use, but the kids shoot more baskets every year. Misguided stomp arrows live in my trees. My driveway has served as a great training ground for young bikers. One weekend per year, the front yard becomes a commercial emporium, as the cousins run the Cool Kids Lemonade Stand. It's been an entrepreneurial success, kick-started with twenty dollars from the grandparents.

Zenith I've had a lot of highs and lows in my life. There's a lot I'm still uncertain about, but I know for sure when I sit in this beach house, when I hear the waves, when this small family bonds here for five days, when the grandkids have gone to sleep, when the parents have gone to whatever rooms they are in, that although I am at sea level, I am at a zenith in my life.

Renay Regardie built, and then sold, a business that provided market research, feasibility studies, and marketing strategy to residential home developers. Later, she published, along with her husband, a business magazine in Washington, DC. Armed with years of business writing, she turned back to her first love, writing, and began taking courses at the Rehoboth Beach Writers' Guild. She especially gives thanks to the guidance and support of Maribeth Fischer. Renay has had stories in both previous Rehoboth Beach Reads books. Her first story, "Refuge," focused on the relationship between a mother, who has Alzheimer's, and her daughter. Since then, Renay has looked at the lighter side of family life at the beach. Each summer, her two sons, two daughters-in-law, and five grandchildren meet at the beach for fun, sun, and sometimes friction. Renay splits her time among Rehoboth, Washington, DC, and Key West.

Judge's Comments

This essay story captures the heartwarming reason why days at the summertime beach are such memorable family bonding experiences, especially for the very young and grandparent-age members—those who, in other words, engage with the beach through play, laughter, and intermittent spats—and those who are indulgently delighted to help the very young explore this world by splashing in the waves and digging in the sand with them.

Somewhere Between Crab Cakes and Cocktails

by Jeanie P. Blair

Syd Reagan was never more content. She sat on the white boardwalk bench, embraced by the warmth of the morning sunrise and the sounds of waves crashing onto Rehoboth Beach and seagulls cackling overhead. As she closed her eyes, childhood memories filled her mind. She was almost certain she could hear her gram's encouraging words in the whisper of the surf, reassuring her that someday she'd realize her dream of turning their family's Laurel Street cottage into a bed-and-breakfast. "I know you'll do it, Sydney," Syd remembered her saying. "It's meant to be. This cottage would make the perfect bed-and-breakfast. There's something very special about it that brings people together. You'll see."

Her grandparents bought the house hoping it would bring their family closer together and, early on, it did just that. Syd's family, along with various aunts, uncles, and cousins, filled her grandparents' house every summer. They'd walk to the beach each day, toting enough gear to fill a U-Haul, grateful the ocean was only a half-block away. Then it was back to the house to wash up, grab some dinner, and head to the boardwalk for games and rides at Funland.

Even off-season trips became a ritual. Syd's family never missed the annual Christmas tree lighting on Rehoboth Avenue, first feasting on Grotto's Pizza and stopping at Dolle's for caramel popcorn. The memories made her smile, though only briefly. After her grandparents passed, the family gatherings stopped, and the traditions ended. Syd's parents maintained the house, but only Syd had a genuine attachment to it, and eventually, she became its primary caretaker. Although satisfied with that role, she never lost sight of her vision to make the home a bed-and-breakfast so others could enjoy it the way she had. Gram's words always kept her on track: "It's meant to be."

* * * * * *

Now that she was thirty-five, Syd couldn't wait any longer. She needed to escape the misery of her broken engagement. In a small town like Newark, Delaware, it was impossible to avoid the two who had betrayed her, and the feelings of anger and humiliation returned every time she saw them together. *Some best friend.* Meanwhile, the corporate grind, with its dreadful commute, was sapping her strength. She had come to loathe Wilmington. Though Rehoboth was barely two hours away, it seemed worlds apart from her problems, and that was where she wanted to live. Eager to realize her dream, she had saved and invested aggressively. She decided it was time to leave her old life behind. Within three months of making her decision, she sold her house, purchased the cottage from her parents, and headed for Rehoboth.

* * * * * *

Though well maintained, the cottage needed to be redesigned to make it work as a bed-and-breakfast. A couple of extra bathrooms were a necessity, and the kitchen had to be expanded to provide adequate entertaining space. Syd even considered adding a rooftop balcony, so visitors could enjoy the breathtaking views with their morning coffee or evening cocktail.

Thoughts of the renovation snapped her back to reality. Time had gotten away, and, if she didn't hurry, she'd be late for the meeting with her prospective contractor. She sprang to her feet, took one more look at the ocean, inhaled a long, deep breath of the crisp salty air, and headed for home.

* * * * * *

As he closed the door of his black Silverado, Brady Morgan paused to examine the potential job site. It was the quintessential beach cottage; a brilliant blue two-story with white trim, white stone flower beds, and a white picket fence. *Straight from the pages of* Coastal Living *magazine,* he thought. As he strode up the brick walkway, he couldn't imagine what improvements this beauty could possibly need. His buddy's dad had referred him, via a vague email with nothing more than the owner's name and address. He climbed the porch steps and tapped lightly on the door, not wanting to startle the old guy who probably owned the place.

* * * * * *

When she heard the knock on her door, Syd took a quick look in the mirror. She snatched an elastic band from her dresser and twisted her wet hair into a haphazard ponytail as she trotted down the stairs. Time had allowed for only eyeliner and lip gloss, but that would suffice. *It's not a date, for heaven's sake.* She yanked the door open, ready to do business with the contractor her neighbor had recommended. An involuntary gasp escaped when she saw the expansive chest of the six-foot-something guy with windblown hair standing before her.

"Hi. I'm Brady Morgan. I'm here to see Syd Reagan." He smiled and looked beyond her, as if he were expecting someone else.

His deep, sandpaper voice was the clincher. Syd felt the redness invading her cheeks. As she pushed open the screen door, she wanted to respond, but suddenly couldn't remember her own name.

Brady offered his hand and repeated, "Brady Morgan—to see Mr. Reagan. Your neighbor, Gus Taylor, sent me."

Snap out of it! She finally found her voice. "Oh—yes. Actually, *I'm* Syd Reagan." She extended her clammy palm, but not before swiping it on her denim shorts, hoping he didn't notice. He gingerly clenched her hand, as if shaking the hand of a child. Annoyed, she returned an extra-firm squeeze. "Please, come in," she said, stepping aside to let him in.

"Thanks. So, *you're* Syd, huh?" he asked.

"Yes. You seem surprised."

"I wasn't expecting a girl."

A girl? She cringed. *Strike two.* "Is that a problem for you?"

"Uh, no, I just expected a guy." Brady pointed to the email on his clipboard and continued. "It's just that—well, Syd is usually a man's name, and Gus didn't tell me—"

"Whatever. Let me show you what I need to have done." Wanting to let him know that she was no frail princess, she added, "I've already done some of the work myself, but unfortunately, some of the tasks require a licensed contractor to meet code."

As he followed her beyond the foyer, Syd tried to act cool but was irritated with herself. She never came unglued around men and was determined that this arrogant ass wouldn't be the exception. *Okay, just chill. It's business. You're not marrying the jerk.*

Room by room, they addressed each item on Syd's wish list. She was pleased to find that Brady concurred with her ideas, and was impressed when he suggested options that made more efficient use of the space. He clearly knew his stuff. When they returned to the front door, he recorded the last few details, then tucked his pen in his shirt pocket.

"Thanks for letting me take a look," he said. "You have a beautiful home here. I'll have an estimate for you soon."

"Great. Can't wait to get started," she replied.

"Same here," he said as he shook her hand, looking her in the eye as he squeezed it firmly.

She pulled her hand back, trying to be cool. "Okay—well—thanks again."

"My pleasure."

Against her better judgment, Syd watched him walk to his truck. He paused as he opened the door and looked back toward her. *Busted.* He grinned and winked at her before sliding in. *He knows he got to me and is proud of himself. Pompous ass.*

* * * * * *

With Brady's help, Syd spent the next few weeks choosing the final materials for the renovation. They made store trips to select paint, flooring, fixtures, and appliances. He even offered to help her prepare the house for the work. Considering her initial impression of Brady and his ego, Syd was relieved that their working relationship was turning out to be surprisingly pleasant.

After significant progress had been made, Syd decided to allow herself a weekend on the beach to reenergize. It was just after Labor Day, her favorite time of year. The chaos of the summer, with its hordes of vacationers, was over, but it was still warm enough to lie in the sun or take a dip in the ocean. She basked in the bright sunlight, her chair set at the water's edge. She rested her head back and closed her eyes, enjoying the harmonious opus of waves and gulls. When she felt herself nodding off, she didn't fight it.

"Well, hey there. I thought that was you. Uh—Syd, are you okay?"

What? It seemed to be raining, but there hadn't been a cloud in the sky. Confused, she opened her eyes and was shocked to find a wet, shirtless Brady Morgan crouching over her, seawater dripping from his lean, tan body.

"Sorry, I didn't mean to scare you," he said. "I was taking a swim and spotted you. Just thought I'd stop and say hi."

"Oh, uh—hi." *Well, wasn't that just the epitome of eloquence.*

"I barely recognized you"—he eyed her head to toe—"in the bikini and sunglasses."

Suddenly feeling naked, she scrambled for her towel.

Brady reached behind her chair. "Looking for this?" he said, her towel in his hand. "Sorry I dripped all over you."

She snatched the towel from him and flung it over her exposed skin. "Oh. No problem." She tried to be nonchalant, but knew she was failing miserably.

"Hey, if you're free later, would you like to grab some dinner? Maybe hit Woody's for some crab cakes?"

What? Did he just ask me out? "Um, I would, but I uh—" she stammered. *Worst. Liar. Ever.*

"I'd really like to go over some last-minute ideas with you. Figured we could grab a bite while we're at it. No strings," he continued.

No. Strings. Two words that were the kiss of death to most women but should be music to her ears. *Should be.* So why was she so disappointed? "Uh, sure. I have no plans." *Great. Way to call yourself a loser.*

He stood and flashed a brilliant smile. "Cool. Pick you up at six?"

"Okay. Sounds great," she said, finally getting a few words out without faltering.

As he jogged away, she checked the time and decided she'd better head home to get ready for her date—er—meeting with Brady.

* * * * * *

Taking one final glance in the mirror, Syd decided she was satisfied with her outfit, a sleeveless floral maxi dress and sandals. Attractive, yet not something she'd typically wear to impress a date. Her loose auburn curls draped her shoulders. She opted for only a light brush of mascara and a swipe of tinted lip balm. When the doorbell rang, she took a deep breath and headed downstairs, pausing to reassure herself. *You've got this. It's just business.*

She opened the door, and her subconscious cheerleader instantly clammed up. *Damn he cleaned up well.* Brady leaned against the door jamb. He wore jeans, a black untucked button-down shirt, and distressed Doc Marten boots. Wavy chestnut hair framed his tanned face, a five o'clock shadow accentuating his strong jaw. When a soft breeze carried the intoxicating scent of Polo Black to her nose, she thanked God he spoke first.

"Hi. Sorry I'm early. Are you ready to go or do you need a few more minutes?"

"Don't I look ready?"

"Actually, you do, Ms. Reagan. I was just about to tell you how beautiful you look."

Wow. Didn't see that coming. She dialed back the defensive. "Oh. Why, thank you. You clean up pretty well yourself, *Mr. Morgan.*" As he swept open the screen door, he flashed a shameless side-smile. As she brushed past him, she couldn't resist another deep, exhilarating whiff, praying he didn't notice.

They spent the ride into Dewey discussing their interests, which she discovered were surprisingly parallel. During dinner they reviewed the final renovation plans. As the conversation carried over to dessert and cocktails, Brady asked about the history of the cottage and how she came to own it. Syd found him unexpectedly easy to open up to. She inadvertently found herself talking about her broken engagement, something she rarely did, as she found it so painful. When Brady's intense gaze turned soft and sympathetic, she froze. The last thing she wanted was for him to pity her. Her eyes shot to her watch. "Wow, it's almost ten. We'd better go. I have an early day tomorrow."

"Yeah, same here," Brady said, summoning their server for the check.

As he examined it, Syd opened her purse. "What do I owe?" she asked.

"Nothing. It's on me," he said, pulling a Benjamin from his wallet.

"I can't let you do that," she protested.

"I insist. Consider it a thank-you for the job."

Oh, right, she reminded herself, *just business.*

"Your treat next time," he said. "We'll grab a cone from Kohr Brothers."

Next time? "Deal," she said, trying not to overthink his words.

As they pulled into her driveway, Brady's phone chimed. He peered at the screen, seemingly puzzled. "Excuse me, I need to take this." He tapped the screen and put the phone to his ear. "Hey, sweetheart, what's up?"

Sweetheart? She suddenly felt a chill.

"Sure I can," he continued. "Tell Mommy I'll be home soon, okay? Love you, too."

What the hell? This bastard is married with kids? He started to speak, but she wouldn't give him the satisfaction.

Angry tears welled up in her eyes as she shot from the truck. "Goodnight." She was barely able to choke out that one word before slamming the door.

Brady jumped out of the pickup calling out to her, "Syd, wait!" He started up the walkway after her, but in a flash she was inside the house, door bolted, porch light extinguished.

* * * * * *

Over the next few days, Brady tried desperately to reach Syd. He placed calls and left messages, none of which she returned. He even scanned the beach each day, to no avail. He needed to know what was wrong. No more pointless phone calls. He *had* to see her.

* * * * * *

After three days of brooding, Syd had no tears left. She was still angry with herself for allowing another man into her head and, worse yet, her heart. One month ago, she could barely tolerate him. Now, here she was, devastated that he was out of her life. *When did things change? Obviously, somewhere between the crab cakes and cocktails.*

Refusing to allow herself to slide any further down the humiliation spiral, she forced herself out of bed and decided it was time to move on. Opting for a run in the fresh sea air to clear her head, she laced up her sneakers and headed downstairs. She opened the front door and almost fell backwards. Standing right in front of her was the infidel himself, fist raised, about to knock. While her initial instinct was to slam the door, she couldn't help but pause when she noticed the concern in his eyes and the worry lines that creased his forehead.

"Syd—" His eyes were wide, as if surprised she'd answered the door.

"I have nothing to say to you," she interjected, and started to close the door.

"Wait," he said, palming the door. "I don't understand. Please. Just tell me what's wrong."

"Seriously? You *really* need to ask?" she snapped.

A couple walking their dog caught her eye. Though she wanted to unload on him, she didn't want her neighbors witnessing it. She sighed, stepped back, and let him in. *Best to get it over with.* "Brady, I've decided it would be best for both of us if I hired another contractor."

"What? You think *that's* what I'm worried about?"

"You bought me dinner. I opened up to you. You even told me I looked—"

"Beautiful. You *did* look beautiful. What's wrong with that? I thought we were having a really good time together," he said.

"We were. Right up until you took the call from your kid."

"My kid?" He paused. "Oh shit, Sydney. I started to tell you about that, but you flew out of the truck before I had a chance. That wasn't—"

Convinced he was lying, she interrupted. "Don't. Just go."

When she started to turn away, he stopped her, gripping her shoulders. "Syd. That wasn't my kid. It was my niece. My sister's lowlife husband took off and left the two of them. She had to sell her house, so they're staying with me until they find a new place. My niece called to ask if I'd pick up some ice cream on my way home. That's it. I swear."

She glared at him, determined to maintain eye contact. He never even blinked. *He's telling the truth.* She suddenly felt like an idiot. "Brady, I—"

He released her. "Look, I know we got off on the wrong foot. But somewhere along the way I—" His blue eyes glared at her beneath his furrowed brow.

"You what?" she asked.

He closed his eyes and turned his head away.

"Look at me. Tell me what you were going to say," she persisted.

"Nothing. Forget it."

"Just say it."

He stood there silent, hands on his hips, staring at the floor.

"Brady, why can't you just be straight with me?"

He inhaled deeply. "Because," he paused, combing his fingers through his hair, "I don't want to lose you."

Confusion flooded her mind. "Lose me?"

"Because. I have feelings for you, Syd." He grasped her hands. "Listen, I know you have no interest in a relationship, and I'll find a way to live with that. But I can't live with losing you completely. If that means we can only be friends, then so be it."

A tear streaked down her cheek. "Brady, I—"

He stopped her. "See, I knew it would upset you. I never should've said—"

"Brady." She pressed a finger to his lips. "I'm not upset."

"Then why are you crying?"

"Because I'm happy, you big dork." She giggled through her tears. "But you said—"

"I know what I said."

"So why the change of heart?" he asked.

"Because I feel the same way."

He took her face in his hands and planted a deep, lingering kiss on her lips. As they parted, Syd smiled. She had suddenly recalled something her grandmother had once said.

"What is it?" Brady asked.

"When we first met, we could barely tolerate each other. But as we spent more time together, things changed."

"Things did change," he agreed. "It must be this magnificent old house."

"It *is* this house," she said, "My gram always said this house was special and that it brought people together. She was right about that. But she also knew that one day I would realize my dream. And she was right about that, too."

JEANIE PITRIZZI BLAIR IS A LIFELONG RESIDENT OF DELAWARE AND CURRENTLY RESIDES IN NEWARK WITH HER HUSBAND, SAM, AND THEIR TWO MINIATURE SCHNAUZERS. SHE HAS HAD A PENCHANT FOR READING, WRITING, AND THE ENGLISH LANGUAGE SINCE SHE WAS A CHILD, WHICH SHE ATTRIBUTES LARGELY TO HER GRADE SCHOOL ENGLISH TEACHERS. THROUGHOUT HER CAREER IN OFFICE ADMINISTRATION, SHE ALWAYS DREAMED OF SOMEDAY BEING A SUCCESSFUL ROMANCE NOVELIST. THANKS TO THE ENCOURAGEMENT OF HER FAMILY AND FRIENDS, JEANIE DECIDED TO ENTER THIS YEAR'S REHOBOTH BEACH READS CONTEST. THOUGH THIS IS HER FIRST PUBLISHED SHORT STORY, SHE PREVIOUSLY HAD A POEM PUBLISHED THROUGH A NATIONAL POETRY CONTEST. SHE CURRENTLY HAS SEVERAL WORKS IN PROGRESS AND HOPES TO HAVE HER FIRST FULL-LENGTH NOVEL PUBLISHED SOON. JEANIE HAS SPENT HER WHOLE LIFE VACATIONING AT THE BEACH, THE INSPIRATION AND SETTING FOR MANY OF HER STORIES. SHE GREATLY ENJOYS SPENDING TIME WITH HER FAMILY IN LONG NECK.

The Debutante Learns to Drive

by Matthew Hastings

When she was twenty-five and her husband was killed in an air raid over Berlin, Charlotte froze with grief. After a month of Charlotte being shell-shocked, Mummy, as she could be counted on doing, decided that enough was enough. She told Charlotte that when people hold on to their pain, they embrace it and cultivate it, the way an orchid lover patiently tends and nurtures his blooms. If they are blessed, it becomes something positive, something beautiful, something precious. But other times, pain is like a familiar ache or twinge. You live with it and tell yourself it is nothing, but it never really goes away; it is always there and you can count on it to leave a vacuum, a burning black hole in your heart, a cancer. Mummy told Charlotte that she should either join a religious order or move on; she was becoming boring.

As years passed, Charlotte Shippen Rush became hard to miss and even more difficult to avoid. She was now somewhere between fifty and eighty, hit five feet tall on a good day, and just might tip the scales at one hundred pounds. She had a signature panda skunk look—with Dusty Springfield thickly mascaraed eyes, and raven-black hair in a color-coordinated beaded snood with a white streak down the middle. On anyone else it would look slightly demented; on Charlotte it was elegant and chic.

During the Rehoboth summer, Charlotte made at least two public appearances each day. At ten o'clock every morning in front of the library, the door of her enormous, mirror-polished 1949 Packard woody was opened by her stately black chauffeur (who was also her butler), and she emerged camera-ready to conduct her errands. Rare was the day when she could walk half a block without being stopped for a chat or asked to pose next to her car with a tourist's family. Thus, she was immortalized on countless Christmas cards.

Few could remember a Rehoboth summer without Miss Charlotte. She was as much a local institution as the Dolle's saltwater taffy sign, the World War II guard towers, and the speed traps. The thing about Charlotte was that she was always delighted to happen upon you. If she had met you twenty years earlier, she would remember you and the conversation. She was interested in whatever was going on with you, your family, or your business. She never judged, and even though she was richer than Oprah, be you the vice president or a waitress, everyone got the same treatment. She was quick to tease, compliment, and encourage. You found yourself smiling and laughing, even when you disagreed with her. You walked away feeling good, feeling optimistic. She was, however, anything but a kind, harmless little old lady. When something occurred in Rehoboth that she felt was inappropriate, it rarely occurred twice.

Her other daily appearance occurred about an hour before sunset. Her bathtub on wheels with its one-digit license plate would sail down Rehoboth Avenue toward its berth.

"Right there," she would direct her driver, pointing to their usual spot, which strictly forbade parking. "Not too close."

People on the beach and boardwalk, thinking a reality TV show was being filmed, would stop swimming, shopping, and sun-burning to watch, as her driver emerged and proceeded to set up the blue-and-white-striped cabana and place matching chairs and enormous hamper on the beach. Charlotte and two plump, indulged Westies, always named Fergus and India, made a little parade following the driver as he gently carried Charlotte's paraplegic brother Lucas Shippen, a frail-looking elderly gentleman in white flannel trousers, blazer, and straw boater, to the Riviera-quality tableau. The patrician siblings sipped ice-cold martinis, talked, and laughed as they nibbled on artisanal hors d'oeuvres, celebrating the end of a fine day together.

The Shippens had always been a law unto themselves—never feeling the need to explain or justify. You were therefore rarely surprised by what a Shippen did or said, but a month after Charlotte's death, when her beneficiaries were made public, even the most stalwart blinked twice. The size of her estate was no surprise. What was outrageous was who got the loot. Charlotte, some said, had gone too far—even for a Shippen.

Two sisters from Manitoba, one a nurse and one a schoolteacher, who could vaguely remember their late parents mentioning some lady in Delaware, hadn't a clue why they were left a third of Charlotte's fortune. The second third—the Packard woody, the eight-bedroom cottage, and the current Fergus and India—went to the children of her butler of sixty years. The final third was left to endow rabbinical school scholarships to honor the late, great Hasidic scholar Simon Burshtin.

Leaving money to strangers and servants is one thing, but leaving it to honor the memory of an arch-conservative leader of Hasidic Jews, who certainly had no time for the liberal, liberated, free-spirited philosophy of someone like Charlotte, is quite another.

Charlotte had spent the war in London, where, as she had been told to say, she trained nurses. She returned home in the spring of 1946 and did what was expected; she resumed her life of responsible privilege in her parents' Philadelphia Main Line mansion. Mummy had decided that what Charlotte needed was a replacement for Angus, her dead war-hero husband. To Mummy, it was a miracle that Charlotte had ever married, and to a Rush at that, without her guidance. Mummy was not waiting for a second miracle.

Charlotte and her mother were not cut from the same cloth. Mummy was silk. Charlotte was boiled wool. Charlotte spoke to strangers, and could do so effortlessly, in three languages. Charlotte's friends were "interesting" and not always in the *Social Register*. She could keep a confidence. She majored in chemistry at Wellesley. She found something fascinating in every person she met. She got right to the point. Kind people said she was "refreshing" and "original." Others simply said "strange."

Mummy was stunned when Charlotte announced there would be no husband-hunting campaign. Her excuse was that no man under forty would marry a woman who could not have children. In reality, no man would measure up to Angus, who as time passed was becoming more perfect in every way. Charlotte announced that she would start her new life by spending the summer in Rehoboth. She would take the butler's son, who needed a job, and Emma, his pretty English war-bride wife, whose cooking was addicting. That Mummy didn't do Rehoboth, she did Isle au Haut, was not entirely coincidental.

Angus and Charlotte had fled to Rehoboth as soon as the wedding bouquet had been tossed. There, they played house until Angus shipped out, never to return. When Angus's will was read, Charlotte learned that Angus had bequeathed her the old Rush family cottage in the Pines and so much money that even Mummy gasped.

Settled in Rehoboth with a brand-new butler and cook, Charlotte felt a little less sad. She gardened, gossiped at the market, took painting classes, played tennis and bridge, read Jane Austen for the umpteenth time, and gave and went to parties. Every afternoon she'd take the butler's and Emma's sweet café au lait son for a boardwalk stroller ride. She secretly enjoyed staring down the disparaging looks and ugly mutters from people who thought the baby was hers. *I should be so blessed*, she thought.

Then. Everything. Changed.

She had seen him on the beach three nights in a row on her sunset walkies with the wee beasties. He stood at the water's edge, fully clothed in a formal dark suit and old-fashioned hat, staring statue-like at the far-off lights from ships and Cape May. At first, she imagined him to be Amish, but then, learned otherwise. On the fourth night, Charlotte stopped and introduced herself. He looked at her as if she had said something obscene. His hair was a shade of red she'd not often seen. The silence was broken only by the waves. Despite being flustered—his manners left something to be desired—Charlotte was not deterred.

She mentioned that he was the first Hasidic person she'd seen in Rehoboth and asked if this was his first summer. His eyes bore into her, saying nothing. Charlotte decided propriety had been met and began to walk away. She was a few steps away when he spoke.

He asked her if she knew the stars. He was searching for Capricorn. His voice was kind, firm, and somehow tender. He apologized for his rudeness. No one had spoken to him in the two weeks he had been in Rehoboth. Charlotte was the first.

He had an eight-sentence life story. He had been a diamond cutter in Antwerp. He had escaped to Cuba and waited seven years for a visa. He was alone; his family had been exterminated. He'd arrived in America six months before. He had been lent a cottage in Rehoboth for the summer by a friend's friend. He was recovering from a drawn-out influenza. He was studying to become a rabbi. He was to marry in September. For one of the few times in her life, Charlotte did not know what to say.

They had nothing in common. She was a war widow. He was engaged to a woman he had never met. She was a grieving twelfth-generation blue-blooded Philadelphia debutante who rode with the hounds, sailed competitively, and took her bridge game a tad too seriously. He was an off-the-boat religious scholar, with no family, in a conservative, almost reactionary, Jewish sect where the men dressed in black with tall hats and distinctive locks of hair on either side of their heads, and the women shaved their heads and wore wigs when they married. She was bright, sparkling, and independent. He was reserved, commanding, and austere. They were chalk and cheese; their worlds weren't just different, they conflicted. To her, his world was strange, forbidding, mysterious, and almost cultish. To him, her world was empty, superficial, and devoid of meaning. He was forbidden from touching or even shaking hands with a woman not his wife. That they would have a love affair was utterly inconceivable.

And yet they did. The next night, she asked him to join her on her beach walk. Soon, they were sharing their most private and intimate thoughts and fears and worries and dreams. While they agreed on nothing, neither could remember laughing so much. After much prodding and encouragement, he agreed to remove his shoes and socks to walk with her in the surf, always in his suit. After the first week, they met nightly at his cottage. Just before dawn after the nights they were together, he walked Charlotte home through the woods. They could taste the salt in the sea mist as they shared their last hidden kiss. Her loss of Angus suddenly seemed bearable. With her, he was a stranger to himself, both frightened and intrigued. They did not discuss the future.

In late August, he said that in ten days he would be returning to Brooklyn. The wedding rituals had to be observed. Charlotte insisted they spend every moment together, day and night, until he left. If her butler and Emma thought there was anything unusual about Miss Charlotte having a Hasidic holy man as a houseguest, they did not let on. Charlotte's friends were so accustomed to her eccentric behavior that, while this fellow was different, he seemed like just one more oddball in Charlotte's ever-expanding world of oddballs. No one could imagine the two of them being anything more than friends. After all, they were from different worlds.

On their last day together, they each took a roll of snapshots of the other. He went to the train station alone and was gone. They had not exchanged addresses. It was over.

After their two months together Charlotte was two months wiser, two months happier, two months less empty. She resumed her life of good deeds and counted the days to confirm what she had been told all her life would never happen. Six weeks later she was stunned when the doctor in Salisbury, diplomatically ignoring the lack of a wedding ring on Mrs. Smith's finger, told her the impossible had, in fact, occurred.

This would be the only child Charlotte would ever have. It would be a child she would never know. Rehoboth was a small town, and her Philadelphia friends had even smaller minds. Suspicion would certainly be cast his way, and such talk would destroy his marriage and his life.

One advantage of being a law unto themselves was that Shippens didn't particularly care what other people thought of them and what they did to secure happiness. Charlotte would have kept the child, scandalizing her world without a second thought, but the risk of destroying the man she loved was too great.

She left before Thanksgiving, and by late June, Charlotte was back in Rehoboth from an extended European tour. She bought a small farm in the countryside that Andrew Wyeth had painted and slowly spun out of Mummy's orbit. Later, when Lucas was crippled in a car accident, he came to live with Charlotte. Always close, now they would be together for the rest of their lives.

Her ginger-haired lover had become a renowned scholar and professor. His books were bestsellers; he was labeled the Jewish Billy Graham and counted Eleanor Roosevelt as a friend. They saw each other only once in sixty years, on the wooden escalators at Macy's in New York. She was headed down; he was coming up. They stared silently at each other as they slowly faded away. Charlotte abandoned her opera companion and fled home on the next train.

Three days after she turned seventy, Charlotte received a letter from Brittle, Manitoba, written by a lady veterinarian making a genealogical inquiry. Only she wasn't. The woman's research had led her to the name "Caroline Smith." She said she hoped Mrs. Rush might have knowledge that she could share.

As it happened, Mrs. Rush did. "Caroline Smith" was the name she'd used when the adoption papers were signed. Despite the layers of secrecy, this woman had found her. Charlotte was excited, terrified, ashamed, and confused—most unlike a Shippen.

She wrote and told the woman that if she was who she claimed to be, then Charlotte was who she hoped she was. She wrote that the woman's father had been engaged to another and had never known she had had their child. She wrote that she had thought of her daughter every day of her life and that she was overjoyed to connect. She asked to correspond before they spoke or met; she wanted to take this slowly. Charlotte was afraid of losing her daughter a second time.

For three months they exchanged two or three letters weekly. They sent one another photographs, sketches, book reviews, poetry, and favorite recipes—well, Emma's favorites. Her daughter never asked about her father and Charlotte never revealed more. She was interested in Charlotte's family medical history. They teased one another about how different they were. Charlotte was shocked, and then pleased, when it became apparent that her daughter was very much like Mummy, only sensitive to others' feelings, and her granddaughters were very much like her, only more self-confident.

The letters stopped as abruptly as they started.

Then a phone call from Manitoba—her daughter's husband. He told Charlotte his wife had died an hour before, after a long battle with cancer; Charlotte was the first to be told. He said Charlotte's letters had meant the world to his wife, filling a hole in her heart. Charlotte felt as she had when Angus had died—numb, then angry, and then resigned. She could not intrude into her daughter's family; her loving adoptive parents and her daughters had never been told about Charlotte. The husband promised to keep in touch and to send news and photos. Her granddaughters would be told Charlotte was a family friend. And that was that.

Ten years later, Lucas and Emma died in the same month. Charlotte could no longer pretend she would live forever. Time was running out. She had put it off too long. He had a right to know. Her lawyers wrote to him, indicating that Mrs. Rush was interested in endowing a scholarship at his rabbinical college. Mrs. Burshtin responded with the news that her husband was quite ill. He had been humbled by Mrs. Rush's generous offer and had asked if they could meet, sooner rather than later.

Charlotte stood in the rain three days later as his wife shyly answered the door. Charlotte was shown into the library of a well-maintained, but very simply furnished, Brooklyn brownstone. He apologized for not rising. She couldn't think of what to say. His wife poured tea and then left the room, closing the door, leaving them alone.

They sat in silence. Suddenly, he spoke. His voice had not changed; it was still soft, still gentle. He asked if she had ever worn a different perfume, he remembered this one so well. He asked if she ever finished the landscape she started on their picnic on Assateague. He asked if she still liked to sing and if she still sang off-key. He asked if she still had the cook whose food was magical. He asked if she had ever admitted that her only fear was that of driving. He asked if she had ever published her beautiful haiku poems and if she still shopped at Macy's. He kept asking questions and Charlotte sat there, saying nothing. Finally, he asked why she had come.

Charlotte opened her purse, and with her hands shaking, slowly removed five photos, three of her daughter and two of her granddaughters, each with the same shade of red hair as his. He took them one at a time and stared intently. His face had been a pasty white; it suddenly became flushed and almost as red as a sunburn.

He knew without being told. He asked what their daughter's name was, and if their granddaughters and she were as spirited as Charlotte. He asked to hear the story. Charlotte told him everything. Her words seemed to have a life of their own. She finished with the death of a daughter neither had met, neither had held, neither had known.

His eyes filled with tears and he reached for her hands. His voice was broken, almost a whisper. He looked her in the eyes and slowly said that in his life two people had loved him and sacrificed their lives for him; his brother who gave him his visa to Cuba and was swept up in the Holocaust, and Charlotte who had given up the only child she would ever have to protect his reputation. He said that he was grateful and undeserving and sad. He looked up and smiled, he said at the same time he was so happy to know that the Lord had created a part of them that would live on.

She asked if he still had the photos they had taken their final day. He smiled, opened a drawer in his desk, and removed his roll of film. It had never been developed. Charlotte reached into her purse and showed him her roll of film, also never developed. They both laughed. All those years, Charlotte thought, and only their memories and their moment at Macy's to hold on to—no photos, no tokens, no souvenirs.

They sat and talked and teased each other as if it were days, not decades, between Rehoboth Beach and Brooklyn. Too soon, it was time to leave. He thanked Charlotte again for her bravery and her love. He began to say that he wished, but then he stopped. It needn't be spoken; they both knew that in a sense they'd never parted, never forgotten. They held one another tightly one last time.

Her sunglasses hid her wet eyes as she walked out of the house into the bright sunshine. She slid into the backseat and hardly noticed as the door was closed and they drove off. A few blocks away she snapped out of her trance and asked her butler to stop. She got out and sat in the front seat. The butler was not surprised; if there as one thing certain about Miss Charlotte it was that you could count on her doing the exact opposite of what was expected. "I'm going to watch you very carefully," she told him. "And when we return to Rehoboth, would you be so kind as to teach me to drive?"

THIS IS THE SECOND OF WHAT THREATENS TO BE A SERIES OF SHORT STORIES BY MATTHEW HASTINGS ABOUT A PATRICIAN, ECCENTRIC, AND RATHER COMPLICATED FAMILY AND THEIR SERVANTS, WHO SUMMER AT REHOBOTH BEACH. THIS PIECE JOINS THE INNUMERABLE LETTERS, STORIES, AND PROFESSIONAL ARTICLES; TWO UNPUBLISHABLE MURDER MYSTERIES; AND FOUR EULOGIES THAT HAVE FLOWED FROM MAT'S KEYBOARD. HE DIVIDES HIS TIME AMONG DC, REHOBOTH, AND A SMALL ISLAND OFF THE COAST OF MAINE. WHILE MAT IS CONTINUALLY ASKED BY TOTAL STRANGERS HOW HE CAN BE SO HANDSOME, SO ACCOMPLISHED, SO DEBONAIR, AND SO WITTY (SMALL MINDS NOTE THAT NONE OF THESE INQUIRIES HAVE EVER ACTUALLY BEEN DOCUMENTED), HE SOMEHOW MANAGES TO REMAIN UNDERSTATED AND HUMBLE—TO A POINT.

I Do

by Glory Aiken

The first postcard arrived on Saturday.

"Remember when we walked on the beach?" the postcard said. "I do."

Like many actors, Russell was used to getting communications from strangers. People he'd never met sent him congratulatory messages, fan letters, sometimes a birthday card. They'd leave flowers at his doorstep, the odd stuffed animal. But a postcard, never. Postcards are not in style, they're hard to find, old-fashioned.

What kind of person writes postcards in this day and age? Russell turned the postcard over. The beach scene reminded him of something. *Could this be Rehoboth Beach? The beach where Leslie vanished, disappeared without a trace more than ten years ago?*

"Jan," he called from the kitchen. "I'm going to the theater now. Short cast meeting, costumes, and then I'll be home. The mail's here. I'm leaving it on the kitchen table." He glanced quickly at the rest of the mail, tossed it on the kitchen table, and headed for the door.

He closed the front door behind him and got into the car for the short drive to the theater. Just as he was about to pull away from the curb, he stopped the car. Opening the car door, he sprinted up the driveway, taking the stairs two at a time.

"It's me again, Jan. Forgot something," he shouted up the stairs as he tucked the postcard neatly into his backpack. "Bye. See you later this afternoon."

The second postcard came exactly one week later.

His fingers slid over the glossy, slick surface. "We sat on the beach and watched the dolphins swim," the script said. "Do you remember? I do."

He sighed out loud as Jan came into the room. "Russ," said Jan, sliding her arm through his, "did someone send you a postcard? I didn't know you liked the ocean—the beach scene reminds me of Rehoboth. Have you been there?"

Russ didn't know how to answer. There was a lot he'd kept from Jan. It was easier to have a secret and not tell. Easier to play the role of a happy, unconcerned husband than to confront the tragedy.

"No," he replied. "I've never been there. I have no idea what this postcard is all about. Probably from a deranged fan with a vivid imagination. Come on, get your coat, we don't want to be late for dinner."

Getting into the car, Russell frowned. *How would anyone but Leslie know about Rehoboth?*

The third postcard arrived exactly one week after the second.

"One last swim before dinner and I'll be happy," it said. "I'll be at the house. Do you remember that night? I do."

Russell's hand shook as he held the postcard. He took a deep breath to calm himself. He remembered that night, the night the fog crept silently in over the ocean. It must have looked harmless to you, my dear wife, harmless, even charming, in a way. A soft pillow that enveloped you as you waded into the warm, shallow water, and then swam past the breakers, into the fog and out of sight.

He recalled his worry when Leslie didn't return from her swim, his panic when he realized the lifeguards were no longer on duty. The feeling, when he ran from the house, stood on the beach, and saw that the fog lay like a blanket over the ocean, its tendrils drifting on the soft wind toward the shore.

Russell held the postcard tenderly between his hands. He felt that he was being called, summoned for something he did not understand and could not explain. He felt an undeniable longing to be in Rehoboth.

"Jan, you're not going to believe this, but a college friend just texted me. I have just enough time to have a beer with him before we go to dinner. You don't mind if I go out for a couple of hours, do you?" Russell didn't wait for an answer. He put the phone in his pocket, grabbed his keys, and got into the car. Ninety minutes, he thought. Just an hour and a half drive to Rehoboth.

* * * * * *

Russell parked the car on Rehoboth Avenue and turned off the engine. Without hesitation, he got out, walked down the street, and turned left into a narrow alley. He strode past the Coffee Mill and then turned right on Baltimore Avenue toward the boardwalk. *Right here,* thought Russell. *The beach house we rented was right on this block. We were so happy, so very happy.*

Russell continued on to the boardwalk and then walked onto the sand. He stopped and looked out at the ocean. He saw the ghostly form of a dolphin as it crested through the calm water. Wisps of fog greeted his outstretched hands. The mist dampened his hair and shrouded his clothing. The rhythmic sound of the waves rippled toward him, inviting him in.

Taking off his shoes, Russell stepped into the water. A peaceful silence enveloped him. He took a few more steps toward the breakers as the fog surrounded him, comforting him, as it quieted the ocean's sound.

Leslie, thought Russell as he felt the saltwater wash over him, *I never wanted to say goodbye. And I remember. I do.*

Glory and her husband, John, moved to Easton, Maryland, in 2012 after living in Michigan for more than forty years. Glory began to write memoir, essay, and short fiction stories after retiring from a career in the pharma/biotech field. She is a member of the Eastern Shore Writers Association. Glory also enjoys facilitating a class for memoir writers for the Academy for Lifelong Learning at the Chesapeake Bay Maritime Museum. "I Do" is her first published work.

New Beginnings at the Beach

by Barbara Nuzzo

"Run, Maddie, run! We've almost got it." I jogged alongside my daughter until the brisk April breeze grabbed hold and whisked our kite into the cloudless sky. "We did it!"

"We did it!" she chorused.

"And you know what that means?"

"It's really spring," she cheered. I helped her give the string some slack, and the colorful kite soared higher, darting left and right over the ocean like a hyperactive seagull.

Thanks to my husband, Brian, spring officially arrives when we fly our first kite of the season on the beach in Rehoboth. He taught me his novel approach to celebrating the end of winter when we were kids. We flew our kites at the beach on the first sunny day our parents would allow us to go, wearing light jackets instead of bulky winter coats. I thought it was a real holiday until I realized we were the only ones there. For Brian and me, it became an annual tradition that lasted through high school, college, courtship, and marriage. We couldn't wait to pass it on to a passel of children.

I'll always remember how Brian rescheduled spring the year Maddie was born. He was on tour in Iraq, so we postponed our first beach outing until his leave came through. I ignored lots of perfect kite-flying opportunities through late March, April, and May. He came home on a hot day early in June. Who cared that it was almost summer? We unwrapped Maddie's first kite and loaded the stroller and our picnic lunch into the car. It was finally time to celebrate her, us, and spring at the beach. That was the only year we ever encountered other kite fliers on our special day.

Brian redeployed for another tour, that time to Afghanistan. We lost him before Maddie's third birthday, and like so many other special memories Brian had inspired, I vowed to carry on his spring ritual.

So here I was, on Maddie's sixth spring-at-the-beach celebration. As the kite rose higher, I took over. Encouraged by the stiff wind, I juggled the spool in one hand and unreeled several yards of string with the other. When Maddie's laughter rang out, I released even more.

I'd left our blanket, Maddie's backpack, and our picnic bag on the sand near the boardwalk. Now that the kite was airborne, I saw Maddie heading that way and realized her squeals of delight had nothing to do with the path of our kite. Her attention was focused on a boardwalk bench several yards away.

"Mom, Bonnie's here," Maddie shouted, running to greet her favorite golden retriever. I smiled, knowing that our neighbors, Sharon and Dan, had arrived.

Edging along in the direction Maddie had gone, I spotted her romping with the dog, but the man holding the leash wasn't Dan, and Sharon wasn't there either.

"No, Maddie," I shouted. *What was she doing? She knew not to talk to strangers.* "Maddie, wait." I dropped the spool and rushed after her, releasing an endless run of string as it fell in the sand. Without warning, a burst of wind snapped it up. The string swirled out of reach and then settled here, there, and everywhere on my body. Whirling around to regain control made things worse. I was becoming ensnared in a mass of string that tightened with every step. Struggling against the pull from the kite and the instability of the sand, I somehow reached her.

"Maddie, that isn't Bonnie." I steadied my hands and held her tight, but my heart thudded. "She just looks like her."

"No, it's really her, Mom," Maddie insisted.

"Excuse me, but she's right. It is Bonnie," the tall, dark-haired man answered. He stroked Bonnie's sleek, golden coat and jingled the red collar she always wore. "I'm Dan's cousin, Larry. He surprised Sharon with a weekend away, so I'm dog-sitting."

"Oh," I said. Relief helped smooth the raw edges of panic. This must be the cousin Dan always talks about. I noticed a similarity to Dan in the shape of his face, but his dimples confirmed the family resemblance the minute he smiled.

He offered his hand, "And you are…"

"Erin," I replied, still breathless and anxious to untangle myself. "And this is my daughter, Madison." I pulled at the string. It clung like a spider web.

"Yes, Maddie. I heard." He glanced at Maddie and knelt to speak to her. "You're a fan of Bonnie's, and I can tell she likes you, too." He extended the length of her leash and handed Maddie a ball. "You can play catch with her, if you like."

After watching them for a few seconds, he glanced in the direction I'd stumbled from and gave a sharp whistle. I spotted a dog digging through the lunch bag on our blanket. It obeyed immediately and bounded to his side. This dog was slightly bigger than Bonnie, but otherwise identical, except for its plain brown leather collar and the chain leash trailing through the sand.

"*Sit*, and mind your manners," Larry scolded. "When food's at stake, that dog could sneak off under the nose of the FBI." Leaving the dog with me, he ran to inspect the damage. I took the opportunity to reel in the kite and attempt to unravel myself while watching Larry's progress.

From what I could see, Maddie's backpack appeared intact, but our bag of sandwiches and snacks looked as if it had been on the losing side of a food fight. Larry shook a shower of sand from the blanket, gathered up our things, and brought the whole mess back to me. This sorry sight would become a banquet for the seagulls.

"I'm afraid he sampled some of your sandwiches," Larry said, aiming a stern look at his dog. "Absolutely shameless."

"No harm done," I said. The dog whined softly and appeared contrite. "No dog could resist such an open invitation." I concentrated on unwinding myself from a section of string.

Larry watched my twirling with an amused grin, but kept a watchful eye on the playful dog to prevent another sneak attack on the food. His steady gaze flustered me. The more I tried to unravel the string, the more twisted it became. The iridescent white strands, blurred by direct sunlight, merged with my white jacket. Following them became impossible.

"Need help with that?" he asked.

"No, thanks. Almost there," I lied. *This is crazy,* I thought, reaching beyond the cluster of string to pull in the kite. I've never been comfortable looking foolish, and today took the prize. There was no easy way to wriggle out of this web. I needed the scissors from the tool box in the trunk of my car.

"We should go," I said.

"So soon? I was thinking you and Maddie could join me for lunch, considering what happened to yours." Larry gave his dog a withering glare and motioned to the food piled on my blanket. "I feel responsible."

"Don't be silly," I replied. "It wasn't your fault. Besides, we have some errands to do." Was it disappointment or relief that flashed across his face? I wanted to escape. There was no way I could have lunch with another man on our "spring at the beach" day.

I tucked the kite under my arm and trudged through the shifting sand to get Maddie. Larry tightened the length of his dog's leash and followed to retrieve Bonnie.

"Well, enjoy your day," I said into the awkward silence.

"You too." He smiled, waved at Maddie, and jogged closer to the water, one dog on each side, matching his pace. I watched them pause a moment, perhaps to shorten a leash, and continue out of sight.

I sighed. "Sorry, Maddie. Things haven't gone very well today."

"Don't look sad, Mom. I had fun."

Off in the distance, a few people strolled on the beach, but the immediate area belonged to us. The lull of low-breaking waves, rhythm of swaying sea grass, and delicate scent of sea salt erased the chaos and calmed my mind. No longer flustered, I slipped out of my jacket. Maddie and I peeled away the string together. Problem solved.

"Let's go to The Greene Turtle for lunch," I suggested. Our kite flight was short, but successful, and we'd still have a nice view of the ocean. We unwrapped the remains of our sandwiches and brownies and set them out for the seagulls. They swooped down in a frenzy of pecking and vying for space. We saw them, still feasting, as we took our things to the car and headed to the restaurant.

After lunch, we stopped at Candy Kitchen for Maddie's favorite gummies. She always explored every inch of that store. We called it our happy place.

Everything was fine until bedtime, when I found Maddie searching through her backpack. "He's gone," she whimpered, finally dumping its contents on the floor.

"Who's gone?"

"Paddington. I brought him to the beach and now he's gone."

"Are you sure you put him in there?"

"I know I did, Mom."

We searched her room, rooting through the closet and drawers. When that failed, I checked the car, but Paddington had disappeared.

"Can you sleep without him?" I held my breath and gave her a hug.
"I don't want to."

"I know, but can you?" I asked, as I tucked her into bed.

"If I have to," she said, close to tears.

I felt the sting of tears, too. Losing Paddington was a double blow. He had belonged to her daddy. I have boxes of Brian's special things saved for Maddie so she has something of his to hold when pictures and memories aren't enough.

* * * * * *

The next morning, I promised Maddie I'd search the whole house. Paddington would turn up. When he didn't, I admitted defeat and went to Browseabout Books and bought a replacement. I perched him on the coat rack so she'd see him the moment she came home from school. As I expected, she ran straight to him. I spied from the kitchen, hoping for a smile.

"Mom," she wailed. "This isn't my Paddington. It's a new one."

"I tried my best, sweetie, but I couldn't find him."

"My Paddington's dead." Maddie's chin trembled. "Just like Daddy!" She ran to her room and flung herself on the bed.

I followed, taking the new bear with me. "Maddie." I rubbed her back, smoothing her long golden curls. She turned over.

"He's never coming back either," she sobbed.

"You know, your Paddington was new to Daddy when he first got it. Maybe you could give this one a chance."

I placed the new Paddington on her dresser and didn't mention him again. Maddie glanced in his direction from time to time while we played Connect Four. She stayed in her room when I left to start dinner.

I'd nearly finished when the doorbell rang. Closing one eye, I squinted through the peephole. Paddington peered back at me.

Paddington? "Who is it?" I asked.

"Larry Walker, ma'am. I think I have something that belongs to you."

I pulled open the door and saw Dan's cousin, dressed business casual, briefcase in one hand and toy bear in the other. "Paddington!"

"Erin?" he exclaimed, wide-eyed. "I found this on the beach. I guess that means it belongs to Maddie."

"Yes! Oh, bless you. She thought she'd lost him forever. Maddie," I called, "Paddington's home."

Maddie charged out of her room. She took Paddington. After a long sigh, she turned him over, examining from every angle. "He's really my Paddington. You found him. Thank you." Smiling again, she ran back to her room, leaving us standing in the open doorway.

"Happy to rescue him for you," Larry called after her.

"Do you realize what a wonderful thing you've done?"

He shrugged. "The card tied around the bear's neck said 'Please Look After This Bear,' so I did. This address was on the back. I had no idea it belonged to Maddie."

"Well, thank goodness for that old wrinkled card." I'd forgotten about writing our address on it. "Please come in. It was kind of you to return Paddington. You can see how much he means to her. This may sound crazy but, because of Dan, I feel like I know you. We were about to have dinner. Would you like to join us? It's the least I can do."

"Thanks, but I can't," he replied. "I came straight from the office and really have to get home. Happy I could help, though. Good night."

"Thanks again," I mumbled, and eased the door shut behind him. *Of course, he has someone to go home to. What was I thinking?* After the fool I made of myself yesterday, he probably wouldn't have bothered to return Paddington if he had known the address was our house. The flush burning my cheeks deepened when the truth hit. That wasn't a real invitation for lunch. He was just being polite because he knew his dog had ruined ours.

I returned to the kitchen. The two places I'd set for dinner looked lost on the large oval table. I felt a lump rise in my throat. After more than three years, I thought I'd put these moments behind me, but I hadn't felt this lonely in months. I called Maddie for dinner. I had someone to be home for, too.

* * * * * *

The doorbell rang at dinnertime again the next day. The peephole revealed only a box with letters too small to read. *What now?* I opened the door as far as the chain lock would allow and saw that it was a large pizza box.

"Sorry, you have the wrong house," I said. "I didn't order pizza."

"Erin, it's Larry again. May I come in?"

What was he doing here? I unhooked the chain and opened the door. He lowered the box and angled it through the doorway. His handsome face showed over the top when he opened the box a crack so I could take a look.

"Half pepperoni and half cheese," he said. "Some of both. Perfect, right?"

"Yes, but you didn't have to do this."

"Sorry about yesterday," he said. "I'm hoping your dinner invitation still stands."

"Well…"

"Here's dinner," he nodded toward the box, "and I have references. Sharon and Dan were happy to hear I met you at the beach. They even told me how you like your pizza. They'll vouch for me."

I laughed and checked my watch. "I'm sure they will, but do you have time?"

"No problem. Clyde's walked and fed already."

I raised a brow. "Clyde?"

"My dog. Surely you remember him. Clyde is Bonnie's brother.

They're great together. Once you get to know him, you and Maddie will love him, too."

Maddie and I? Love? I thought of the encouragement I had given Maddie about giving the new Paddington a chance. My heart warmed to the idea. I smiled and led the way to the kitchen. After I set an extra plate and Larry added the pizza box, the table no longer looked so large and empty. Perhaps I should follow my own advice. Doesn't spring bring new beginnings?

BARBARA NUZZO GRADUATED FROM RUTGERS UNIVERSITY. YEARS LATER, AN AD FOR A COURSE IN FICTION AWAKENED HER LONG-NEGLECTED WRITING MUSE AND LED TO MORE COURSES, WRITING CONFERENCES, AND NATIONAL ORGANIZATIONS. SHE'S A FOUNDING MEMBER OF SISTERS IN CRIME'S CENTRAL JERSEY CHAPTER AND WRITES MYSTERY, ROMANCE, AND NONFICTION STORIES THAT HAVE APPEARED IN *WOMAN'S WORLD* MAGAZINE, *U.S. 1 SUMMER FICTION* NEWSPAPER, THE *CUP OF COMFORT* BOOK SERIES AND VARIOUS ANTHOLOGIES. HER POEMS HAVE BEEN FEATURED IN THE *U.S. 1 SUMMER FICTION* NEWSPAPER AND SEVERAL POETRY ANTHOLOGIES. BARBARA AND HER HUSBAND, RAY, MOVED TO DELAWARE ALMOST THREE YEARS AGO AND ARE STILL EXPLORING ITS MANY TREASURES. WALKS ALONG THE REHOBOTH BOARDWALK ON COOL, BREEZY DAYS OF PERFECT KITE WEATHER PROVIDED THE INSPIRATION FOR THIS STORY.

JUDGES' COMMENTS

This romantic story revolves around the inherent optimism of those who live at the beach: a magical place situated between the land of our remembered past, and the ocean of our as-yet-unknown but hoped-for future. A mother and her young daughter, grieving the loss of a husband and father in Afghanistan, meet someone while flying a kite on the beach who may help them begin to live a new life.

Oksana and Carly

by Fran Hasson

Oksana was feeling particularly homesick that morning. She and her friend, Aisa, were the only two international students from Kalmykia who had been chosen for the summer program at the beach, but Aisa had been hired in Bethany while Oksana's job was in Rehoboth. There were other Russian students as well, but Oksana did not quite share the same cultural experiences with them. She didn't look like the European Russians, either. Her Mongol ancestry set her apart. Though her appearance was more like that of the Thai or Chinese summer workers, she also didn't fit in with them.

No one who met her would ever have suspected her of being lonely. She smiled quickly, was polite and friendly, could converse in English, Russian, French, and German—and, of course, Kalmykian—but she always remained in the background. Her reticent nature and dedicated work ethic made her an ideal employee, but she was lonely when not at work.

That morning, she thought about her sister, Natalya, who had written her a long letter, begging her to return home and saying that she missed her big sister more than she could bear. Oksana cried softly as she reread the letter and looked at the detailed drawing Natalya had made of their Buddhist temple with its prayer cans. Natalya had drawn a line pointing to a can and confessed that she had stuffed it with pleas to bring Oksana home.

Oksana had spent a year in England, where she had made friends easily. Of course, there she went to school with others her age, and there were many opportunities to mingle—parties, field trips, the dorm, and daily classes. In Rehoboth, she had attended one picnic sponsored by a local church especially for international students, but she had gone alone and left early. She did not know there would be no other opportunities once the tourist season began.

While she busied herself at work cleaning the ice-cream freezer, stocking sugar and waffle cones, wiping down the counter where the customers paid for their purchases, and tidying the storage area, another lonely girl, one who was Natalya's age, was having problems of her own.

* * * * * *

Everywhere that Carly went, her cat was sure to go.

Carly hummed the line to herself to the tune of "Mary Had a Little Lamb" as she fought to push her cat into the carrier. He reminded her of the cartoon character Wile E. Coyote, smashing through a solid door, leaving the imprint of widespread arms and legs. This kitty was a tough customer who would rather follow her like a free-range chicken than travel as a caged tiger.

Today, Cream Puff was making his first trip to the beach and Carly was taking her first solo outing. She lived only a few blocks from the ocean, so she packed the cage into the little wheeled metal cart her parents used to haul their umbrellas, water cooler, blankets, and towels when they went to the beach. Her dad was at work and her mom was still sleeping—she worked until closing at Fins Fish House and often did not get home before two in the morning.

It didn't occur to Carly that she shouldn't go alone to the beach, and with her cat, to boot. She was ambitious for a nine-year-old and quite strong. She had just completed fourth grade at the Rehoboth Elementary School and was ready in every way to be a "senior" there, her last year before entering middle school. She sorely missed her big sister, Melanie, who was spending the summer in France as an exchange student. Melanie would often take Carly to the beach, but now her best friend was Cream Puff.

After loading the cart and heading toward the beach, Carly began to wonder if this was a task she could handle alone. The first problem came at the corner of Second and Christian Streets. The cart began to shake. Carly struggled to right it, wedging the Sherpa carrier into the cart's wire basket. The carrier had been placed on the top shelf of the cart until an impatient driver's horn blast had given poor Cream Puff the shakes. Carly opened the zip-top entry panel to soothe him, but he was having no part of it and tried to spring out of the carrier. Since she had thought ahead to put his harness on, Carly was able to grab the restraint and stuff him back into the carrier. She zipped it tightly, resolving not to open it again until she'd reached the beach.

She pushed the cart along, thinking how Cream Puff would love to watch the seagulls, oystercatchers, and crashing waves at the beach. If they were lucky, they might even come upon a sand crab, which he would track attentively and pounce on before it could burrow. *Would it pinch his nose?* She was glad she had a leash for the harness so she could wrest him away before the scrabbling crustacean could nip him.

As she pressed on past the ice-cream shop and headed toward the boardwalk, Carly decided to stop for a treat to cool her already parched lips. This was hard work, shepherding a thirteen-pound cat down Wilmington Avenue. Wheeling around to backtrack for some ice cream, she crashed into a bench outside the shop. Cream Puff lurched. She could see him through the three ventilated sides. His golden eyes were wide as he scrunched down, as small as he could make himself, and peered out all three sides for a possible escape route. She saw him hunch his muscles and ripple them in preparation for a leap.

"No!" Carly called to him. She petted him through the outside of the carrier, hugging him as best she could, making the Sherpa bag collapse around him. "It's okay, Cream Puff. We're almost there."

* * * * * *

Oksana saw the unfolding drama as she stood on the porch of the shop during her break. She went out onto the sidewalk and helped Carly pull the cart up the three steps and into the ice-cream parlor. As Carly was placing her order, they heard a woman who had just entered the shop gasp, "Is that a cat in your cart?" Her tone rose on the word cat.

Carly turned and cradled the carrier protectively. "Yes, of course." She thought that was such a dumb question. What did it look like? A raccoon? She eyed the woman, apprehensively. She decided the woman was too old to be the fun grandma type and too young to be the kind and caring type like her grandma. She looked from the woman's short mousy hair down to the too-tight shorts to the puffy white legs ending in scuffed Crocs. For a brief moment, she felt sorry for the woman. She thought she must be very uncomfortable on a day this hot.

"Well, you need to turn right around and get it out of here," the gruff woman demanded.

Carly decided she was not sorry after all. "But I want to buy an ice-cream cone," she explained. "And he's no trouble. He's in his carrier."

The woman put one hand on her hip and pointed with the other to the sign, which held multiple commands regarding smoking, shirts, shoes, and the last one—No Pets Allowed. "Can you read, little girl?"

Cream Puff seemed to understand the insult. His tongue flicked in and out, while his tail thumped against the fleece floor of the carrier.

Oksana spoke to Carly in a quiet and kind voice. "I'm sorry, but she's right. If you just wait outside, I'll bring your ice cream to you."

Oksana helped Carly get the door open and carefully bounced the cart back down the steps while the hateful woman watched, tapping her foot as she tsk-tsked. Soon, the woman came out licking at a triple-dip chocolate cone. Carly wished the scoops would topple onto the pavement.

Oksana appeared with a gigantic strawberry cone in one hand and a closed fist that she opened to reveal six little cat treats. "I am so sorry," she told Carly. "You have a very fine kitty. He's well behaved. He would have been no problem." She opened the flip-top panel just enough to drop the treats inside without letting the cat out.

When Carly dug into her cutoff jeans pocket for money, Oksana flashed her white teeth and brushed her long dark hair back, pushing the money away. "No, this one's on me," she said. "Have fun today with your kitty." She sat on the bench with Carly. "I still have ten minutes left on my break. Can I spend it with you?"

Carly was delighted. "You're nice," she told her new friend. "You remind me of my big sister."

"And you remind me of my little sister," replied Oksana. "And your kitty reminds me of my own cat. She has golden eyes like your kitty. Where I come from, cats are a sign of good luck. Whenever someone moves into a new home, they must have a cat with them. Another thing—your cart reminds me of my town and my *babushka*. She always goes to the local shops with a cart like yours."

"Your babush-what?" laughed Carly.

Now it was Oksana's turn to laugh. "*Babushka* is Russian for grandmother."

Carly's cell phone rang. She saw that it was her mother.

"Carly, where are you? And where's Cream Puff? I've been worried sick looking for you."

"I'm on my way to the beach with Cream Puff, but right now I'm at the ice-cream shop with a new big sister. Can we keep her until

Melanie comes home?" She looked at Oksana, hoping she'd want to be kept.

There was silence while her mother seemed to process this bit of news. "What do you mean you're there with a new big sister? Wait right where you are. I'm coming with the car."

Carly pictured her mother shaking her head while Oksana laughed at the thought of her own mother having such a phone conversation with Natalya. Of course that couldn't happen because even though modern technology had reached the tiny country along the Caspian Sea, she didn't know of any nine-year-olds who had their own cell phone.

* * * * * *

Even though Carly never made it to the beach with Cream Puff that day, she remembered it as a turning point. Carly's mother invited the personable young woman for dinner that evening, and soon she was coming over nearly every night. Carly's mother and father talked it over and decided to ask Oksana to stay with them. Carly's mother went to Oksana's landlord, who was a frequent customer at Fins, and got him to allow her to break her lease.

Oksana moved into Melanie's room for the rest of the summer and into September, even spending a few days sharing the room with Melanie when she came back from France. In addition to gaining a new big sister, Carly formed a fast friendship with Natalya after the two became pen pals. This helped Natalya deal with the absence of Oksana, knowing she was well cared for, although she still marked the days on her calendar until her sister would return home.

As for the tan kitty with the golden eyes and white belly, Cream Puff was happy to be back home and out of that cage! He never knew what he was missing at the beach, but he purred contentedly in both Oksana's and Carly's arms the rest of the summer.

Fran Hasson, a retired educator, began writing as a hobby after thirty-two years of teaching physical education and English. Her two novels, *Allawe* and *Mothers and Other Strangers*, were written as a result of contact with the Rehoboth Beach Writers' Guild. Her selection, "Oksana and Carly," came about as an outgrowth of her involvement with international student workers at the beach resorts. Her church hosts picnics every year, and this is an activity she has always enjoyed, as it provides an opportunity to interact with students, especially ones from countries she visited while working in Europe. Her character, Oksana, is based on a Kalmykian student she met while competing in a Chess Olympiad in the Republic of Kalmykia.

Judge's Comments

"Oksana and Carly" stood out with its kind, sympathetic portrait of a familiar character we don't often read about: an international student spending a lonely summer earning money in Rehoboth Beach. Oksana misses her little sister; she bonds with Carly, who misses her older sister. Their easy friendship reminds us how similar we are to each other, no matter where we're from.

Time in the Sun

by Terri Clifton

It was an ordinary Tuesday, the kind I took advantage of to stare at the ocean and read a book. I had a new mystery from the bookstore in town, and the usual iced black coffee. The tide was out, but turning, so I chose a spot above the tide line.

I liked weekdays because there was plenty of room. Even later in the day it still wouldn't be jammed the way it was on weekends, when a path to the water had to be picked between sunbathers and coolers, umbrellas and towels. When you could barely hear the gulls over the people. I had stopped coming on weekends years ago. Weekdays were my beach days. I was older now and I deserved such things.

Just as I got settled I spied the man and his children, and eyed their approach with some trepidation. Children are noisy and their parents don't watch them.

Two boys—I guessed five and eight. They both helped to spread a faded blanket several yards down the beach. The father opened a blue umbrella from the rental stand and anchored it deep in the sand. As they began to arrange their myriad belongings, I was hoping against hope that they wouldn't be too disruptive to my peace. I was surprised to find that I'd read three chapters without incident, so I looked to see where they were, and saw them a little farther down, wading in a tide pool. The father pointed, and two golden heads bent to look at something. I went back to reading, knowing I should enjoy it while I could, and I was right. Soon they were back, pulling off T-shirts and heading into the waves.

I was as vigilant as any lifeguard, sure that this young father wouldn't take seriously the potential dangers of waves and undertow. I sat ready in my chair.

The three of them held hands, the little one in the middle, and they didn't go out very far. They squealed a bit, but not the shrieking sound I'd come to associate with overindulged children. It sounded more like I'd remembered children in my time, back when there was innocence. I settled back, thinking that perhaps the waves weren't very big at all today, and though I'd picked up my book, I must say I watched them over the edge of it, maybe because their laughter was the most honest thing I'd heard in a long time. The older boy rode waves on a bright yellow boogie board while the younger stood clapping on the wet sand, the father's watchful eye on one, his helping hand on the other.

They ate sandwiches and grapes and read a book under the umbrella while I did virtually the same under mine. When their Frisbee landed at my feet, the older boy fetched it, with an apology and a smile. I nodded as I shook off a bit of sand. Not nearly as rude as I'd expected. I hoped he wouldn't grow out of it in a few years.

After my walk down the beach, I came back to a sandcastle, with construction of moats and turrets under way. Watching them build, I expected them to get bored or do something destructive, as boys will do, but they worked the afternoon away, quietly talking as they added shells and reeds and driftwood to create an imaginary kingdom. I heard their talk of caves and treasure, saw their careful selection of twigs for an orchard, stones to build a staircase.

I expected them to bombard it or jump on it before leaving, but they left it standing. Halfway to the dune crossing, the little one looked back at it one more time.

They had seemed like decent children and, despite my initial fears, hadn't disturbed me at all. I counted myself lucky they hadn't been older and more rambunctious.

In the parking lot I caught up with them, their car next to mine under the partial shade of the pines. The boys were shaking their beach towels while the father packed the car. I opened my trunk as he closed his. He looked over.

"Sorry about the Frisbee," he said. He brushed his hands together, dusting away the last granules stuck there. "My youngest is just learning to make it fly. We are working on direction." His smile was open and friendly, but he looked tired.

"There are plenty of beach days left for practice." I fit my chair next to my lunch bag.

"Yeah." He looked over at the boys in the car, the older helping the younger to buckle in.

I thought he'd go, but he didn't, lost in a moment of his own.

"I have them for the whole summer this year."

I thought I understood then, a divorced father, but he kept talking.

"The last one I'll get."

It sounded like a confession. I frowned, beginning to feel uncomfortable.

"I'm sick," he said, in little more than a whisper. "Cancer. I've got until winter, or maybe a little longer."

I couldn't help glancing over his body. He looked healthy.

"My brain," he said, as if to answer my inquiring eyes.

I'm sure I blushed, as I looked away, thinking about the selfish thoughts I'd had earlier.

A burst of laughter from inside the car brought his eyes back to his children. "I want it to be a summer they remember. I don't have the time to teach them all the things I wanted to."

I didn't know why he was telling me these things. Maybe he just needed someone to say it to. I thought about all I'd seen of him that day. The care, the kindness, the humor. He'd read to them and hugged them. They had laughed together and played. I had tried, but been unable, to find fault.

I had to clear my throat. "Long after you and I have passed from here, I think—I know—your sons will be fine men. It doesn't take much imagination to see them here, with their children someday."

One of the boys laughed again and the father smiled.

"Thank you for that."

Inside I felt a need to thank *him,* but I wasn't sure for what, so I just nodded.

His keys jingled as he waved, and I turned, pretending to readjust the beach chair in my trunk. The radio began to play and they were all singing as they pulled away.

The bright green bucket seemed to glow in the long afternoon shadow. It was the one the littlest boy had carried. Inside was a clam shell, some pebbles, and a piece of blue sea glass. I waited, to see if they'd realize the loss and come back, but they had probably forgotten all about it. Soon, there was only the sound of waves, muffled by the dune. I ran my thumb along the once-sharp edge of the sea glass, weathered by ocean, and sand, and time.

TERRI CLIFTON IS THE AUTHOR OF *A RANDOM SOLDIER,* A MEMOIR. HER NOVEL *RED BALLOON* WAS THE BASIS FOR HER 2013 DELAWARE DIVISION OF ARTS FELLOWSHIP AWARD IN FICTION LITERATURE, AND SHE HAS RECENTLY COMPLETED A MIDDLE-GRADE NOVEL. HER STORY, "STOLEN HEART," WAS INCLUDED IN *THE BOARDWALK* IN 2014. SHE IS CURRENTLY AT WORK ON A NOVEL SET IN THE FICTIONAL DELAWARE TOWN OF ZWANENDALE. IN ADDITION TO WRITING, SHE SPEAKS ON ISSUES OF LITERACY AND THE IMPORTANCE OF STORIES, AND TEACHES WORKSHOPS ON CREATIVITY. A DELAWARE NATIVE, SHE LIVES ON A HISTORIC FARM AT THE EDGE OF THE DELAWARE BAY WITH HER SON, RYAN, AND HUSBAND, RICHARD, AN INTERNATIONALLY KNOWN WILDLIFE ARTIST. SHE IS AN ACCOMPLISHED PHOTOGRAPHER AND LOVES TO TRAVEL. SHE IS ALSO THE DIRECTOR OF A FOUNDATION BENEFITING VETERANS.

Beach Daze

by Margaret Farrell Kirby

The Sea, once it casts its spell,
holds one in its net of wonder forever.
–Jacques Yves Cousteau

She woke to the sounds of rolling waves, squawking seagulls, and laughing children—the soothing background noises of the beach that had lulled her to sleep. Napping on the beach, enveloped by the warm sun and gentle breeze, was one of Anna's great pleasures. It was a Thursday afternoon in the middle of August, the second day of her five-day escape to Rehoboth Beach. As the elusive fragments of her dreams ebbed, she returned to the flow of life around her.

After she yawned, stretched, and pushed herself awake, she ran to the water and dove through the waves. Fully awake and invigorated, she floated on her back and gazed at the lone red kite bobbing high in the blue sky. Sleep and warm sun had penetrated her exhausted mind and body, bringing her senses alive to the textures, colors, and smells of the beach.

After she returned to her chair, Anna noticed a man sitting a few feet away. Tanned and handsome, with salt-and-pepper hair and a light gray beard, he reminded her of George Clooney. He glanced at her and smiled. Embarrassed to be caught staring, she dropped her eyes and picked up her book.

"Time for a swim," he said, as he stood and took off his shirt and sunglasses. "Are you on vacation?"

"Just a long weekend," she said, as she studied his face. He really did look like George Clooney.

"Where are you from?" he asked.

"Washington. I try to come every month to decompress."

"I do the same, every few weeks. I'm from DC too, but I also have a townhouse in Bethany Beach. Where are you staying?"

"The Atlantic Sands." She pointed to the hotel. "Why do you come to the beach in Rehoboth if you have a place in Bethany?"

"The beach is bigger. Bethany gets packed in the summer, so I come here when I want to spend a day on the beach. I love to go to Grotto, get a slice, have some fries. Not the best diet in the world, but I can't resist." His smile was warm.

"I know. I love Thrasher's." She watched as he jogged to the water, and then she leaned back and closed her eyes.

Anna, a lawyer, worked fifty to sixty hours a week and savored the beach weekends as her time to rest and recharge. She sometimes came with friends, but for the most part traveled alone. In her twenties and early thirties, she joined summer group homes and came to Rehoboth every weekend. By the time she was thirty-five, tired of the noise and chaos and getting home exhausted every weekend, she started renting a hotel room by herself for a long weekend each month.

Still single at thirty-eight, she'd had a few long-term relationships, but none seemed worth sacrificing her career for. Most of her friends had married and started families. They eventually stopped trying to set her up on blind dates, told her she was too picky, looking for perfection, for the impossible. Perhaps she was, but after spending an evening listening to married friends bickering over petty things—like loading the dishwasher—she was happy to go home to her predictable life.

On her last date, a few months earlier, Anna went out to dinner with an attorney from her firm, and knew from the start it was a mistake. He treated their server like a servant, waving his arm when he wanted another drink and keeping the poor guy standing at their table waiting for their order while he perused the wine list. He liked to talk, so she let him. She asked innocuous questions that kept him chattering about himself. It got her through the meal. He wasn't perceptive enough to sense her boredom. Drained by the end of it, she hadn't gone on a date since.

She opened her eyes when she heard the creak of the man's chair. He looked at her as he pulled on a T-shirt and said, "I'm heading to the boardwalk to get some Thrasher's. Do you want some?"

Anna checked her watch. Four o'clock. "I'd love a small one, let me get my wallet."

"No. It's my treat. I'm Ben, by the way." He stood and pulled on a baseball cap. "How much salt and vinegar do you like?"

"Lots of each. Thanks. And I'm Anna." She watched him walk to the boardwalk. Tall, tanned, lithe.

When he returned, he handed her a cup of fries and moved his chair closer to hers. "What do you do in DC?" he asked.

"I work for a public interest law firm. Long hours, but I love it. What about you?"

"I have a consulting firm. We deal with healthcare policy issues. I can work from here some of the time." He picked up her book. "You like to read?"

"Yeah, I love reading, but can't find much time for it. So I save books to bring to the beach. The first day I keep falling asleep, but by the second and third I can get through a few."

After they finished their fries, he moved his chair back to his umbrella, and they picked up their books. The whistle of the lifeguards signaled the conclusion of their workday. This hour, at the end of a beach day, was her favorite time. The beauty of the softened glow of the sun on the water and sand added to her languid and mellow mood. Anna returned to the ocean and floated in the gentle water. A perfect beach day, she thought.

Ben was watching her as she came back to her chair, dried off, pulled on her cover-up and slipped her feet into her flip-flops. "Hope you have a nice weekend. Thanks again for the fries." she said.

"Would you like to have dinner tonight?" he asked. "There's a neat place across the street from the Sands. I've been a few times. Thursday night is steak night and they have a cool bartender who sings while she makes the drinks."

Anna had bought a bottle of red wine on the ride into Rehoboth and planned to order a pizza from Nicola and watch TV. She debated. He seemed thoughtful, kind. His brown eyes were mesmerizing. She didn't notice a ring.

"Sure, that sounds like fun," she said, surprised at herself for stepping out of character, for doing something unexpected.

"I'll make reservations—the restaurant is called Café Azafrán. Is eight OK? I'll meet you in your hotel lobby."

"No, I'll meet you at the restaurant," she said. "At eight."

Back at the hotel, having second thoughts, she looked at the TV and the bed. But she was hungry and, she had to admit, intrigued. She showered, dressed in a black sundress, and let her long curly hair dry naturally. Back home she'd have spent an hour to blow dry and tame it, to look professional and conform to the image of her law firm.

When she entered the restaurant, she saw Ben standing at the bar with a martini, wearing jeans and a black T-shirt under a gray blazer. The bartender sang "Unforgettable" as she mixed drinks. Near the tables, a musician accompanied her on a keyboard.

"Do you want one?' he pointed to his icy glass. "She makes the best in Rehoboth."

"I'd love one. Vodka, extra-dry, with a twist," she said to the bartender, who nodded and smiled as she sang.

Their table in the front window had a candle and small vase filled with yellow daisies. As she sipped her martini and listened to the music, Anna relaxed. The day at the beach had softened her brittle edges. Ben was easy to be with, present and attentive, with a great smile and easy laugh. They talked about life in DC, politics, the gridlock in Congress, her law firm's work on immigration, his work with healthcare reform.

"So, Anna, tell me." His warm brown eyes focused on hers. "Are you single, dating, married, divorced?"

"I'm single, not in a relationship now," she answered, and tried to calculate his age. With a few wrinkles around his eyes, the salt-and-pepper hair and beard, she figured him to be in his late forties, maybe early fifties, so probably about ten years older than she was. "And you?"

"Divorced," he said. "Been quite a while, now."

As she began to ask him more, their server came to the table. "Hey, let's order," he said. "Would you like a steak?"

As she watched his movements, the way he treated the server—nice, friendly, considerate—she relaxed even more. After they ordered their steaks and a bottle of Malbec, she asked, "How long were you married?"

When he didn't answer right away, she wondered if she had offended him. He took a sip of wine and looked out the window. "About ten years," he finally answered.

The crack of thunder was so sudden, she jumped.

He laughed. "Are you nervous?"

"No, I just didn't expect it." She shivered and pulled her shawl around her.

"So, tell me about the book you're reading," he said, as the waiter served their dinner.

"The title is *Saturday*. It's by Ian McEwan, set in London over the course of a day, an ordinary day, in the life of a man. It's after 9/11 and protests against the Iraq war are going on in London as he goes through his day thinking about the world, his job, his family, his fears. Then, an unexpected event happens that changes his life. I've been thinking about it all day. The randomness of life, how we go along with our illusions about our lives, our neat, tidy lives, how something can be just around the corner that changes everything. Nothing the same afterward..." She stopped, thinking she was babbling.

"Is your life neat and tidy, Anna?"

"Probably too much," she said. And in truth, the book had evoked introspection about her life—how she had crafted it to keep it ordered, and safe. "What are you reading?" Anna asked as she sipped her martini.

"A book by George Pelecanos—crime, mystery, set in the DC area. Nothing neat and tidy in his books," he said with a smile. "I love them, love how he paints the scene, you feel like you're right there."

"I've wanted to read a book of his," she said.

Jagged bolts of lightning lit the sky outside the window, beautiful and scary at the same time. Like she did as a child, she counted the seconds until the thunder clapped to see how far away the storm was. Three seconds. Getting closer.

While their waiter picked up their plates and the empty wine bottle, Ben asked, "Would you like a nightcap? We don't want to get soaked." Rain pelted against the window. He hummed along with the sultry voice of the bartender singing "The Way You Look Tonight."

As they sipped their cognacs, she smiled at him. "Why are you staring at me?"

"I'm trying to think of who you remind me of. Oh, I know. The actress who starred in *Groundhog Day*. I can't think of her name. She's beautiful."

Andie MacDowell, she thought, but didn't say it. And didn't tell him he reminded her of George Clooney.

As the bartender sang "You Go to My Head," Ben put one hand over hers on the table and held his drink with the other. "Want to spend another beach day with me tomorrow? We can get lunch, walk to Browseabout. I'd like to get the book you're reading."

"I'd love to," Anna said. "You can help me pick your favorite Pelecanos book." Dazed, she smiled and it was as if she were outside herself, in a movie or a dream. As she gazed at his hand over hers, it took a minute for her brain to compute and connect. Then the recognition hit her like a bolt. His left hand. The empty pale place on his tanned ring finger. The place a ring had been not long ago. Faint, but unmistakable. She stiffened and pulled her hand away.

"What's wrong?"

"Nothing." Anna's face felt hot. How gullible and naïve she had been, seduced by the attention, by the drinks, by the romantic songs.

She stood. "Would you excuse me for a moment?" In the bathroom she leaned against the sink. Was anything he'd said true? The lawyer in her wanted to interrogate him, to ask him, "How often do you pick up women on the beach? Where is your wife?" But she knew she wouldn't.

She returned to the table. "This was a great place. The bartender's amazing." She took out her wallet and a credit card.

"We don't want the night to end, do we? The rain stopped. Let's go to the boardwalk; there's a bar a few blocks down on the boardwalk."

"Probably not a good idea. You don't want to get pulled over on your way back to Bethany," she said.

"Maybe you'll let me stay at the Sands with you? It'll save me having to drive back tomorrow for our beach day."

So that was how he had planned it. He sounded so sure of his chances. He'd set it up perfectly.

"After all, we've had a great day, haven't we?" He smiled.

"Unforgettable," she said and stood up, smoothing her dress.

She walked across the room, resisting the urge to turn, to see the look on his face, the confusion breaking through the confidence. As the bartender sang "I'll Be Seeing You," Anna smiled and walked out into the rain, away from the lure of the shimmering illusion, and back to the script of her neat and tidy world.

MARGARET FARRELL KIRBY WORKED FOR THIRTY YEARS AT SO OTHERS MIGHT EAT (SOME), AN ORGANIZATION IN WASHINGTON, DC, THAT WORKS WITH THE HOMELESS. WHEN SHE RETIRED THREE YEARS AGO, SHE BECAME A MEMBER OF THE REHOBOTH BEACH WRITERS' GUILD AND HAS TAKEN CLASSES IN WRITING DIFFERENT GENRES. SHE RECENTLY ATTENDED THE ECKERD COLLEGE WRITERS' CONFERENCE (WRITERS IN PARADISE). "BEACH DAZE" IS HER THIRD PUBLISHED PIECE IN REHOBOTH BEACH READS BOOKS. SHE DIVIDES HER TIME BETWEEN SILVER SPRING, MARYLAND, AND REHOBOTH BEACH. SHE IS APPRECIATIVE OF THE TALENTED AND SUPPORTIVE TEACHERS AT THE WRITER' GUILD, AND ALSO FOR THE WRITING OPPORTUNITIES AND ENCOURAGEMENT FROM CAT AND MOUSE PRESS.

The Dead Man's Sendoff

by J.L. Epler

TRUDY M. BING
P.O. BOX 2243,
REHOBOTH BEACH, DE 19971

June 4, 2015

Dear Gil –

I hope you don't mind me writing to you, seeing that you are trying to put this all behind you. But when you left yesterday, well, I felt it was wrong how you left. It wasn't your fault, or anyone's fault, really. But as I watched you head up over the dune to your car, you seemed still caught in an undertow of anger. I know I'm just the old lady who happened to live next to your dad. It's just that I'm the one who found him, and I'm the one who called you to deliver the bad news, so it kind of links us in a way that most folks can't lay claim to. I should have noticed the mail piling up—but I try to mind my own business. When Sal (the mailman) came to the door with that concerned look on his face, it never, and I mean never, crossed my mind that your dad had passed.

If you can bear with me, I just want to tell you a few things I've thought of since you left. Forgive me if I sound a bit unsettled myself. As I walked my dog this morning, the turkey vultures that usually circle high above our development actually landed on your dad's chimney. Three of them. I could hear their claws scraping at the siding as they tried to grip it. Don't fret—the house is fine and all, but it seems like something is lingering.

First, I hope you didn't find me too overbearing these last few days. Your dad's request was unique. I mean, leave it to Jon to want to celebrate the end of his life by having us set up his usual spot on Deauville Beach. Habit being strong like it is, I guess I shouldn't be surprised that this is how he'd want to be sent off to the next life, or whatever he believed. Your dad was an unconventional man. I'm not letting out any secrets here or saying anything you don't already know. Sometimes I envied his ability to live his life in such a carefree way. I'm just not made up like that, and from what I could tell during the past few days, you aren't either. Organizing something so unusual—or maybe informal is the better way to put it—well, I figured it was going to be uncomfortable for you.

I do chuckle when I think about his list, though. I saw the envelope taped to the cabinet with red duct tape as I called for help that morning. "In Case of Emergency," it said. Finding your father facedown on the floor with his half-eaten breakfast still on the table sure did constitute an emergency in my mind. So naturally I had to open it. I guess Jon wasn't convinced you'd come to help, or even if he still had your right phone number, so he left the list with the instructions for anyone who opened it. But I knew right then and there it was my job to get you down here. And my next job was to help you through this ordeal. Anyway, I hope someday you look back at the list as some sort of keepsake (I've enclosed it here). It was like your father thought you had never been to the beach and wouldn't know what to bring. But I think it was his way of reminding you of the past.

We must have looked a sight—you in your starched shirt, suit pants, and loafers, and me in my ratty retired-lady clothes, digging deep into his musty old shed for beach chairs that hadn't been used since your last visit here. What was that, fifteen years ago now? You might have been thirteen or so the last time I saw you. I wish you had borrowed one of your dad's old shirts like I suggested, especially since you had to go into the crawl space to retrieve those two pathetic boogie boards. I guess those things all had sentimental value to your dad. Oh, that reminds me—the quilts we used as blankets yesterday—I've washed them and stored them in plastic for whenever you decide to come down to get the place ready to sell. I assume you are selling it? I believe those quilts are heirlooms, like I told you when we dug them out of the closet. One has a tag on the back of it. Looks like it was made for your bed when you were a boy.

Back when you were young, your dad and I weren't as friendly as we were in recent years, so I don't remember too much about that time. I do recall you and your dad doing projects together, like painting the mailbox pole at the end of the drive with purple paint (which was painted over as soon as you left that summer) and the two of you heading out to the beach most days on rusty bikes.

But that first year you didn't come for the summer, your father, well, he never really got over it. He'd spend any day that held the least bit of sunshine at Deauville Beach, hauling all that stuff—that same stuff we had to haul yesterday for his "funeral." I guess he was hoping you'd magically appear. He never said what got between the two of you. I can only guess that he wasn't caring for you and your mom like he should have. Any young man can sense that and has to take a stand one way or the other. It's part of growing up.

I don't mind telling you that I worried about you getting home last night. I know you were confused and angry. But you also hadn't eaten a thing all day as far as I could tell. Frank & Louie put out some good sandwiches. I wish you had taken something for the road, but I understand it must have felt overwhelming having a bunch of strangers trying to press you with food and make you take some of your dad's things (I brought his towel and baseball cap back with me and put them on the kitchen table for you, in case you change your mind). Those folks didn't mean any harm by it. Only a few know the real story is my guess.

I gave the leftover food to Tre and Darryl (the tall one

who did all the handstands on the beach). Your dad has been helping them out. And that's what I hoped you learned yesterday morning, Gil. Your father—whatever he did to you and your mother—was a caring man here. These people (an odd assortment, I'll agree with you there) all had faults, maybe like your dad did. But he cared for them in a way that others around here wouldn't. Maybe he was paying old debts, or making himself forget whatever drove you away, but these people came to rely on him. They gave him a chance to do the right thing, or at least that's the way I see it.

The party (it wasn't really a party, either, now was it?) went on for a few hours after you left. I had plenty of help breaking down the chairs and packing things up. You'll be glad to know I was able to give everything away except the stuff I snuck in my bag to save for you. People got a little "festive" (your dad's saying) toward the end of the day after the case of beer was gone. Some were trying to ride the waves with those old boogie boards, which broke into pieces pretty much right away. Every now and again there'd be a loud chorus of "To Jon!" That certainly caught the attention of the lifeguards. But that's how this group seems to operate— shunning the "to do" lists and any sort of normal routine to have as much fun as possible. I certainly can't do that kind of thing. Stuck in my ways, I guess.

Your dad would try to include me sometimes, though. He'd call me up many an evening and invite me over to his backyard when the beach party broke up and several of those misfits followed him back to his place. I knew when the string of lights he wrapped around the tree branches went on, it was going to get "festive." Your dad thought if he invited me over ("Little Miss Quiet," that's what he used to call me), any noise they made would be okay. "Trudy," he'd say, "gonna get a little festive over here tonight. Why don't you join us?" I never did, or at least hardly ever did. Your dad and I had different lifestyles. I didn't judge him for his, and he didn't judge me for mine. That's probably why we were such good neighbors.

Back to yesterday, though. Just before we packed up the last of his things, the high tide started to nip at the base of the sandcastle. I wish I had had a camera to capture the look on your face when you saw it. It was a nice tribute to your dad.

Word spreads quickly around here. I expected as much, but I'm guessing your dad's celebrity caught you a little off-guard? He was a legend over at Deauville. Young and old flocked to him, I guess because he was just a fun person to be around. That and the box of books he used to bring every day. As you know, he loved to read, but he had a "book bin," a sort of lending library that he carted to his spot every day. People knew him for that, too. "Here comes The Book Man," they'd say.

He'd been in the paper once or twice too. Did you know that? Nothing special—just a photo with a caption. I wish I had kept them now, to include in this letter. Anyway, a year or two ago, there was a great picture of him leaning over the side of his chair with one hand in a sand bucket and the other holding a book. Next to the hand in the bucket were these elaborate sand towers he had created just by letting the wet sand drizzle off his fingertips as he read. The caption, I think I'm remembering this correctly, said they were called dribble castles. Strangest thing I ever saw.

So like I was saying, the poetry and tributes started after you left. Folks stood up and said some nice things. I'll try to jot down what I can remember and keep it for you when you come back to close up the house. And yes, I know it was hard to figure when to leave. When you came over to me after people started eating, asking me if I thought it was over, well, I knew it wasn't. Even though there was no agenda or anything like that, these people just made a day of it like they did any other day. I was hoping the longer you stayed, and the more you heard about your dad from these folks, the more your mind might start to shift about him. Kind of like those days at the beach that are still and buggy and miserable, and then, all of a sudden, the wind changes direction and the currents shift, and it's like a completely different experience—a new day. I had hoped that would happen for you. Maybe it will in time, but then again, maybe not.

Oh, and the last thing I wanted to say—I'm sorry about the Twizzler incident with Marianne. I know it isn't me who should be apologizing, but I could see how upset you were. Sometimes Marianne doesn't know when to let things be. I hadn't known your dad brought Twizzlers to the beach as a memorial to you. When I saw "Twizzlers" on his "bring to the beach" list, I didn't get the significance. Sure, it is candy, and it doesn't melt, and it is pretty hard to mess up, but Marianne seemed to think it was your favorite candy as a boy. You see, she started hanging around your dad more and more after you stopped coming for the summer. They weren't a couple or anything like that, but she had lost someone close to her, and she probably knew how your dad felt losing you. I guess he told her about taking the candy to the beach every day in case you decided to show up unannounced to mend fences with him. She shouldn't have tried to force you to take the candy with you when you left. You could probably tell she has an issue with the booze. Once the vodka gets working, her penchant for telling people the truth goes into high gear. Jon could forgive her for it. I'm not sure I would have been so generous. And believe me when I tell you I've seen her in bad shape, but Jon always got her out of the view of others to salvage any semblance of dignity she had. That's the kind of man he was. I know I'm getting off-topic now, but these stories about your dad may help you get some sort of peace about this whole thing. At least I hope it does.

Anyway, if anything, you have a good story to tell the people at work (and sorry for sending this to your work address, but I saw your business card on the kitchen table). Tell them that you were part of the most unusual funeral anyone has ever seen. A day at the beach. Anyone who came to that section of Deauville was part of it. And your dad's chair, empty except for a towel laid across it and his hat in the seat, was in the center of it all.

I imagine your dad got what he wanted when he planned it all out that way, right? He got one more day at the beach with you.

PS: You left this picture on the mantle. Perhaps you intended to, but just in case you didn't, I've enclosed it here. You look all rough and alive—wind-blown hair, suntanned. It's a treasure. Your dad looks great in it too.

Yours truly,

Trudy Bing

PPS: Maybe you will keep the place? I'm a good neighbor. I'll keep the key for now just in case. BTW—It's calm and clear out now. Looks like the weather has shifted and sent off whatever attracted those vultures.

In Case of Emergency

You are reading this letter because something has happened to me. Please contact my son, Gil, at the number below. I hope you can find him. If not, please ask my neighbor, Trudy Bing, to pass this note along to friends. She'll know how to do that.

Sendoff for Jon, a.k.a. "The Dead Man"
(pardon the dark humor)

Please set up my usual spot on Deauville Beach with the items I've listed below. Set up by 10:00 or 10:30 A.M. Those who know me will know how to find me. Anyone is welcome to join in. No one should be turned away.

BEACH CHAIRS. The one I use all the time is on the porch; I have several orphan chairs in the shed that you can bring. They'll need some cleaning.

A DOZEN OR SO PAPERBACK BOOKS. Go to the used-book aisle at Browseabout—you can get them for a good price there. I use the crate by the back door to carry them onto the beach.

SUNSCREEN. Hawaiian Tropic is my preference.

PADDLEBALL SET. In bin by the side door.

PLASTIC BUCKETS AND SHOVELS. Also in bin by the side door.

BOOGIE BOARDS. There are two underneath the porch—just remove the lattice and they are right there.

TWO COOLERS. Trudy Bing next door should have one you can borrow and I have a large one in the shed. One cooler should be for drinks. I have a case of beer (cans) by the basement stairs. Don't forget the "cozies" to make it less obvious. The other cooler should be big enough to hold an order of twenty or so sandwiches from Frank & Louie's. Get an assortment and have them cut them in half. I have a prepaid account there.

A BAGGIE FULL OF DOLLAR BILLS FOR THE WATER ICE LADY. There is a roll of dollar bills in the left kitchen drawer. She won't have lots of change on her. Tip her with anything that is left over.

TWIZZLERS. Red only. Four or five large bags should do.

BLANKETS. I usually don't bring a lot of these but I have three quilts folded up in the hall closet. Please take all three. There are beach towels in the same closet. The one I always use should be near my beach chair on the porch with my Phillies hat.

When the party is over, leave no trace of it. Give everything away.

Cheers,
Jon

JENNIFER EPLER IS A MEMBER OF THE REHOBOTH BEACH WRITERS' GUILD AND IS ACTIVE IN OTHER AREA WRITING AND CRITIQUE GROUPS. HER SHORT STORIES HAVE APPEARED IN *THE BOARDWALK* AND *THE BEACH HOUSE*. HER CREATIVE NONFICTION STORY "SECRET ADMIRER" WON FIRST PLACE FOR PROSE IN THE DELAWARE LITERARY CONNECTION'S 2015 SPRING PROSE AND POETRY CONTEST AND WAS PUBLISHED IN *THE BROADKILL REVIEW*. IN 2014, SHE WAS SELECTED TO PARTICIPATE IN THE DELAWARE DIVISION OF THE ART'S CAPE HENLOPEN WRITING RETREAT. SHE RESIDES IN WILMINGTON AND REHOBOTH.

JUDGE'S COMMENT:

A poignant story about family reconnections after many years, and this one is laced with a certain humor that gives it depth. Splendid use of short story form, creative, clever, witty, engaging, and enjoyable to read. Bravo.

The Wineglass Clue

by Nancy H. Linton

Bronson Adair inspected the monogrammed cuff of his pale blue shirt. It coordinated perfectly with the discreetly striped wool suit he had chosen to wear for his book launch today at Browseabout Books in Rehoboth. Some might say that his attire was a bit much for the informality of the beach community, but Mother had always insisted that he set an example of what the well-dressed gentleman should wear throughout the seasons. After all, his family's clothing store, Gordon's Apparel for the Discriminating Man, had been a fixture in the Rehoboth community for decades.

Bronson's collection of short stories about Rehoboth and many of its residents had languished for months on the local fiction shelf, but now that he was chairman of the Rehoboth Beach Writers' Guild, he had fought to make his own book launch a priority. This was just the first of his plans for the Guild. He had waited years for this opportunity; at last his work would finally receive the attention it deserved. The mysterious death of the previous chairman had worked out very well for Bronson Adair.

"Is all to your liking, Your Highness?" Norman's mocking would not rattle him today. Norman had been the manager of Browseabout Books for years, and Lou, the new owner, had simply continued with that arrangement. As one of the judges of the short-story contest run by a local publisher, Bronson was spending a great deal of time in the bookstore. He suspected that Norman was listening in while the judges held their meetings in the community room. All comments the judges made about the entries were supposed to be confidential. The other judges had not complained, but none of them had known Norman in high school. Bronson still seethed when he recalled how he, as third-period hall monitor, had been bullied by Norman, star quarterback.

"Yes, Norman. Well done, I say. I think the podium adds a bit of flair, don't you?" Bronson placed his notes on the stand and glanced toward the doors. The crowd would arrive soon.

Norman was already heading back into the store when he heard a familiar voice.

"Norman! I got your message. Is the book you reserved for me at the register?" Emma Walsh, another Guild member and contest judge, shared Norman's love of a good mystery. A few months ago, he had recommended the Murder Around the Clock series, which featured a clever sleuth named Harriet. Since then, Emma and Norman had read all of the books in the series and had tried to solve each case before Harriet did. Now they were eager to begin book 13, *Lights Out at Eleven*.

"What's happening here today?" she asked. "I see that the community room is open." Emma fished her credit card out of a tote bag stuffed with yarn, needles, and a notebook. When she wasn't reading or working on her own writing, Emma knitted samples for the local yarn shop and she carried her projects with her wherever she went.

"It's Bronson's book launch, remember?" Norman rolled his eyes as he handed her the receipt and her purchase.

"Is anyone there?" she whispered. Before Norman could answer, she heard Bronson's nasal twang.

"Emma, good of you to come!" he called from across the store. "We'll be starting soon, so don't dawdle."

Emma looked at Norman and sighed. "At least I can get some knitting done."

On her way to the community room, Emma stopped by the coffee bar and ordered a large latte. She hoped she would have a chance to talk with Lou, the new owner, but he seemed to be busy in his office. Lou was a mysterious new presence in Rehoboth. No one knew much about him. There was a rumor that he kept a gun in his desk, but why would a Rehoboth bookstore owner need a gun? Her next-door neighbor, Marla, had said he was another government retiree from Washington. Thinking of Marla was still painful. She wished that Harriet could come to Rehoboth to help her sort out all the odd details of Marla's sudden death.

Two weeks ago, Marla, who ran the short-story contest for the publisher, had called a meeting of the judges. This year's theme, "Beach Days and Nights," had drawn hundreds of submissions. It was a challenging task for the judges, but Marla, using her experience as an editor in New York, guided them through the process. Her perceptive, caustic comments about the entries had enlivened the hours devoted to selecting the winners.

Still thinking about her friend, Emma grabbed her latte and entered the community room. Much to her relief, she saw three other Guild members sitting in the front row.

"Welcome. Welcome, everyone." Bronson opened his binder and began, "This book is a collection of my observations of our little community and its denizens over the years. I always—"

Emma barely heard him. She stared at her knitting and wondered why she had stopped in the middle of a complex crossed cable over multistrands stitch. Then she recalled the horrible night Marla died.

They had walked home together after a judging meeting, but Emma had declined Marla's offer of a glass of cabernet at her place. Instead, she had returned to her own home and had just started knitting when she heard Ezra barking. Marla's schnauzer was moody and occasionally aggressive toward visitors. As Ezra continued barking, Emma went to the window and looked across the yard at Marla's house. Marla's drapes were drawn and the lights were on; perhaps she was sharing her bottle of wine with someone else. Emma put her knitting aside and decided to finish it the next morning.

During the night, something roused her. *Ezra again. Why was he barking at 3 A.M.?*

The next morning, Marla's curtains were still drawn and the porch light blazed in the morning sun. Emma knew something was wrong. She rushed over to Marla's house, knocked on the door, and shouted her name. The only response was Ezra's frantic yelping. She took a deep breath and pushed the door open. Ezra dashed by her and scrambled into the backyard.

Marla was slumped on her white leather sofa. One look confirmed Emma's worst fears. She grabbed the phone and dialed Rehoboth's police station. The voice she heard was that of her upstairs tenant, Carrie Beth, assistant to the chief.

"Carrie, it's Emma. I'm at Marla's. I think she's dead! She's just slumped over on the sofa. What should I do?"

"Don't touch anything, Emma. Wait on the porch. We'll be right there."

Emma headed for the door but she turned to look at Marla again. The coffee table, usually littered with books, coffee cups, and wine glasses, was clear. Emma shook her head. *How unlike Marla. Where is her bedtime glass of wine?* She stepped into the kitchen. As she expected, one of Marla's favorite reds was uncorked and waiting on the counter. At least two glasses had been consumed. But where was the glass? That mystery was quickly solved. Marla's favorite wineglass from one of her New York adventures was rinsed and drying in the rack.

"Emma! Where are you?" Carrie Beth burst into the house, followed by the EMT team and Chief Harvey Harris.

The EMTs quickly assessed Marla's condition and retreated to get the gurney. The chief sauntered around Marla's living room, scowling at the odd collection of art and photographs on the walls.

"That woman…what a nutcase," he muttered. "I don't know where she got some of her wacko ideas. Probably from the firewater she consumed. Woman drank like a fish."

Carrie Beth turned away from her examination of Marla's body.

"Chief, I don't see any evidence—"

"Oh, for heaven's sake, Carrie Beth. She probably just had a heart attack. Hey, Emma," he said, finally noticing her standing by the kitchen door. "What are you doing here? Did I tell you me and the missus are taking us a two-week cruise to the Caribbean next week?"

Emma nodded weakly. Everyone in Rehoboth had heard about the cruise for months. Carrie Beth squeezed Emma's shoulder in sympathy. "Don't worry, Emma. We'll sort this out. When did you last talk with her? Weren't you two at Browseabout last night?"

Before Emma could answer, the chief bellowed, "Come on, Carrie Beth. We're done here. Let's check on what's happening at the diner."

Carrie Beth sighed. "We'll talk later."

As Bronson droned on, Emma sipped her latte and wondered once again about what had caused Marla's sudden death. According to Carrie Beth, the chief had suggested a heart attack as the cause when he phoned Marla's nephew in Chicago, but there had been no real investigation. The nephew had had no contact with his aunt in years and hired Thad Wyman's law firm to settle her affairs for him. Ezra was adopted by neighbors down the street, and now Marla's home was dark and silent, but Emma could not forget about the wineglass sitting neatly in the rack. *What would Harriet say about that?*

A few nights later, Emma was awakened by Carrie Beth's hurried footsteps down the stairs outside her bedroom window. Now that the chief was away on his cruise, Carrie Beth was officially in charge. Emma hoped this emergency was not another mysterious death.

The next morning, Carrie Beth delivered the shocking news.

"Emma, I can hardly believe this but Bronson—" She drew a deep breath. "He was found dead and may have been murdered!"

"What? What happened?"

"You know the Martinez family—the ones who own Boardwalk Burgers? Well, their son locked up the store last night and took a shortcut home through Bronson's yard. He noticed fumes around the garage and called 911. We found Bronson in his car in the garage with the door closed. Emma, it doesn't make any sense. He had just finished a book reading at the Century Club and those nice ladies even bought several copies. Why would he commit suicide? We checked the garage door and there's no problem with the mechanism."

Emma felt a cold dread. *Was someone targeting the short-story contest judges?*

"Anyhow, I called Steve from the state police and requested help. I know the chief wouldn't want me to do that, but we have two mysterious deaths and no suspects. And there's one more thing—I noticed a lump on the back of Bronson's head. The EMT said he might have fallen earlier, but I don't think so. The medical examiner will tell us more, I hope." Carrie Beth gulped the rest of her coffee and rushed out to her car.

Emma locked her door carefully after Carrie Beth left. *Who would want to kill Bronson? And if it was murder, did the same person kill Marla?*

Friday was Emma's day to volunteer at the Rehoboth Beach Museum. The cool, rainy day kept visitors away, so she had time to catch up with Harriet's latest adventure. She couldn't wait to discuss it with Norman, and she decided to stop by the bookstore for a latte and a chat later that afternoon.

When she entered, she saw Norman and Lou in deep conversation with the chef of Figaro, one of Rehoboth's trendiest new restaurants. Later, she found Norman stacking the chairs in the community room. She could see right away that he was upset.

"What's wrong, Norman? Did you hear about Bronson?" she asked.

"What? Bronson? Oh, yeah, that's too bad. No, the chef wants to know where the cookbooks are for the benefit tomorrow night. I told Lou that I delivered them to Marla before she died. I guess they're still in her house. What am I supposed to do about it? The place is locked up, isn't it?"

Emma decided to choose another time to discuss Harriet's case, so she returned to the counter to pick up a copy of the *Cape Gazette*, and, as an afterthought, she added a copy of Bronson's book to her purchase.

When she arrived home, a Delaware state trooper's car was parked outside her door. Steve and Carrie Beth called to her to join them at the curb.

"Hi, Emma," Steve began. "Look, this case of Bronson's requires state investigation. Carrie Beth is right; this is no suicide. So we'll be running the investigation from now on. But you need to be extra-vigilant now."

He turned to Carrie Beth. "I know you blame yourself for not investigating Marla's death, but there was nothing you could do. The chief closed the door on that—but this is different. If we find Bronson's killer, I think we'll also solve Marla's case."

When Steve left, Carrie Beth sighed and headed back up to her apartment. Emma locked her door, poured a glass of pinot grigio, and pulled her knitting from the bag. Bronson's book fell on the table. She picked it up and felt a twinge of guilt. *Why hadn't she, as a fellow member of the Guild, been more supportive of his work?* No one had really taken him seriously. An hour later, she closed the book and poured a second glass. Bronson's attempts at describing

Rehoboth's vacation atmosphere, with its beautiful beach and bustling boardwalk, were flat and colorless. His descriptions of its residents, however, were sharp and cruel.

Emma immediately recognized Marla in his biting, sarcastic portrayal of a power-crazed writer whom he called Marva. He wrote about her fondness for wine, her cruel critiques of amateur writers, and even her annoying dog, Ira. Emma had not realized that Bronson hated her friend so much. *Enough to murder her?*

And who had hated Bronson? His scathing attacks included a chef he described as a low-life who made his money in the drug trade, an art gallery owner with a crew of attractive adolescent assistants, and—here Emma could hardly continue. Bronson's description of Norville, a high school football star and bully who became a store clerk with dreams of writing a bestselling mystery, could only be Norman.

Emma could not imagine Norman as a murderer. *Had Norman read Bronson's book?*

The next morning, Carrie Beth phoned with the results from the medical examiner.

"Steve says Bronson was knocked unconscious with a bat or a cane—something like that. His attacker put him in the garage with the car running to make sure he was dead and so that we wouldn't investigate it as a homicide."

"What about fingerprints on the car or the garage?" Emma asked. She knew that's what Harriet would have asked.

"They're looking at that today, but Steve says it's unlikely to give us anything. I keep thinking about Marla, Emma. What am I missing?"

Emma wanted to tell her about Bronson's book, but first she needed to make a trip to Browseabout. Tonight there was a lecture about Chinese porcelain in the community room. That would give her an opportunity to launch an investigation of her own.

Emma found a seat in the last row just as the program began. At the end, she hurried out of the community room and down the aisle where the mysteries were shelved. Norman was nowhere in sight. She located the shelf where the Murder Around the Clock series was stacked.

She ran her fingers along the shelf until she found book 7. Yes, this was the one in which Harriet had solved the case of the beautiful debutante whose champagne had been drugged with one of those date-rape drugs. She skimmed a few sections. The debutante's escort didn't know that she was diabetic and that the combination of "roofies" and diabetes had changed a nasty prank into murder. *Was Marla's glass of wine drugged?* Her diabetes was a well-known fact, and the murderer must have known that the drug could have deadly results if ingested by a diabetic.

And then there was Harriet's case of the corrupt congressman. He was knocked out in the parking lot, stuffed into his Mercedes, driven to his garage, and left to die in—

"Emma! What are you doing?" Norman's tone was sharp; his eyes glared at her with a new hostility.

"Oh, just browsing." Emma knew her shaky voice was not convincing. "You know that I'm always looking for new authors."

She slipped by him and headed out the door. For a moment she was tempted to call Carrie Beth to take her home. Rehoboth Avenue was empty and the rain had left a glistening, slippery surface on the sidewalk.

"Emma!" Norman's shout clutched at her heart. *What did he want? Was she imagining the danger she felt?*

Emma turned reluctantly and saw Norman waving a knitting needle. "Hey, Emma! Wait! You dropped this in the store!"

Emma saw the needle and her first thought was to shout back that it wasn't hers, she was using circular needles on this project.

But Norman was closing the distance between them rapidly. The look on his face told her that what he held was not a knitting needle. Harriet had solved a similar case in book 9. In that one, the needle was really a slim spike sharpened into a murder weapon—very much like the one Norman was brandishing at her!

Emma wanted to scream. She wanted to run. Instead, she stood rooted to the sidewalk, watching Norman run toward her.

"Stop, Norman! Drop that thing. I'm a good shot—don't tempt me."

Lou spoke with cold authority, as did the gun he pointed at Norman. Emma thought it might be a Glock, like the one Harriet had learned to shoot in book 1.

The spike clattered to the sidewalk as Norman sagged to his knees, putting his hands behind his head. Emma sank down on a nearby bench and Lou kicked the spike out of Norman's reach.

Suddenly, the street was alive with sirens and flashing lights as Carrie Beth arrived in her patrol car, followed by Steve in his. Carrie Beth rushed toward Norman.

"Norman, what were you thinking? Why Emma?" she demanded.

He glanced guiltily at Emma. "Because she figured it out. She knew I was the one."

"Carrie Beth," Steve's voice held a warning note. "We'll take care of him. Please see that Emma gets home safely." Steve resumed his conversation with Lou while two other troopers handcuffed Norman and led him to their patrol car.

The next morning began as a day as gloomy as Emma's mood. She had spent a restless night thinking about Norman. Emma turned off the TV; she was already tired of hearing the young reporter from WBOC breathlessly recapping the events of the previous night.

Suddenly, the doorbell rang. Much to her surprise, her caller was Lou, balancing a carrier filled with Browseabout cups and a pastry bag.

"I thought you could use a latte and a chocolate croissant," he smiled as he offered the tray. As he settled back on the sofa, Emma asked him if he had any news about Norman.

"I spoke with Steve early this morning. Norman gave a full confession." Lou shook his head. "He was really a better store manager than criminal."

"If only I had read Bronson's book earlier," Emma said sadly, "so much of this might have been avoided. The chapter about Norville was brutal."

"And Norman heard that Bronson had read that chapter at his first speaking engagement at the library two weeks ago," Lou added. "He was sure that everyone knew it was about him. When Bronson was the featured speaker at the Century Club, Norman slipped into the back of the room just long enough to hear him reading the Norville story once again."

"So he was waiting with a baseball bat when Bronson returned from the club," Emma said, figuring it out as she went along. "First he hit him with the bat, then put him back in the car, and left the car running with the doors closed."

"Yes, it sounds like the plot from a novel. Maybe that's where he got the idea."

Emma felt a slow flush creeping onto her cheeks. *Did he know about Harriet?*

"I have a big regret about this, too," Lou continued. "During her visits at the store, I heard Marla teasing Norman about how he could use one of the Guild's writing workshops. I know that he had submitted a story to the contest about his experiences as a lifeguard and that he had overheard her comments about his work."

Emma sighed. "I wondered about that. It seems like Norman was always close by when the contest judges met. Marla could be cruel at times. I wish I had spoken up about it."

"But here's the part I don't understand, Emma." Lou placed his cup on the coffee table. "I heard Norman tell Carrie Beth that he came after you because you knew. He said the same thing in his confession. Carrie Beth said you two have known each other for years. So why did you suspect him of murder?"

This was the moment Emma had dreaded. Apparently, Norman's confession did not include the role that Harriet and the Murder Around the Clock cases had played. Instead, he had transformed Emma into a detective just like Harriet, and soon everyone would be asking her about the case—maybe even the reporter from WBOC. She and Norman had frequently wished that they had a case to solve, and now it was here.Emma smiled and turned to face Lou. "It was difficult to think that anyone would want to kill the contest judges, and even harder to see Norman as a murderer. But I knew the clues were all there, and for me, the first one was Marla's wineglass."

LIKE EMMA WALSH, NANCY LINTON IS A MYSTERY FAN AND OFTEN READS EVERY BOOK IN A SERIES. "THE WINEGLASS CLUE" IS THE FIRST MYSTERY SHE HAS WRITTEN, ALTHOUGH SHE WONDERS IF EMMA WILL SOON FIND HERSELF ENTANGLED IN ANOTHER CASE. NANCY'S STORY "FOR SALE" WON A JUDGE'S AWARD AND WAS PUBLISHED IN THE FIRST REHOBOTH BEACH READS ANTHOLOGY, THE BEACH HOUSE. SHE AND HER HUSBAND RESIDE IN GARNET VALLEY, PENNSYLVANIA.

Synchronicity

by Gail Sobotkin

I was on my knees, photographing a seashell that had washed ashore. Tiny water bubbles trapped inside it glistened in the sun. I captured the shot from different angles, enjoying the solitude of Rehoboth in fall, until a long, thin shadow eclipsed the brilliant sunshine.

Annoyed, I looked up and glared at the stranger towering above me. "Can't you walk someplace else? We're the only two people on the beach and you're ruining my photo shoot."

"Sorry. I thought you had fallen and might need help getting up."

The man's voice was smooth as a baritone sax and the notes sounded vaguely familiar. I stood, shielded my eyes from the sun, and tried to get a better look at his face. As soon as I saw the thick dark lashes framing his sepia eyes, I realized it was Joe, the guy I'd fallen madly in love with the summer after my high school graduation. Oh, how I'd envied those lashes. Even with mascara, my own were pathetically thin by comparison. Time had certainly been kind to his looks and physique. His hair had receded a bit, but except for a smattering of gray around the temples, it was still dark, and the only lines on his face were narrow crow's feet. Heart fluttering like a hummingbird's wings, I squealed, "Joe Woodruff?"

His thick, full lips broke into a wide grin. "Well, I'll be, if it isn't little Sarah Mills! You've hardly changed at all. Bet I can still sweep you off your feet."

Before I could protest, he picked me up and swung me around, magically transporting me to the summer of 1969, when he'd swung me around on this very beach.

"Put me down!" I had said, and when our eyes locked, I had half feared and half wanted him to kiss me.

"People are staring at us."

He put me down, and when I ran away, he charged after me. For a few moments we were like two sandpipers, zigzagging in and out of the water's edge.

Suddenly, a black cloud came over us and rain begin to fall. We dove under the boardwalk for shelter. Joe took off his T-shirt and spread it over our heads to protect us from the rain coming through the cracks.

Within a few moments, the shower turned into a light drizzle, so we huddled under his shirt. I was acutely aware of his bare, muscular chest, and the fact that we'd only known each other since last week's bonfire on the beach. He had to be the most handsome boy I'd ever seen. This was our first official date, and sitting so close to his half-naked body seemed disturbingly intimate.

After an awkward silence, he said, "I love the sea. I've always dreamed of joining the navy and becoming a Seal. I've already spoken to a recruiter."

"Aren't you afraid of being sent to Vietnam?"

"My dad's in Vietnam, and he's my hero." Joe sat up straight. "He's a naval officer who's had a great career, and he always said if I wanted to join the navy, he'd support me on it. I'm not changing my dream just because some people don't like the war. Besides, I think Nixon will end it soon."

"But what if he doesn't?"

"I'll defend my country, just like my dad."

I nodded. "I've always wanted to be a pediatrician. My older sister got polio and died just before the vaccine came out. I was really young and don't really remember her, but I remember my parents crying. When I was four I said I was going to be a doctor, and that seemed to make them happy. Now I'm going to NYU, premed, starting this fall."

We looked at each other, realizing we were doomed to years of separation and any romance was unlikely to survive. I sensed that his thoughts matched mine as he leaned down to kiss me, but it didn't stop the feelings of passion. His kiss was long and lingering.

A loud bark startled me.

Joe whistled and a golden retriever came bounding toward him. "Meet my trusty partner, Lucky. He loves beautiful ladies, don't you, boy?"

Lucky barked twice and I laughed. "I see the two of you operate as a team when picking up ladies."

"You bet. He's got my back and I return the favor when he meets a female dog. Give Sarah your paw, boy, and a proper hello."

Lucky extended his paw, and as I bent to take it, he licked my salty face with his scratchy tongue. "He's quite a charmer."

Joe picked up a small piece of driftwood, threw it in the ocean, and watched Lucky run after it. "I see you're married," he said, noticing the ring on my left hand.

"Widowed a few years ago after thirty-five years."

"Sorry to hear that. Must be tough being alone after so many years together."

I nodded, then changed the subject, afraid I'd tear up if I talked about my beloved Sam. "And you?"

"Not the marrying kind. Tried it once, but my wife divorced me three years later—military life is hard on a woman. Retired last year. That's when I adopted Lucky from a local shelter. Figured that'd be easier than trying to live with a woman after so many years of single life."

When Lucky came back with the stick, Joe took it and rubbed his neck. "I've always envied couples who were together for decades like you and your husband. You grow up together, not just get older, at least that's how I imagine it would be."

We walked in silence for a while. *So many years.* He had joined the navy as planned, and I had gone off to NYU. After he got shipped to Nam, we exchanged letters for a few months, but then his letters stopped. I tried to call his dad, but the phone number was no longer in service. I contacted the navy, but since I wasn't his wife, no one would tell me Joe's status or location. Heartbroken, I had focused on my studies.

Joe broke the silence. "I never forgot you. Even tried to look you up when I got released from the POW camp and had been back in the States for a while. That was when my dad gave me the stack of letters you'd written a few years earlier."

"Why didn't he tell me what had happened to you? I didn't know if you were dead or alive."

"He didn't have the heart to tell you I was MIA. He thought it would be better if you forgot about me."

"Well, why didn't you contact me when you got back?"

"After reading your letters, I came down to Rehoboth, made a few discreet inquiries about you, and found out you were engaged."

I was stunned. What would I have done if he had found me back then and told me why he'd never written back? In my heart I instantly knew the answer—nothing would have changed my love for and commitment to Sam.

"I'm sorry to hear that you suffered so much."

He shrugged. "It wasn't what I bargained for, but as you know, enlisting was my choice. I had no one to blame but myself."

I touched his arm. "You did what you had to do and I respect the sacrifice you made for our country—and your decision to not intrude on my relationship with my husband."

A shadow came over his face and I noticed his eyes looked glassy. "Do you think things would have been different if I'd been able to answer your letters? Sorry to put you on the spot, but it's a question that's always haunted me."

I paused, trying to collect my thoughts, knowing I owed him a truthful answer. "I don't know. What I do know is that learning to live in the present, one moment at a time, is the way one gets through grief, and right now, what I'm feeling is grateful that you found me here today."

He smiled and reached for my hand. "Me too."

We walked a little farther down the beach, and then he stopped suddenly. "Have you had lunch yet?"

"No, and I'm starving."

"Good. Let's drop Lucky off at my condo and I'll take you to Grotto's. You still like pizza, don't you?"

"Yep. Some things never change and my love for Grotto's pizza is one of them."

GAIL SOBOTKIN EARNED A BSN DEGREE FROM WILLIAM PATERSON UNIVERSITY AND IS A MEMBER OF THE REHOBOTH BEACH WRITERS' GUILD. SHE'S A RETIRED NURSE WHO LOVES WRITING MEDICAL AND TRAVEL ARTICLES, AND SHORT STORIES. HER WORK HAS BEEN PUBLISHED IN THE *AMERICAN JOURNAL OF NURSING*, *DELAWARE BEACH LIFE*, *CHICKEN SOUP FOR THE SOUL: FIND YOUR INNER STRENGTH*, AND *DELMARVA QUARTERLY*. SHE COEDITED *MYSTERIOUS & MIRACULOUS BOOK II*, A COLLECTION OF ARTICLES ABOUT PARANORMAL EVENTS AND MIRACLES (MOST OF THE BOOK'S PROCEEDS GO TO SUPPORT HOMELESS VETERANS). GAIL'S STORY, "SYNCHRONICITY," IS FICTION, BUT THE MAIN CHARACTER WAS INSPIRED BY HER HUSBAND, FRED, WHO IS A VIETNAM VETERAN. THEY HAVE BEEN MARRIED FORTY-ONE YEARS AND MOVED TO SOUTHERN DELAWARE IN 2001 TO LIVE NEAR THE OCEAN.

Witchy Women

by Connie L. McDowell

Emerging from the infernal heat of the boardwalk bar, Tristan stumbled across the boards, hoping to clear the fog infiltrating his brain. A nip in the autumnal air on this final Thursday evening in October forced a momentary shiver from him. His body's internal thermostat struggled to readjust to the drastic temperature change. Wisps of vapor emanating from his nostrils formed a feathery mist as his lungs sucked in cold air and exhaled warm.

The moon glowed like a lantern overhead, casting thousands of tiny crystals of light across the sea. Reminiscent of a virgin snowfall, the sand glistened on the moon-blanched beach. Waves crested and crashed, as the water tugged at the shoreline.

While gazing at the idyllic scene, Tristan spied a sudden movement. Three shadowy figures streaked across the sky, in triangular tandem formation, their shapes silhouetted in sharp relief against the full moon. Tristan gasped.

I must have more of a buzz on than I realized, he thought. *That can't have been what it appeared to be.*

Behind him, Tristan heard a loud *wh-o-o-sh* and the boards under his feet vibrated. He whirled around. There stood the most incredibly vile creatures he'd ever encountered. "Oh, God, help me!" he cried.

The trio advanced toward him. "Somebody, please help me!" Tristan's frightened pleas went unheard. Between the blare of the music and the frenzied chatter inside the bar, there was simply too much noise. Tristan retreated until his back was against the railing. Out of room, no place to hide, nowhere to run. Recoiling, he waited for them to strike. Instead, they halted, inches away. Shuddering,

Tristan peered through first one eye, then the other.

Clad entirely in black, all three wore pointed hats and shoes. Their gnarled fingers, straggly hair, crooked teeth, and chartreuse skin peppered with warts made Tristan cringe. One of them muttered, "It's colder than a witch's tit in a brass brassiere down here." Cackling wildly, they parked their broomsticks beside the light pole.

The second one piped up, "Believe it or not, it's supposed to be in the sixties on Parade Day."

"Not *too* hot, I hope, or you know what'll happen. We'll become mere puddles in the street," said the third one.

Tristan feared his legs, now as wobbly as Jell-O, might fail him. He plopped onto the nearest bench and stared at the boards, willing the spectacle before him to disappear. His brain registered a sexy voice asking his name and his head snapped upright. The unsightly crones had mysteriously vanished; in their stead stood a trio of statuesque sirens. A fiery redhead, her shimmering locks highlighted with shots of liquid copper, reminded Tristan of his favorite brand of rum. Beside her towered a stunning brunette, whose long satiny hair, the color of Kahlua, flowed across her unblemished shoulders. Rounding out the threesome was a stellar platinum blonde, with pale golden curls that sparkled like expensive champagne. Tristan shook his head and shut his eyes. When he reopened them, the enticing visions remained.

The alluring redhead appeared to be in charge. Leveling her eyes at him, she said, "I asked you your name. What's the matter, cowboy? One of our cats got your tongue?"

Force of habit compelled Tristan to remove his Stetson, exposing his sweat-drenched head. He finally managed to say, "I'm...I'm... Tris-tan." He wiped aside the stubborn strands of hair plastered to his forehead.

"Pleased to make your acquaintance, *Tris-tan*. What a marvelous moniker. I'm Della. The blonde's Stella, and this one's Esmerelda. In case you hadn't noticed, we're triplets; not identical, but close enough to give people fits, if we choose."

Tristan stammered, "I'll bet!"

Although hair color differed, the women's overall appearance was essentially the same, their facial features startlingly similar. Their dresses, though not exactly alike, hugged their curvaceous figures in the same way, clinging in *all* the right places. Forget your clichéd blond bombshell. This was the D-Day invasion.

Spellbound, Tristan couldn't help gawking—and wondering what the heck was going on. But before he could think of what to ask, one of the—what—apparitions?—began to explain.

"We flew in for the Sea Witch Festival," said Della. "Most of you mortals prefer baking yourselves to a crisp on the beach during the summer, but we don't handle hot weather well. This is *our* idea of a beach vacation. We intend to have fun this weekend, but primarily we came for the costume parade."

"Uh, 'mortals'?" Tristan recalled the hideous crones that had mysteriously vanished at exactly the moment the beautiful trio materialized and made the connection. *The Sea Witch Festival.* Leery about asking, he eventually summoned his courage. "So you're—"

"Witches. Yes."

Tristan stared at Della. He wondered what kind of costumes they planned to wear to the festival. If they could change back to the way they'd looked when he first saw them, they'd scare the bejesus out of everyone, but certainly have a lock on the most authentic costumes.

As if reading his mind, Stella said, "We figure there'll be enough mortals masquerading as witches, so we're planning to wear human disguises. Won't that be a hoot?" In her most beguiling and breathiest voice, she murmured coyly, "Hi. I'm Marilyn Monroe." Sidling up to Tristan, she crooned the infamous "Happy Birthday, Mr. President," then kissed him on the cheek.

Della said, "I'm portraying Rita Hayworth, movie star temptress and World War II pinup girl. And darling Ezzy is—"

Flinging out her arms, Esmerelda replied in her sexiest growl, "I'm Liz Taylor, famous for my violet eyes and my penchant for expensive jewels."

Tristan nodded his approval. "You just might win. I think I'll stick around and see what happens. Where're you staying?"

"Esmerelda found the perfect spot," said Stella. "Tell him, Ezzy."

Smiling, Esmerelda said, "The Bewitched and BEDazzled Bed and Breakfast, on Lake Avenue."

Tristan guffawed. Then he said, "You're pullin' my leg."

"No, she's not," said Della. "Come see for yourself."

Tristan accompanied them to the address, where two ordinary-looking houses appeared connected by a communal backyard and deck. Artfully designed Halloween decorations and lights were anything but spooky, and nothing suggested the places were haunted. Tristan didn't understand what the sisters found so appealing.

"The online pictures of the interior attracted me," said Esmerelda. *Witches use the Internet? Now that's a scary thought.*

Ezzy continued, "The first house, resembling the one from the sitcom *Bewitched*, has rooms named after the TV characters. The other home's designed to fit the sophisticated movie star image from the thirties and forties, with rooms bearing the names of famous actors and actresses." Della and Stella agreed. Ezzy couldn't have chosen a more enchanting place.

"We're sleeping in Aunt Clara's room, one of the few with enough beds," said Stella. "As true witches, we believe in the rule of three. We won't be separated, not ever." On that note, they turned to go inside, but not before inviting Tristan to join them for breakfast.

"But I'm not a paying guest," he said.

"No problem. We'll brew something for you in our cauldron—it's bubbling in the backyard," said Della. Watching his horrified expression, she shook her finger at him, emitted a wicked laugh, and shrilled, "Gotcha!"

Tristan's attraction to this curious trio conflicted with his normally wary nature. Drawn like a magnet to metal—like the proverbial moth to a flame—temptation trumped distrust. He wavered briefly, then said, "O-K...I guess. I'll see you gals at eight."

Tristan noticed they carried no bags, but before he could mention it, they wiggled their noses. Suitcases appeared in each of their hands. His mouth agape, Tristan shook his head again, then he strode down the street toward his truck and drove to his motel on Route 1.

* * * * *

Tristan awoke to the sun streaming through the window. The clock display read 8:37. Leaping from his bed, he dove into the shower. Less than ten minutes passed before Tristan gunned his old truck and headed for Lake Avenue.

The innkeeper responded to the insistent ringing of the doorbell. Trying to appear unconcerned, Tristan inquired about the triplets. The innkeeper said, "O-oooo. If you're Tristan, you're in hot water."

I might become acquainted with that bubbling cauldron yet, he thought.

"Those gals were mighty peeved at you for missing breakfast. I'm afraid they've already stomped off. I think they were headed for the boardwalk."

Tristan paced up and down the boardwalk and back and forth on Rehoboth Avenue. Everywhere he ventured, he asked if anyone had seen the triplets. No one had. Then he spied three little girls pointing and snickering at him from a bench near Dolle's. They looked about eight years old—one with brown hair, one with red, and one with gold. Marching over to them, he fumed, "Not funny. I've wasted two hours hunting for you. Now I'm starved." Della raised her arms, her hands hidden behind a puff of smoke. When it dissipated, she held a tray containing a lavish breakfast. Tristan sat and wolfed it down. After polishing it off, he asked, "How'd you do that?"

"Magic, my dear. Magic."

"So I s'pose that also explains how you were gorgeous women last night, but today you're just little girls."

Esmerelda grinned and said, "Partly, that was your punishment for missing breakfast, but mostly we transformed ourselves because we want to participate in some of the kids' events."

This wasn't how Tristan had envisioned the day. He'd planned on squiring three drop-dead gorgeous women around town, doing grown-up activities like hitting the bars, or maybe even something more interesting. Attempting to mask his disappointment, he asked, "Like what?"

Esmerelda said, "We'd like to ride the ponies to compare them with our usual mode of transportation. There's not much room on those brooms of ours, you know." They trudged across the sand to the person collecting money.

"Pony rides—five dollars apiece," said the guy slouched in the chair.

The triplets looked at Tristan expectantly. "We don't have any money," admitted Stella. "Please, please can we ride the ponies?" she whined in a childlike voice, for the benefit of the ride guy.

Scowling, Tristan peeled a ten and a five from his wallet. He grumbled, "What happened to your magic?"

"We could be arrested," replied Della. "You *know* it's a crime to manufacture money, Tristan; that's counterfeiting."

Tristan watched sullenly, while the girls clambered into the stirrups and settled onto the saddles. They appeared almost angelic riding along the shoreline. A smile spread across Tristan's face as he watched them cavorting among the waves. By the time they dismounted, everyone's mood had improved, the morning's unpleasantness forgotten.

At lunchtime, Tristan and the sisters feasted on "broasted buzzard" and "petrified pork sand-witches," a.k.a. turkey and ham. "Batwing stew," a soup of thinly sliced beef and noodles, was enjoyed by all. Their beverage of choice was "slime-ade," a grass-green potion that tasted suspiciously like lemon-lime soda.

While they were eating, Della said, "Mortals sure are weird, Tristan. Why do you use such strange names for your food and drink?"

He gulped. *How can I explain without offending the girls?*

Before he could respond, Stella came to his rescue. "I don't think they really use these names, ordinarily. They've just renamed their food in keeping with the spirit of the festival."

Tristan heaved a sigh of relief and nodded.

"Well, I certainly hope that's true. It's not like we're from a different planet," said Della indignantly.

After lunch, the group trooped down to the beach for the games. Finding it impossible to balance a peanut on their noses, they came in last in the "peanut on the nose walk." Della complained, "We would have done better with our witches' noses." But then they wowed the crowd with their aerial acrobatics in the "frog hop," bounding and leaping their way into the top five. Confidence restored, they moved on to the final event, the "whacky broom toss." Although dismayed to learn that use of personal brooms was forbidden, the girls' supernatural powers served them well. During her turn, Stella intoned, "Life's a witch, and then you fly," as she threw her broom. She placed third, tossing it seventy feet, triple the length of her nearest competitor. Esmerelda propelled her broom into the air, uttering the words, "If the broom fits, fly it," and nailed down second place with a throw of seventy-two feet.

Della, the final competitor, stepped forward. Preparing to launch her wood-and-straw missile, she chanted, "Something wicked this way comes." It blasted from her hand, leaving behind a trailing cloud of smoke. Onlookers oohed and aahed as Della's broom catapulted into space. It vanished from view, then quickly reappeared. It zigged to the right, then zagged to the left, before centering itself, landing an amazing eighty feet away. Della was declared "Boss of the Toss." Holding her broom-shaped award, she quietly boasted to Tristan, "I could've hurled it all the way to Florida if I'd given it my best effort, but that would've been showing off." Eyeing her sisters, she added, "Since we won the top three spots, I guess one could say we 'swept' the broom event."

Tristan couldn't refrain from joining in. "Very punny," he said, setting off another round of giggles.

Plodding across the sand, the girls informed Tristan they were entering the bike race on the boardwalk. "But you have nothing to ride," he protested. No sooner had he spoken than three bikes miraculously appeared.

"Why don't you race with us, Tristan?" asked Esmerelda.

"I can't. Even if I had a bike, competitors must be eight years old or younger."

The instant the words rolled off his tongue, Tristan felt the boardwalk rise up to meet him. People of ordinary height morphed into giants. Turning toward the girls, his puzzled brown eyes collided head-on with three matched sets of sparkling emerald-green ones. The girls had shrunk Tristan to the size of a young boy. A shiny blue bike stood before him. An adult's hand ushered Tristan toward the starting line; the triplets followed suit. When the starter pistol sounded, Tristan pedaled, pouring every ounce of energy into the race, focused solely on the finish line.

"Whoa, cowboy! You can stop now. You won by a country mile. I'm surprised there's any rubber left on them tires. They're practically smokin'."

Tristan looked around, then tilted his head upward. Some old codger, grinning broadly, handed him a small trophy with a bicycle on it. The girls crowded around and chorused, "Let's see. We want to see your prize."

"I didn't actually earn this. You girls are responsible."

"Don't be silly," said Stella. "*You* put the pedal to the metal!"

Laughing, Tristan confessed, "Okay, it was kinda fun, you know, reliving my childhood, but if it's not too much trouble, I'd really like to be *me* again."

In seconds, he was back to his normal six-foot-five frame. Deciding playtime was over, the girls transformed into adults again. Their metamorphosis elicited admiring glances from Tristan. "The local landscape sure has become much more interesting. Everything was so flat; now there are lots of peaks and valleys." The triplets pretended not to understand, but he caught the sly glances they exchanged.

Della said, "Come back to the house, and we'll concoct a spooktacular dinner for you."

"And afterward, we'll catch the outdoor movie—*Hocus Pocus*," added Stella.

They watched the movie, and after it ended, Tristan escorted them to their room. "I'll grab breakfast on my own," he said, "but I'll be at the convention center at 10 A.M. to take pictures of the parade."

"We'll be waiting," said Esmerelda.

Stella said, "I'm so excited. I doubt I'll sleep a wink."

"Don't be late," warned Della.

Retiring to his motel, Tristan's last thoughts before falling asleep were of the similarities between the movie and the events he was experiencing. *Three witch sisters had returned to Earth after being dead for 300 years. One was a redhead, one was a brunette, and one was a blonde...*

* * * * * *

Tristan was punctual, but a huge crowd had already gathered, making it difficult to locate the sisters. Finally, he heard Esmerelda calling him. Following the sound of her voice, he discovered them on a side street. Tristan stood, transfixed. Each one's hair was styled like that of the "star" she portrayed, makeup flawlessly applied, with dresses and accessories perfectly tailored for her character. Tristan snapped multiple pictures of the threesome, as well as individual shots.

The parade took hours, due to a record number of entries and the length of the parade route. While the triplets anxiously awaited the results of the costume contest, Tristan treated them to lunch. Eventually, a horn sounded and the crowd converged on the bandstand. The names of the winning bands in the competition were announced first. Next came the winners of the motorized division. At last, individual contestants who'd won prizes were named. The triplets had tied for first place. They went crazy—yanking on Tristan's clothing, jumping up and down, and screaming.

* * * * * *

Tristan felt himself being jostled. A faraway voice shouted in his ear, "Tristan, wake up, man. What're you doing? It's freezin' out here."

Slowly, Tristan sat upright on the bench. Groggy and disoriented, he asked, "Where're the girls?"

"What girls? There aren't any girls out here. They're all inside the bar." His buddy, Joe, eyed him oddly.

"No. I mean the *triplets*—Della, Stella, and Esmerelda."

"You're the only one *trip*-pin'," said Joe. "I don't know what you've been drinkin' or smokin', but when I came outside looking for you, you were passed out here, dude. Out cold and a-l-o-n-e. I'm telling you again, there were *no* girls."

"The weirdest thing happened, Joe. You'd never believe me if I told you. I can hardly believe it myself."

"Bring it on," said Joe.

Tristan recounted the details of the previous two days. Joe cracked up and said, "Sounds like you went to the *S-e-e* Witch Festival. You really tied one on, pardner, having a whacked-out dream like that. I sure don't want none of whatever you were drinking."

"I can prove it! I took pictures of them in their costumes," said Tristan. "Wait, I'll show you." Grabbing his camera, he searched frantically for the photos, but there were no images. Then he recalled hearing that manifestations, like ghosts and witches, were impossible to capture on film.

Was Joe right? Did I pass out from too much booze, conjuring up, whatever—an eerie dream, or a weird hallucination?

Returning his camera to the truck, Tristan spied something shiny on the mat. He retrieved it, realizing it was the trophy he'd won. He set it on the seat—atop a napkin stained with lipstick—the one he'd used to wipe away Stella's lip print after she kissed him. Slamming the door, he sprinted to Lake Avenue. The Bewitched and BEDazzled Bed & Breakfast did indeed exist, just as he'd remembered it. A piece of paper fluttered from the windowsill of the room in which the triplets had stayed. Picking it up, Tristan read: "We shall return. D/E/S."

A note from the girls—*he wasn't going bonkers after all.*

As Tristan walked slowly back to his truck, he gazed up at the sky. Three shadowy figures streaked across, in triangular tandem formation, silhouetted in sharp relief against the full moon. Unlike before, they didn't come down to Earth. Instead, they appeared to plant themselves in the western sky—a trio of twinkling stars. Stars that seemed to be winking at him.

Tristan smiled and winked back. He continued his stroll, whistling the tune "Witchcraft," from *Hocus Pocus,* already looking forward to next year's Sea Witch Festival.

CONNIE MCDOWELL IS A NATIVE SUSSEX COUNTIAN AND A FORMER ELEMENTARY TEACHER AND SPECIAL EDUCATION COORDINATOR IN THE WOODBRIDGE SCHOOL DISTRICT. RETIREMENT AFFORDED HER AN OPPORTUNITY TO DEVOTE MORE TIME TO ONE OF HER MANY INTERESTS— WRITING. "WITCHY WOMEN" IS HER FIRST PUBLISHED WORK. THE STORY, INSPIRED BY THE SEA WITCH FESTIVAL, BEGAN AS A CONVENTIONAL, STRAIGHTFORWARD NARRATIVE, BUT IT MORPHED, TAKING ON A LIFE OF ITS OWN. CONNIE WOULD LIKE TO THANK CAT AND MOUSE PRESS AND BROWSEABOUT BOOKS FOR SPONSORING THIS CONTEST. THEIR ENDEAVORS PROMOTE AND SUPPORT ASPIRING AND ESTABLISHED WRITERS WHILE HIGHLIGHTING THE NATION'S SUMMER CAPITAL— REHOBOTH BEACH. KUDOS ALSO TO THE PANEL OF JUDGES FOR TAKING TIME FROM THEIR BUSY SCHEDULES TO PARTICIPATE.

Waiting for Summer

by V. K. Dorner

As she ran along the beach, her long, golden ringlets bounced with each step, shimmering in the brilliant sunlight. *An angel,* I thought to myself. I was only five, but that vision of her was forever etched in my memory.

She skirted along the water's edge before spying me on the wet sand. She ran up and sat down beside me, announcing in a prim voice, "Hello! My name is Summer Stevens. You are going to be my friend."

And so I was. Her family was vacationing on Rehoboth Beach, the beach I called home. We spent the days building sandcastles and collecting seashells.

"I want to stay here forever," she said on her last night in town. "Just like you."

"I wish you could," I sighed, fiercely holding onto her hand. "Then we could play together every day."

"Are you going to miss me?"

"Yes. Are you going to miss me?"

"With all my heart."

"You'll come back, won't you?"

"Definitely. You'll wait for me, won't you?"

"Always."

She smiled and gave a small nod, pleased with my reply.

"Summer, time to go," her father yelled.

"Good-bye, Jared."

"Good-bye, Summer."

She leaned over and quickly kissed me on the cheek. She did not look back as she ran away, but that was the moment I knew. I was in love.

Summer and I grew closer over the years, as her family regularly rented the house next door to ours in Rehoboth Beach. Beginning the first morning of summer break, I would look out the window, checking to see if she had arrived. Sometimes, it would be a short wait, mere days before she and her parents pulled into the drive next door. Other times, the days dragged on and she didn't come until nearly the end of the season.

If I was there when the car pulled in, I would rush over. Even before the car came to a stop (much to her father's dismay), she would fling open her door and bound out of the car. True to her name, she brought warmth and joy that made me glow inside.

Each year it grew harder to say good-bye. We took to hiding under the porch, prolonging the time before her father called for her to go home.

When I was thirteen, it was particularly hard to let her go. Perhaps I had a premonition. Perhaps I was just experiencing the pull of hormones for the first time.

"Summer, time to go," came the dreaded words from her father. We huddled under the porch, holding hands. I couldn't stop admiring her long, tan legs.

She leaned over and whispered in my ear, "I gotta go."

"No," I pleaded. "Don't go. Stay here with me."

"I wish I could."

I stared into her deep, green eyes and saw the same longing I felt. Instead of a quick peck on the cheek, she pressed her lips to mine. *Cherry lipstick.*

"Summer," her father warned from above. "Now."

We broke apart, smiling at each other.

"Will you wait for me?" she asked, as had become our custom farewell.

"Always."

She leaned over and gave me another kiss before she crawled out from beneath the porch, leaving me staring at her in amazement and grinning like an idiot.

During the long wait until the next summer, I imagined our next kiss. I daydreamed about her, and when I found a shell I thought she would like, I fashioned it into a necklace, etching "J ♥ S" on the underside.

When the time finally came and her father pulled into the driveway, I ran upstairs and retrieved the necklace before rushing next door. The back door flung open and out stepped a young girl with shiny, black hair. Confused, I looked back at the driver. Yes, that was Summer's father, but that was not Summer's mother, and that was not Summer.

"Hey, Jared," Mr. Stevens called, as he climbed out of the SUV.

"Where's Summer?" I blurted, panic crowding out politeness. Her father glanced quickly at the woman in the passenger seat, his neck reddening.

"Uh, Summer will not be joining us this time. She has decided to stay—with her mother."

"What do you mean? Summer is supposed to be here."

He came around the car, put his arm around my shoulders, and led me away.

"Look, son. Summer's mother and I have separated. She is spending the holiday with her mom. Hopefully, she will join us next year."

But she didn't. Not the next year, the following year, or the year after that. I lost count of the number of times I wanted to yell at her father for ruining my life. Summer was not summer without Summer.

As the years passed, I stopped looking out the window, stopped anticipating a reunion that would never come. In high school, I dated off and on. Nothing serious. Every girl paled in comparison to the memory of Summer. I would lie in bed at night and remember our last good-bye, the sweet kiss, and the promise to wait.

Waiting was hard, but I never gave up hope.

After high school graduation, several of my classmates planned a party on the beach. It was a last good-bye, as most were going off to college. Not me. I would be taking over my parents' small gift shop on Rehoboth Avenue. It would not make me rich, but I could live at the beach.

"Are you sure you don't want to go? Mom and I can watch the shop," Dad asked from behind the cash register, worry etched on his brow.

"Nah. I am good," I replied, shooting him a quick smile before continuing to place the suntan lotions on the shelf in front of me. I was so engrossed in my task that I didn't hear the door chime, or the slap of flip-flops on the floor.

"Excuse me. Do you have any SPF 30?"

Starting at the neon pink toes and working up the long, lean legs, I looked at the girl—no, the woman—standing before me. Golden curls were pulled back into a high ponytail and when she pushed her sunglasses to the top of her head I stared into familiar green eyes.

"Summer?"

"Jared?" We locked into each other's gaze.

"Oh, my God!" I cried, as I dropped a bottle of lotion and reached for her. She jumped into my arms and held tight as I swung her around.

"I didn't think I would—"

"Ever see you again," I completed her thought.

We hugged, and if not for the watchful eye of my father, I would have kissed her then and there. After all, I had been imagining it for five years.

"What are you doing tonight?" she asked, a blush creeping up her cheek.

"Uh…" I looked back at my dad. He just gave me a knowing smile and nodded. I turned back with a grin. "Going to a party. Wanna go?"

"Sure!"

"Come on," I said, holding onto her hand, partially dragging her to the door. "Oh, wait. Don't forget this." I reached back with my free hand and grabbed a bottle of tanning lotion off the shelf. We slipped out the door and into what I believed would be the best day of my life. We talked for hours, catching up on all the missed time.

"I'll be going to college in Baltimore next year."

"You will?"

"Yeah. They have a really good art program."

"Are you going to be a famous artist?"

"Maybe. Someday. But mainly I just want to paint."

"Do you use naked models?" I asked, wiggling my eyebrows.

"Why? Are you volunteering?" she asked, with a blush.

"Maybe. Someday."

"You're a goofball," she said, punching me lightly on the shoulder.

"But the good news is that you will get to see this goofball more often. Baltimore is only a couple hours from Rehoboth. You could come here every weekend—or I could go see you!"

She laughed at my enthusiasm. "That would be great."

I stopped walking and turned her toward me, grabbing both hands. "Summer."

"Yes?" she asked hesitantly, confused by my sudden seriousness.

"I…"

The words suddenly stuck in my throat. *I have waited five long years for you. You are beautiful and sweet and funny. I think I am in love with you.* I cleared my throat and tried again.

"I…I…I think…the party is about to start."

"Oh. Okay," she said with a smile. "Let's go."

As we headed toward the growing crowd, I shook my head. *I am an idiot. I should have told her.*

The cool sea breeze washed over the shore like a lazy wave, leaving Summer shivering in its wake.

"Burr," she said, rubbing her bare arms. "It's colder than I thought."

"I'll run to the house," I said, "and get you a jacket."

"Do you mind?"

"Of course not. I'll be right back. Will you wait for me?"

"Always!" she said with a laugh.

I ran toward the house, navigating past clusters of tourists to the less-congested neighborhood streets. When I got home, I opened the door and raced upstairs. As I snatched a hooded sweatshirt out of my closet, I caught my reflection in the mirror above my dresser. I had a goofy grin that refused to go away. I turned away to head back out when I spied the shell necklace on the desk. I picked it up and looked at our engraved initials. I tucked the necklace in my pocket.

The party was now fully under way. I searched the crowd for Summer and finally spotted her. She was chatting with a group of people, but one particular guy was close by her side. As I watched, his arm casually dropped across her shoulder. He looked a couple of years older than we were—hair buzzed short, muscles highlighted by a tight shirt. I had to fight back the urge to rush up and push him away.

"Hey, Summer. There you are," I called out as I walked over. "Here's the jacket you wanted."

"Thanks, Jared, but I'm okay now," she said with flushed cheeks. As if unaware of the anguish this was causing me, she continued, "Jared, this is Bryan. Bryan, this is my good friend, Jared."

Friend. Friend? How could such a kind word cause so much pain?

"Hey, dude! 'Sup?" Bryan said with a nod.

"'Sup with you?" I said, mirroring his chin jerk. Summer shot me a questioning look.

"Bryan, how do you know Summer?"

"We just met," Summer answered.

"Yeah, dude. I saw this pretty lady all alone, and that wasn't right. I had to swoop in and steal her before someone else did."

"Well, actually," I said, grabbing her hand, "she isn't alone. She's with me."

"Whatever. I'm gonna get a burger. Summer, you should join me." He turned and walked away.

She stared at him the way I stared at her, and I knew I had lost. She turned back to me with a hopeful look. "You don't mind, do you, Jared? He's in the army," she said, as if that explained everything.

I could push, but I sensed it would get me nowhere. "Go ahead. I gotta get back to the store anyway."

She hugged me tight, whispering in my ear, "Thanks, Jared. You're a really great friend."

"Always," I whispered, fighting back tears.

As I turned, I heard her say, "Hey, Bryan. Wait up."

I thought that would be the last I saw of Summer. During the next year or so, I sometimes wished it had been, so my heart could mend. Instead, I saw her all the time.

I watched her date Bryan and then had to listen when she talked about it with "her friend Jared." While he took her to movies and dances, I helped her study for finals. I shed tears of joy when she graduated with honors and then tears of heartache when she accepted his proposal that same night. I stood as groomsman when the woman of my dreams married the man of hers.

I saw her stand strong as she said good-bye to Bryan when he was deployed and was there to catch her when she received the news of his death. I was at her side for the funeral and the depression that followed. Then I watched her slowly recover, forever changed by the loss. I encouraged her to paint again and find new hope.

One day, as we were watching the sunrise over the beach from my patio, she leaned over and placed a shell in my hand.

"What is this?"

"I found it when I was helping you clean out the garage."

I turned it over and found the engraved initials. "Oh…"

"Why didn't you tell me?"

"I was scared and stupid. And then you met Bryan…"

"Oh, Jared," she cried, as she placed her arms around my neck and hugged me. "I'm so sorry. I should have known. It must have been terrible for you."

I gave a small smile. "I was glad to see you happy. That had to be enough."

"How come you never moved on? Never married?"

I pulled back, cupped her face in my hands, and looked into her eyes. "Because I love you. I have always loved you, from the first day we met. You are my best friend, but you are also my love." We kissed, and her lips were just as I remembered.

Her breath caught. "Wait, Jared," she said, as she pulled away. "I—I don't know if I can do this. I loved Bryan. I can't tell you I didn't or that I felt this way for you the entire time…"

"I'm not asking you to," I said, pulling her back into a hug. "I know you loved Bryan. He was a good man. I am not asking for your past. I am asking for your future. I promised you I would wait for you, and I will—for however long it takes."

She pressed her lips to mine once again.

I had waited for that kiss for fifteen long years, but Summer was worth the wait.

* * * * * *

As she ran along the beach, her long, golden ringlets bounced with each step, shimmering in the brilliant sunlight. *An angel*, I thought to myself. *Just like her mother.*

V. K. DORNER LIVES IN HUMBLE, TEXAS, WITH HER THREE CHILDREN. SHE LOVES TO TRAVEL, BUT NO MATTER WHERE SHE GOES, SHE ENDS UP IN THE EXACT SAME SPOT: THE LIBRARY! SHE LOVES TO READ. BOOKS HAVE HELPED HER THROUGH SOME ROUGH TIMES, OPENED HER EYES, HEALED HER HEART, AND SET HER FREE. SHE HOPES HER STORIES WILL DO THE SAME FOR OTHERS. ALSO WRITTEN BY V. K. DORNER: *THE LITTLE LAMBS AND THE RAINBOW ZEBRA, TWISTED TALES: THE DOWNFALL,* AND *LAZARUS.*

JUDGE'S COMMENTS

What struck me first about "Waiting for Summer" was how quickly I became invested in the central character. Romantic tales told from the man's point of view are rare, and in this case, a nice bonus. Yes, the prose was clean and tight, and the setting an integral part of the story, but the driver here was excellent character development over an unusually long time frame for a tale so short.

The Tell-Tale Coin

by Wayne Hughes

"Thank you, sir, and please come again," Charlotte said to the young gentleman who had finished his meal, paid the tab, and left a generous tip—although it was all in change. Charlotte scooped it up to add to the rest of the tips of the day.

It was the summer of 1942 in the popular beach vacation spot of Rehoboth, and although the war had been raging for eight months, it was beginning to resemble any other summer, with just a few exceptions. Car headlights were covered halfway, making them look as though they were sleepy, but keeping them from giving away locations to an enemy that could be patrolling the coast. Window shades were dark blue or green to prevent light from glowing through the windows. During the warm and humid Rehoboth Beach summers, it was often a choice between pulling the shades down and being able to have lights on, or sitting in the dark with the shades up and getting some measure of relief from whatever breeze might waft through the window screens.

This particular summer's day had been a long one for Charlotte. She had worked a shift and a half at Merton by the Sea—twelve hours, total—because Charlotte's friend and coworker, Marie, was assisting Miss Jeanette, the owner of the inn, in getting rooms ready for vacationers. But now, the working day was over, and Charlotte bussed the last table, tip money jangling in her apron pocket.

As Charlotte shut and locked the front door, she waved to Bernie, one of the local Civil Defense volunteers. "Don't forget to pull the blinds," he reminded her, and went on his way. She nodded and turned the cardboard sign on the door to "Closed." She heard Marie and Miss Jeanette enter from the back and give a tired sigh as they walked through the kitchen to the restaurant area.

"How did things go while we were gone?" Miss Jeanette asked Charlotte, whose arms were burdened with dirty dishes. "Did you have any trouble taking care of the customers?" The restaurant had only ten tables, but with just one waitress, things could get overwhelming.

"Everything went well," Charlotte replied wearily. "But I can tell you, there will be no walking on the boardwalk tonight. I just want to go to my room and change into my pajamas. It's been a long day."

Miss Jeanette chuckled. "All right. Why don't you and Marie go up to your room now. I'll take care of the cleaning up."

The teenagers gratefully plodded upstairs to the small third-floor room with twin beds and a window that overlooked the backyard. The converted attic was sweltering in the summer, but the room was free for as long as they worked at the Merton. The ceiling was slanted, forcing them to stoop over when getting into bed. Beside each bed was a small nightstand with a lamp and a Gideon Bible.

"Whew! I can't wait to get into bed tonight," Marie said. "I'm glad we can sleep in a bit tomorrow."

"Me too," Charlotte said with a yawn. "But I think I'll count my tips before I turn in."

The coins clattered on the varnished dark wooden tabletop as Charlotte emptied her apron pocket. There were a couple of one-dollar bills, but everything else was change. Charlotte neatly folded the ones and put them in the wallet she had bought from a small store on the Rehoboth boardwalk. Her old one had gotten wet and fallen apart when a wave had caught her and Marie by surprise while they were walking knee-high in the surf early one morning.

"Twenty-five, fifty, seventy-five," she counted out loud, but softly, as she pulled the quarters from the handful of coins. "Two dollars and a half in quarters," she said, louder. Next, she counted dimes and nickels, leaving the pennies for last.

Marie was already in bed, but not yet asleep. She turned on her side and said, "At least you got some tips today. All I got was exhausted from washing linens and preparing rooms."

Charlotte just nodded her head as she continued counting and pulling the coins from the table into her hand. Suddenly, she stopped and just stared.

"What is it?" Marie asked.

"Look at this. Have you ever seen one of these before?" Charlotte handed the coin over to Marie, who reached for it from her bed. She examined it and sat straight up.

"No, I haven't, but it's not difficult to tell where it's from," she said, turning the coin over in her hand.

"Where?" Charlotte asked.

"Well, by just looking at the picture on the front, I'd say Germany. See—it's Hitler's profile. And there are German words written around it. Where did you get it?"

Charlotte thought for a moment and said, "I'm not sure, but I think the last customer gave it to me when he left a tip all in coins." She paused again. "Peculiar. I wonder where he got it. Oh, well. It will be a souvenir of the summer of 1942." And she left it on her nightstand. The other coins she would turn in at the bank for dollars, but she wondered to herself if this coin was something she should show Bernie, the Civil Defense volunteer. After all, what would someone in Rehoboth be doing with a German coin?

Charlotte rubbed her eyes. "I can't think about it anymore. I'm much too tired." With that, she bent over so as not to bump her head on the low ceiling, and got into bed. She and Marie turned off their lamps and were soon asleep.

When Marie woke up, she shook Charlotte, who managed to open one eye and ask the time. "It's nine. Let's take a walk on the boardwalk before our shift starts." Both teenagers washed, dressed, and got downstairs in record time.

The sun was shining brightly, and the temperature was already in the upper seventies. They could hear the waves crashing on the beach and the seagulls screaming for tourists to toss them French fries. The girls stepped off the porch and headed toward the boardwalk with nothing on their minds except enjoying summer at the shore. When they returned to school for senior year, their friends would be so jealous!

They glanced at the beach and saw some vacationers plodding through the sand to erect an umbrella and thereby establish their claim to a few square feet of shaded beach to protect them from sunburn. It was still a bit early, but in another hour, the beach would be crowded with tourists who had traveled from surrounding areas to spend their one week off from work here at the shore.

Charlotte and Marie were buying a fresh-squeezed orange juice when Charlotte noticed the restaurant patron from the night before. She nudged Marie and whispered, "There's the man who I think gave me the German coin last night." As both girls watched, he entered one of the boardwalk pavilions that faced the beach just opposite them and sat down. In a moment, another man came and sat down beside him and they began to converse.

As they spoke, it became clear to the girls that this wasn't a friendly "how are you doing?" type of conversation. The men seemed to be speaking with some intensity. Charlotte suggested that they walk by the men and try to hear what they were talking about.

Marie said, "I have a better idea." At that, she pulled Charlotte by the arm and went down one of the wooden ramps from the boardwalk. They walked to where the beach dropped several feet, thereby making a space under the boardwalk—space enough for two teenage girls. "Come on," Marie said, "We'll listen to them under the boards."

Charlotte hesitated. "Aren't we a bit too old to go crawling under the boardwalk? And besides, it's filthy. Food gets spilled and falls through the spaces. People get sick and— No. I'm not going." But before she had finished her sentence, Marie had grabbed her arm and pulled her under.

It was a strange feeling being under the boardwalk. Light peeked through where the boards were separated and made a striped design on the ground below. Footsteps echoed from the walkers above, who were unaware of anyone's presence beneath.

"How do you know where to go?" Charlotte asked Marie as they crawled on hands and knees through a mire of half-chewed candy, soda straws, discarded trash, and the occasional spider.

"Trust me," Marie whispered back. "I've been here before."

"When?" Charlotte asked with an impish smile.

Marie stopped and turned around to face Charlotte, blushing slightly. "Just you never mind. I've been here, and let's leave it at that."

Charlotte grinned, and the girls resumed their crawl. After a few more feet, Marie held her finger to her lips and pointed upwards. "This is where they are," she whispered in a voice so soft Charlotte could barely hear her. The girls kept perfectly still and strained to hear the men's conversation.

Most of what the two men said was drowned out by passersby, but it was clear they were having a serious conversation. After several minutes of eavesdropping, Charlotte tapped Marie on the shoulder and whispered, "Come on. We can't hear anything and I'm feeling more and more ridiculous the longer I stay here."

Marie turned to her friend, shushed her, and whispered back, "Just a couple more minutes. I can make out some pieces of what they are saying." Charlotte nodded in agreement but couldn't hear anything that seemed significant. In fact, it seemed the two men were just sitting, watching the tide bring the breakers closer and closer on the beach.

Just then, Marie gave a start. The men had stopped talking. One of them said, "Did you hear something?" Charlotte could see through the gaps in the boards that they had stood up and were looking around. The girls froze, waiting several very uncomfortable minutes. Then the men sat back down, and their conversation continued.

Marie stared at Charlotte and was silent for a few more seconds before she motioned to leave. As the two girls emerged from their secret listening spot, Charlotte was one step behind Marie, who had taken off toward the main street. "Marie, what's wrong? Why the rush?"

Marie looked back over her shoulder at Charlotte and stopped dead in her tracks, almost causing Charlotte to bump into her. "You know what? Those guys are Germans!" Marie said with an edge of fear.

"What—what are you talking about?" Charlotte replied. "It's probably just some local people who speak a little German. Lots of people came from Germany after the last war and lived here. What's the problem?"

"Well, I don't like it," Marie responded.

"What did you hear that made you think they were German?"

Marie paused. "I heard them speak German words, and I don't mean 'gesundheit'!"

"Well, what then?" Charlotte asked as they started to walk back to the Merton.

Marie gave a puzzled expression, stopped again, and said, "One word I heard was 'strand' and then something like 'aussie' something with 'storm' on the end."

"Maybe they were just talking about the weather or something." But Charlotte could tell that Marie was worried. There were warnings on the radio to watch for spies and signs in the post office that said "Beware of Infiltrators." Charlotte thought. *Maybe...*

She looked at Marie. "Tell you what. We still have some time before work. I was going to show Bernie my coin, but instead, let's go to the candy shop on the corner and ask Anna if she can help us with the words you heard." Marie nodded in agreement and they were off.

Anna Kluge was a second-generation German American. She lived nearby and worked in her parents' candy store just a block down from the beach. Her parents had come to the US just before World War I and settled in Delaware. They had spoken German at home, so Anna was bilingual.

When the girls entered the store, Anna was busy refilling the bins of saltwater taffy that vacationers loved so much. "Can I help you?" she asked, without looking up.

"It's only us, Anna," said Charlotte. "Do you have a minute? We would like to know what some German words mean."

"Okay," Anna said, "I'll give it a try. What are they?"

Charlotte said, "One word was 'strand,' and the other was—" Turning to Marie she said, "What was the other?"

Marie said, "I don't remember it all. I think it was 'aussi' something. I can't remember the rest."

Anna said, "Well, *strand* means 'beach.' That one is easy. But I don't know what you're talking about with the other one. Can't you remember anything else?"

Marie shook her head. "Sorry."

"Well, it seems as if whoever said it was talking about the beach. Probably just a tourist."

The girls heard the door open behind them as another customer walked in. Marie said to Anna, "Thanks anyway. Or should I say 'danke'?"

Anna smiled and asked the gentleman who stood behind the girls if she could help him. Charlotte and Marie turned and stopped dead in their tracks. It was the man who had given Charlotte the German coin in her tip last night at the restaurant.

"So, you girls know some German?" he said, as he glared at them.

Anna hastily jumped in. "They were just asking about some German words they overheard on the boardwalk. Now, what will it be?"

The man watched as the two girls hustled out of the store. They kept walking toward Merton by the Sea, not saying a word to each other. After a few blocks, Charlotte said, "Do you think he recognized me?"

"I don't know, Charlotte," Marie said. "Let's just get to work."

Charlotte and Marie were kept busy all day—not frantic, just busy. But by closing time both girls were really tired. While Marie bussed the last table, Charlotte went to the door to turn the sign from "Open" to "Closed." As she did, the door was yanked open and an arm reached in, grabbed her by the wrist, and pulled her outside. It was the man who'd had the German coin.

He pulled Charlotte around the side of the restaurant where the shadows were darker and said, "So, you want to learn some German, huh? Well, I'll teach you some German—after we take a little ride."

"Oh, no, bud," came a voice from behind them. "You'll be the one taking the ride!" And immediately, Bernie and two others grabbed the man and restrained him. Charlotte broke away from the man, while Bernie and his friends struggled to keep hold of the attacker, who was fiercely trying to break away. During the tussle, the men were being thrown about, bouncing off walls and falling into bushes, but Charlotte's attacker was no match for Bernie and his friends.

After gathering her senses and realizing what had just happened, Charlotte almost collapsed. Anna ran over to her and caught her before she fell to the ground. By this time, Marie and Miss Jeanette had heard the commotion and had come out of the restaurant to see what was going on. In a flash, a military jeep pulled up and two men in US Army uniforms got out and ran toward them.

"We'll take it from here, folks. Which one of you is Bernie?" one soldier asked.

"Uh, I am," Bernie said, a bit sheepishly.

"Well, thanks, Bernie. I'm glad to see you Civil Defense guys are on the ball. But how did you find out about this?"

Marie interrupted and told the soldier about the coin and how she and Charlotte had eavesdropped on the Germans' conversation. Then she related how they had gone to the candy store to speak with Anna about the German words they had heard, and that's where they saw the man again.

"But how did you know to come here and just in time?" Charlotte asked in a weak, shaky voice.

Bernie replied, "It was Anna who deserves the credit for that. Tell them, Anna."

"Remember when you asked me about the word *strand* when you stopped in?" Anna asked. "Well, that was easy. It means 'beach.' But you couldn't remember the other word. You said it was 'aussi' something. I kept thinking about it during the day, and then it hit me—*aussichtsturm*. That means 'watchtower.' I put the two words together, realized they were saying 'beach watchtower,' and got worried. Why would someone speaking German use those words together? I thought it was important enough to report it to Bernie."

Bernie took over from there. "After Anna told me about the words, I decided to bring her and my team over after the restaurant was closed to ask you more about it. I had one of my guys stay back and call the military, explaining what had happened. We got here just in time, I guess."

The first soldier spoke up. "We had been notified of a German plan to sabotage some of the watchtowers along the coast. If they knocked them out, it would allow sufficient time for infiltrators to land quietly on the beach and make their way to Washington. At first we didn't think we had anything to worry about, but after we got Bernie's phone call, we came in a hurry. We'll be very interested in what this fellow has to say."

At that, the two soldiers hustled the handcuffed man to the jeep.

"There is at least one more of them," Charlotte shouted as they pulled away.

"Thank you. We'll take over from here," the soldier shouted back.

After a few moments of silence, Charlotte began thanking everyone for their efforts in saving her. Then the group dispersed. Charlotte and Marie went back to the restaurant. Miss Jeanette told them to go to their rooms and lie down—kitchen cleanup could wait until morning.

The girls climbed up to the third floor and flopped on their beds. Charlotte reached over to turn on the lamp on the side table. There, glistening in the light, was the coin—the one with the German writing and Hitler's picture.

"I'll never forget this summer," Charlotte said aloud. She turned, ready to say more, but Marie was already asleep. As she stared at the coin, Charlotte realized that the war had become very real to her. Remembering the blackout rules, she turned off the light before raising the window shade. She smiled as she felt the cool sea breeze drift into the room.

WAYNE HUGHES HAS A BS FROM TOWSON STATE COLLEGE AND A MASTER'S FROM WESTERN MARYLAND COLLEGE. HE TAUGHT SOCIAL STUDIES AND LATER CHAIRED THE SOCIAL STUDIES DEPARTMENT AT OWINGS MILLS HIGH SCHOOL, WHERE HE TAUGHT HISTORY AND GOVERNMENT. HE HAS WRITTEN CURRICULA AND AUTHORED SCRIPTS ON THE HISTORY AND GEOGRAPHY OF MARYLAND FOR A MEDIA COMPANY. A FEW YEARS BEFORE RETIRING, HE SERVED AS ONE OF THE TEACHER REVIEWERS FOR A HIGH SCHOOL HISTORY TEXT PUBLISHED BY *WEST PUBLISHING*. HE IS THE AUTHOR OF TWO MYSTERIES THAT ARE AVAILABLE ON AMAZON KINDLE. THIS STORY WAS INSPIRED BY HIS MOTHER-IN-LAW'S EXPERIENCE AS A WAITRESS AT MERTON BY THE SEA IN THE SUMMER OF 1940—QUIETER TIMES THAN THOSE DESCRIBED IN THE STORY.

Molting

by Kathleen L. Martens

The early beach sun creeps up over my deck railing and spills liquid gold into my art space. It's quiet, except for the incessant tick-tick of the Thomas Tompion clock on the mantle and the scrape of my palette knife across the canvas. The cadence of the minutes passing echoes in my vaulted ceiling—and I paint. I stroke, press, and drag my brush until the blue paint oozes and leaves the perfect thick and thin lines that I somehow know will read as ripples in the waves from across the room. My wrist nods and flows like a conductor directing unheard music. I step back to see how the enlivened water eerily moves, and I smile because it works—yes, it works. It's the only time I feel my life works—here, near my love, in these still moments on the other side of the bridge.

It's the only time I feel I am in command, conducting some small part of my life away from the years of running charity events, slicing oranges for soccer games, and playing the many roles that draw my blood, my strength, my *me*. In those few precious fleeting hours in the meniscus between light and dark, night and day, in the "just befores"—just before bed and just before our beach house full of guests awakens—I molt. I drop my mantle of motherhood and wife to release the hidden artist inside me.

I should be grateful, Oprah and my meditations tell me. I should be grateful for the pin that holds me in place, like a rare butterfly, for everyone to admire. I'm not; I'm desperately lonely, while relentlessly surrounded.

Even though we arrived late last night after the usual frantic

Friday escape into traffic, I am up before dawn. I leave my husband snoring in the darkened room to prepare to see my "Mr. O," as I've come to call him. I have no guilt for this uncontrollable love affair with the ocean and the shore. It is an irrepressible passion. I think of him, close my eyes, and smile unashamedly—even while sitting next to my husband, Daniel, in our overloaded SUV at the top of the Bay Bridge.

I can feel the ocean comforting me, listening to the whispers of my soul. It never fails to free me, and I feel myself transform, casting off my shell of perfection—the perfect mother, the perfect wife—to walk barefoot in the sand with unkempt hair, unpolished toes, and dreams of a life free to be myself with Mr. O. He likes the raw me, the *real me,* the me before the messages took hold that told me how to be, the me before my life of tennis whites at country clubs and hair swept back in bows.

I think of the Old Masters, whose apprentices did all the painting while the Master took credit for the final piece. I feel like that, never holding a brush to create the details of my own life, only appearing in the end, to add my name on the bottom right corner to signify this was my creation. But, it wasn't handmade by me, I confess. It was made by the hands of others: my children, my husband, even a five-pound puppy that made his paw marks on the canvas of my life.

For now, I luxuriate alone with my brushes and the acrid scent of the oils on my palette: six shades of blue, three greens, a touch of red, and some golden yellows for her hair. I mix just the right shade with an urgent tapping of my brush, with one ear listening to the lapping sounds from the open window that call to me, and the other for the footsteps and flushes in the ceiling above. I take in the selfish aroma of my one-cup hazelnut Keurig, not wanting to wake them with the alluring scent of a full brewed pot. I raise my shoulders, not yet ready for the clarion call to relinquish my selfish time in my secret world, to take on the cloak of mother, the role of wife, the demands of host, queen of the beach house.

I'm conflicted, wanting the morning to move on so I can see him in the new light, but I don't want my creative process to be rushed. After all, it's from the ocean that I've learned to set my boundaries, demand my space, and feel my worth. I've learned it, although I've yet to live it. He's strong, dependable, and steadfast, yet he allows his natural moods to flow freely with no apology. I need to learn to do that; I adapt myself to suit the moods of others.

I work wherever I please on the canvas, unfettered in my rare freedom, and she takes shape. Surfacing from the blotches of color, she flashes the shimmering scales on her tail, and her blond hair with bits of shell and tiny fish dances on the canvas with wild abandon. The foam and bubbles push her forward in the powerful flow of the sea that surrounds her. It makes her reach out, unashamed of her nakedness, as if she could swim into your arms. I angle the easel closer to the emerging natural light and add a final touch of glimmer to her captivating green eyes, quickly cleaning up a tiny splatter of oily evidence from my immaculate wide-plank hardwood floors. Her look comes together—tender, enticing, yet pure and full of heart. My own heart beats faster, and I inhale deeply. It's good, *no, it's very good,* I tell myself, and I push aside my usual self-doubt.

Tonight, I'm throwing a party for my seventieth birthday and our forty-fifth anniversary. It's our summer's requisite hoorah. Even my birthday is overshadowed by my husband. He isn't to blame; he is just as much a victim of this life of routines and rules, this cardboard box we share. It's all he's ever known. I'll order this and arrange that, and celebrate myself and the years of birthing and bonding to this man who gave me his name, waiting on friends, cooking, cleaning, and toasting my seven decades living as a crustacean who has never learned to molt.

I think of the quote that inspired me to paint this seaside siren who calls desperately to me to live out loud, to find my true self, to audaciously create in broad daylight. "I must be a mermaid," Anaïs Nin wrote. "I have no fear of depths and a great fear of shallow living." Yet, I still paint in shadow, thinking my true self would not be welcomed in my daylight world.

I have lived in this fear of shallow for all of my adult years, so why did I succumb to the demands of my affluent suburban life? I was enticed by the neatness of it all, the comfort of the rules, knowing just what to say and do, with marker pen poised to slash the white space from my children's calendars. I should be grateful for this safe and perfect life with perfect shoes.

Her face has come clear now with the final touch of my brush. She wears a look of serenity that I don't share except in these precious, guilty, stolen moments when everyone sleeps and no one asks me: "What's to eat?" "Where's my suit?" "There's a button missing; can you sew it on?" "Where'd I put my keys?" "Can I borrow the car?"

I rip off my painting shirt and store it with my mermaid in my secret place. Someone has brought a puppy without permission. He stretches and lumbers to my side. His tiny sharp tooth lodges itself in the leg of my yoga pants, signaling it's time to go. He drags along behind me, and I pry his little jaw open and release him. The symbolism doesn't elude me. I open the sliding screen door and silently close the latch. The whine of the little dog and the first upstairs flush fade behind me, and I'm free just in time.

The salted air lures my hurried barefoot steps along the dunes to the south end of the boardwalk. With my water sandals swinging in my hands, I stop to fill my lungs with salty anticipation. For good luck, I touch the rough gray splintering railing that marks the boardwalk's end, and my fingers register the feel of its ridged and rugged texture. I save it in my memory for my art.

I notice that my blue, size-small "Life is Good" T-shirt is stretched tight across my middle. Some weakness this season has made me surrender too often to the long-forgotten beach food; I have returned to Thrasher's. The punishing gulls swoop down to attack my familiar oversized salted cup of fries scented with apple cider vinegar, trying to prevent my sin, screeching, "No, No, No!"

I have much to ask Mr. O today. He's always there to listen to my aching heart, and today I need his wisdom. I need his arms around me. I fear I am disappearing into a dark place.

I pick up my pace. *One mile of boardwalk exercise, then my illicit escape awaits me,* I tell myself. I slip on my shoes and hypnotize myself with the thumping sound on the boards beneath my impatient feet. A sticky glob of ice cream, a stray Funland ticket, and a Dolle's saltwater taffy wrapper connect me with my jealousy, thoughts of husbands who don't golf all weekend and dreams of mothers who don't plan their own birthdays, but then I think, *I do it so well.* My tears begin.

I stop to pick up a lost hermit crab, its natural shell decorated with the painted helmet of a Redskins player. I know what it feels like to live beneath a label. His claws neatly line up, like fingers on a praying hand, and he pulls back in embarrassment, as if he feels my eyes on him. The smell of dying rises up from his shell, and I reach through the boardwalk railing to place the escapee on some dune grass with hope.

I have my love in my sights in the distance beyond a rounded wall of sand that was sucked up from the ocean floor in one of his unexpected moods last night. I turn right and follow the winding fenced-in path. I am almost there. I run to him, my wonderful ocean. He thunders today at the sight of me. Unlike my husband's moods, he doesn't make me pull into my own shell. He allows me to be real, and to bravely bring to him whomever I am each day. It's a freedom I feel with no one else, except maybe Helen, my best art college girlfriend, who accepts me as I am but lives a freer life and struggles to relate.

I am alone along the early shore, empty as far as I can see, two far-off concrete towers half-wrapped in morning shadows like paper around an ice-cream cone. I feel some brief relief as my feet sink into the cool sand. I watch a horseshoe crab soothe itself in a cooling massage of foam, encrusted with dependent travelers— shells, barnacles, and tiny misled crustaceans clinging for dear life, like me. I nudge it until it catches the current of a rescuing wave.

Something is different today. I am being swallowed by all the expectations in my life. The errand-filled planning of my own party opened a wound in me that has been festering all week. The sun is pushing through the bank of gray along the horizon. It's a westerly insistent wind that lifts white wisps from the crest of each wave, and I see Mr. O is also in an agitated mood. Still, he will always listen, so constant, so deep in his understanding.

He often leaves me with a feeling of resolve that melts like the secret cup of Kohr's custard that I sometimes indulge in on my walks home. The sugar high readies my lioness to leap. Each time I enter my door, my courage to change somehow dissipates, and I keep my paintings and my feelings locked up like a secret lover in a closet where no one goes. Instead, I take out the frying pans to prepare the brunch— omelets for thirteen, me and the one dozen sets of sunburned legs and arms sprawling on white organic cotton sheets upstairs.

Today is different; I've reached a point. Walking beside him and confiding in him isn't enough. I've never actually gone in the ocean in all the time I've used him as my secret confidant. I've never let go of my fussy concerns about the cold, getting my hair wet, the grit, the undertow, the excuses that prevent me from feeling him raw and real. I step lightly through a half-moon of old crushed memories, broken chards and shells left behind by the tide. Only one familiar woman and her curly-haired white dog are in the distance, too far away to see my sin.

A sudden blanket of foam sizzles over my feet, draws back, and I follow. Ankles, calves, knees, and the swell of my belly chilled by his hands make me hesitate, but he entreats me. My feet lift off the coarse bottom. I turn to see the watery arc above me and I give in, pulled under by his power. Sun, churning sand, I'm tumbled in the foaming bubbles, my long graying hair, like my mermaid's tresses, dancing in the restless water. I feel my breath needing to escape, to be replenished, yet I stay, marveling at the sound of the pounding waves, caught in the hydraulic of confusion.

I am drawn farther and farther from my contrived life, and I'm transformed into the woman I was—hopeful, youthful, creative, unfettered and alive. I see my tail growing and shimmering with blue-green scales, my youthful breasts lifted by the current, my long silky hair with bits of shell and tiny fish playing joyfully around it like an alluring coral shelf.

I feel the current taking me deeper. His desire for me pulls me farther out, and I succumb to the freedom. I watch the bubbles of my final breath rise up above me to the surface. I see my daughter's pleading eyes, my son's search along the shore, my grandchildren's tears, my husband's regretful face changing with kind promises, my friends begging me to love them enough to stay. The sun reaches through the water surrounding me, and I rise up with a sudden understanding. I push my way through the final crushing wave that holds me, and it pulls off my mermaid tail, freeing my legs.

My cheek rests in the gentle foam, safely on the sand, and my rapid breath slows. My hand lies next to a set of bird footprints, and my eyes follow their silly drunken tracks that wander off in any direction, at their whim. *Nature is so wise,* I think.

I walk along the shore for hours, gathering stares in my disheveled state, meandering where I please. I'm not concentrating, just giving myself time to absorb. I'm boldly molting in broad daylight.

The sun goes high, turns down toward the horizon again, and urges me to return. I walk up onto the deck of my oceanfront home. When did the cedar shakes turn from silver to brown, I wonder? Imperceptibly, over time, just as I had slowly weathered? Just as my husband has slowly gone bald? I am the reverse; my aging has turned my sandy brown to silver beneath my camouflage of blond.

I look through the sliding doors and I see them standing silent, staring—the entire gang. I imagine how I must look. I don't care. Even the caterer is frozen in place, waiting for the tap of my baton. My nervous guests are dressed so stylishly, champagne in hand, standing in my precious predawn art space that has magically turned into the family room again.

"Bridget, where *were* you?" Daniel steps out behind me and talks through teeth under his breath. "The guests are here; they're hungry," he says through a smile intended for those watching at a distance, but not for me. I laugh to think there is one hundred dollars' worth of food per person, waiting within reach just over the granite counter, to save them from starvation. My perfect husband stands tanned, tall, and trim. I smile. I am not the only one who suffers from the disease of perfection. "Have you seen yourself? Have you looked in the mirror?" he asks.

I think the same, have you, have *we*? "You were worried about me, weren't you?" I translate, touching his face. Without a word, I walk across the room and drag out my easel from the storage closet. I dramatically whip off the cover, which is actually my daughter's forty-year-old baby sheet.

My friends and family draw in their breaths and everyone applauds. "Oh, it's beautiful."

"Spectacular."

"Is that your gift from Daniel?"

"Oh my, Daniel, where did you get it?"

"Who is the artist?"

"Do you mind sharing? I *have* to have one of his works for my collection!"

They examine my painting, step back, and then lean forward with concentrated appreciation. They are silenced by her look. My mermaid emerges from the blue and green of the windy sea with arms that promise to hold you, heal you, love you as you are. The water moves and undulates around her. Her vibrant green eyes look deep, catch the light just right, and electrify her admirers.

My friend Helen, the only one who knows my secret, walks toward the painting, which is as tall as she. "Well, let's see," she says, and winks at me, an understanding gesture that makes me glad to be alive. She bends over to examine the lower right-hand corner. "Bridget King McDaniel," she reads, in three distinct words, and I feel the last of my shell peel away and clatter to the floor.

I accept a loving hug and kiss from Helen, who kindly plucks a length of seaweed from my wild hair. In my peripheral view, I see my children's faces, lit with amazement, and watch Daniel walk toward me with a look I haven't seen in many years. He studies me intensely with wonder, and his eyes flicker, searching mine.

"Danny." I smile, calling him by his college nickname to instantly rewind us in time. I so desperately need him to remember two imperfect, optimistic dreamers: he, the dedicated architect who rebuilt villages after earthquakes, and me, the promising artist who secretly painted colorful seaside murals on dreary city walls. Can he see himself tenderly plucking that dab of turquoise paint from my hair nearly half a century ago? Can he remember the deep connection and convictions we once had? He glances at the painting and then at me, and pauses for a painful minute.

Tick-tick is the only rebounding sound, and I wait. Then, he shakes his head, grinning, and I know he sees me. He looks through the mess that I've become—weathered beauty, unknown artist, shells and tiny fish in my hair—to see his mermaid. He steps forward and kisses me with lips that taste of long ago. All along it was I who had to change, to change my world around me. I am the artist of my own life now, and I step back and smile because it works, yes, it works.

KATHLEEN LANGMAACK MARTENS IS AN ACTIVE MEMBER OF THE REHOBOTH BEACH WRITERS' GUILD. WITH A BA IN ENGLISH LITERATURE AND SOCIOLOGY AND AN MA IN EDUCATIONAL PSYCHOLOGY FROM THE UNIVERSITY OF CONNECTICUT, SHE PURSUED A CAREER IN INTERCULTURAL COMMUNICATIONS. KATHLEEN LIVED AND WORKED AS A CORPORATE EXECUTIVE AND ENTREPRENEUR IN THAILAND AND INDONESIA, AND TRAVELED THROUGHOUT SOUTHEAST ASIA AND CHINA. SHE IS NOW PURSUING HER PASSION FOR WRITING STORIES OF WOMEN RISING UP AGAINST ADVERSITY, WHICH RESULTED IN THE MEMOIR OF MARGARET ZHAO, A SURVIVOR OF THE CULTURAL REVOLUTION UNDER CHAIRMAN MAO, *REALLY ENOUGH: A TRUE STORY OF TYRANNY, COURAGE AND COMEDY*, WHICH WON THE SHARP WRIT BOOK AWARD FOR BEST BIOGRAPHY/MEMOIR FOR 2012. SHE IS CURRENTLY WORKING ON A NOVEL SET IN THE JUNGLES OF INDONESIA, AND A BOOK OF SHORT STORIES.

The author's first-sentence "hook" brought me immediately into the tension of the story. It's quiet, yet strong. The story progresses from a calm opening to a strong sense of struggle for the character. There is a feeling of weightiness to the visit to the beach, and that feeling grows as the character is drawn to the water and struggles with the strength of the ocean. The author brings the story around full circle, returning from the internal and external struggle with the ocean and the character's personal growth, to her artist's palette and acceptance of herself. A good read!

Seven Scenes

by Hyl Norman

An ensemble cast illustrates love and desire in a beachside setting.

Soundtrack: audience members who are senior-discount eligible will hear The Drifters; those younger than fifty will hear contemporary pop, also available as a Spotify playlist (search "Seven Scenes in Rehoboth Beach").

Title: There Goes My Baby (Adventure)
Location: Beach, late morning
Props: mass-market paperback, blue sand pail,
healthy sandwiches

Marianne was old-school, reading the latest Jennifer Weiner in a substantial paperback, thick and satisfying and somehow like an avocado, about which she now thought as she scanned the beach for Peter. It was time to collect him, protesting or not, and put some lunch into his little six-year-old stomach. The whole-grain wraps with avocado, sprouts, and garlic aioli were calling. Calling her, at least.

"John, clear the top of the cooler and get the kale chips from my tote, please," she said, still scanning.

John put down his e-reader and knelt by the ice chest with a tranquil expression. "The weather report said there might be a fast-moving summer storm this afternoon, but the sky sure is clear now," he remarked.

"Where is Peter? Can you see him?" Peter was not where he had been. Not fifteen feet away, his blue pail bobbed in the moat of the ragged wet sandcastle built by a long morning of child labor. She stood abruptly, and the Weiner book fell with a thud onto John's foot.

"Where are the Snowdens?" she asked frantically. "They're here, aren't they? Maybe Peter's with Corey."

Please let him be with Corey, she thought, as she jogged north to the Snowdens' usual spot. John said, calling to her disappearing freckled back, "He wouldn't go in the water alone, Mari. He wouldn't. He's just lost."

Just lost. There's no *just lost* if you're six. Being lost was the most frightening nonpermanent thing that could happen. But it couldn't have happened. Peter was such a cautious child, almost timid. He hung back and watched adventurous children. She couldn't imagine him wandering away. *What could have possessed him*, she wondered, stopping with a rush of panic as she came in view of the Snowdens' umbrella. Corey sat alone, calmly eating hummus off celery sticks, his eyes fixed on the eternal, hypnotic Atlantic.

Title: Losing It (Connection)

Location: Hotel roof, morning

Props: plastic stacking chairs, cigarette, headphones

Andrew had been on the hotel roof for an hour. The people below looked like ants, if ants could be imagined wearing straw hats and sunglasses, pushing strollers, and carrying totes and canvas chairs.

It was the third morning of their second trip to the beach this summer, and Andrew, for one, was sick of the place. The rest of his family had gone down with their towels and chairs and skimboards early, to get a good spot. Andrew had gone up to the roof looking for some privacy and a chance to sneak a cigarette. The roof was a radiant plane of reflected brilliance, empty but for three enormous HVAC units and two plastic chairs for smokers. It was heaven's field of nothing, of subdued noise and color-draining glare.

The happy beachgoers weren't really very antlike. The hotel was only three stories tall. He could see the people below quite clearly, even their faces. Right now he saw a young girl, maybe ten years old, mugging at her reflection in a shop window. Her brother steadily ate Thrasher's fries from a big paper cup.

Across the avenue, a yoga session was ending in an airy second-floor studio with wooden floors. The yoga instructor rolled her mat and pirouetted across to the exit, where she turned off the light switch with her foot. Everywhere Andrew looked was transparency, people letting themselves be seen as they were. He wanted to cry. He wanted to kick something.

Instead, he crushed his cigarette filter to shreds and flung it off the roof, unhappily aware of himself playing the ironic self-conscious depressive. What Andrew wanted to find was someone close to his age, which was seventeen, someone young enough to enjoy music, to understand his struggle to be open and real, someone else racked with hope and longing. She needed to meet him here, though, and soon, before he lost it completely in these mindlessly happy crowds of summer people, people who were definitely not thinking about what kind of time they were having.

Title: A Season in Hell (Despair)
Location: Rehoboth Avenue, noon
Props: the *Baltimore Sun,* straw panama

Scott was suffering the kind of misery that made everything drab—a banal canvas, but also the kind of misery that unsettled one's insides, the kind that probably caused cancer. Everything was either dull or actively unpleasant since the breakup. To add insult to a surfeit of injury, the sunny sparkle of Rehoboth Beach presented vistas that were mere mirage, because they were in the past: A faint crystal drift of sand washed up on a perfect tanned ankle, iced glasses of cocktail hour, damp waves of hair touching the top of a crisp white shirt over dark skin, a certain moody amethyst glitter, the gleam of youth, spark of smile, bright eyes, dark lashes.

The prepaid rental week was truly a season in hell, with this and more in his mind's eye, out of reach.

The nadir of this awful week was that he had become, in the space of a morning, quite infatuated with a woman. While he was picking up the *Sun*, of all things. A woman, of all things. Nadya with a vanishing whisper of a Russian accent, Nadya of the dance studio, Nadya of the storm-blue eye, who coaxed a promise to visit the studio from his reluctant mouth; Nadya who had admired his quick feet as he sidestepped her on the packed street, Nadya who intensified the scents of salt breeze and roses, Nadya who had said his trilby was "debonair," with a little musical trill of the final *r*, and then said, "I'd like to dance with you, and I will wear a feather to match the grosgrain," with two more perfectly rolled *r*'s.

"Who are you?" he'd asked, after she had told him her name.

Her bright eyes glittered and she said with a wink and a laugh, "I'm the goddess of summer, of course!"

It was impossible that this had happened, that anything could have distracted him from his misery. All Scott had wanted was a week to not think and not remember, and instead everything reminded him of Hector and nothing was Hector and now here was this vaguely exotic woman, not particularly young, whose eyes, darker than the slow clouding sky, said to him, *I know you.* He wanted to call Hector and tell him all about it.

Title: The Mermaids of Rehoboth (Joy)
Location: A dune fence, midday
Props: unlimited

Delice and Bette conjured magic as much as they could, as best as they were able. Flushed and sweating, inspired, they danced around the suggestion of a maypole. Plastic daisies represented their access to the beauty of the world: horses and crystals and the flowing skirts of modern witches, the sweet smell of blue cotton candy, and the sharp blue of a June sky. Behind them, wares of the souvenir and beach-supply shop fluttered and jangled, a kaleidoscope sectioned by gaps in the boards. Everything necessary was present.

Toward the water, two of the mothers and one of the fathers were talking and listening to the radio, sitting beneath floppy hats and a striped umbrella. They were supposedly enjoying themselves, but they showed no sign of the fever-dream of sensuous delight the girls were experiencing. How could they, when they had to be coaxed to stand, to dig in the sand, to get their hair wet? Incredibly, they just talked. About sunscreen and baseball scores and, proudly, of their prodigious naps.

Bette put a cricket in a bottle. Delice dashed to the parents' space and brought back juice, and they filled their mouths with tart orange. They clung to the fence posts as a storm threatened to capsize their imaginary ship. A bit of driftwood raised its terrible fin above the sand, revealing shark-infested waters all around. Hot wind rose and rose to sting their cheeks, charging the rapture of their play to a higher pitch. Soon they would have to race straight into the blue-green water, where they might, if they were spectacularly lucky, turn into mermaids and meet the terrible sea king.

Title: Give Me Sunshine (Loneliness)
Location: The boardwalk, midafternoon
Props: bicycle, backpack, a slice of pizza

Fairchild, who went out in the world using only one of her names, had biked the last thirty-eight miles yesterday, reaching the bustling town just at sunset. Her bicycle was chained to a lamp post on the boardwalk, but she had moved herself and her pack several yards away, into the shade. This morning, at sunrise when the wind was cooler than the water, she had raised her arms above her head and stood in the surf wearing all her clothes, everything but socks and duct-taped shoes.

The wet sucking sand had shocked her feet. She changed into a dry tank and hung the wet shirt on her bike, where it flapped steadily. When the vacationers started to arrive with their playpens and mesh bags of sandy plastic toys, she retreated peacefully and alone. Her shoulders were already smarting from the sun. In the distance, a narrow smudge of cloud marred the perfection of the summer sky.

She was not thinking about anything, but was hungry for experience. She didn't know quite what she wanted, but she was sure she would recognize it when she found it. The smile that broke and rode over her face was involuntary, disarming passersby as she watched the boardwalk traffic. Her twisted hair was knotting itself into dreadlocks, an act of cultural identification that came out of both its own heritage and Fairchild's neglect. She would take care of it soon, restore it to her army cut. For the moment, she was happy to sit and watch, but inside, a restless feeling was growing.

She enjoyed a half-slice of cheese pizza in late morning. No money had been required. She had met the eye of a young girl about to break into a run toward Funland who first needed to lose the thing sagging from her Grotto's napkin. Fairchild stepped toward her and held out her good hand, palm up, and the child happily made the transfer. Fairchild saluted her with her prosthetic arm, but the girl was already gone. *A friend*, she realized as she ate, that was one of the things she wanted.

Title: When I'm with You (Nostalgia)
Location: The arcade, late afternoon
Props: eyeglasses, Skee-Ball prize tickets

Louis couldn't identify the strains of late, melancholy Springsteen coming from somewhere nearby. It wasn't yet dusk, but the shadows were long. Debra walked beside him, comfortable shoes matching strides, taking it in but not speaking, insulated by the chatter and bustle of the crowd.

The open-sided arcade was just as it ever had been. She tugged his arm, pulling him in with surprising energy, and said, "Skee-Ball! Goodness, how many games did we play? And the carousel, the beautiful, beautiful carousel!" Her eyes were shining.

"Can you believe how long it's been since we've been here? Thirty-five years, forty? So many things still the same!"

He smiled at her. The lights inside were suddenly turned on and they were in the glamour and magic again, fifteen years old and on their first date. "So many things different! Look at the people!"

"They're the same—the same, Lou. The bandstand! Dolle's taffy!"

"The movie theater is gone—the Beachwood. Remember it?"

Her face fell. "Don't remind me of what's changed."

He leaned in. "Look at those two kids. That was us." The pair he pointed to were holding hands, scarcely moving, eyes on each other, leaning on the bumper-car fence. She tipped her glasses down her nose and watched them a moment. "I'm surprised he isn't wearing a

Jim Morrison T-shirt," she finally said, acknowledging the accuracy of his comment.

Still, he despaired of re-creating the emotions of their youth.

They played a few games of Skee-Ball and tossed the tickets to the ground. A few warm raindrops splashed them as they wandered back to the boardwalk.

More teenagers, in twos and threes and fours, scurried toward the arcade or slouched under awnings, nervous and idle. A tall boy with a sunburnt nose and floppy hair was alone, staring intently into faces as he walked furiously, but without purpose. Nearby, a young woman with long twisted curls and a forearm made of metal and plastic was saying under her breath, "Why not, why not?" She might have been staring back at the solitary boy.

As they stood indecisively in front of the bandstand, a child of about six appeared amid a sudden crack of thunder as if deposited from the sky like a ghostly streak, a barefooted shimmer of motion racing toward the avenue. Debra took Lou's hand and laughed. He rejoiced in the pure sound that was so deep and full, so much the same. They followed the running child, ambling toward the old cinema building as the cobalt sky opened up with a gust of hot rain.

Title: Dance with Me (Promises of summer fulfilled)

Location: A dance studio, end of day

Props: fairy lights, red carpet, mirrors, a potted tree

People scurried for cover. The rain fell sideways and there was the sound of things blowing away. An old wooden door street-side blew open and several people took shelter inside. An encouraging voice above them invited them to come up. By the time they climbed the wide wooden stairs, the rain was already dwindling. Above, so many roof tiles had lifted off in the wind that the deepening sky of early evening was visible through the holes. Clouds dissipated into thin streamers like the bubbly wake of a boat.

An invisible hand, belonging, perhaps, to the owner of the kind voice, had turned on a string of lights that ringed the room over the mirrors. In one corner was a fig tree in a pot and a piece of red carpet on the floor, remnants of a theatrical set.

The twinkling lights, real stars beginning to peep out above, and then: music. A young man and young woman walked together to the corner of the room and sat cross-legged under the tree, sharing a single pair of earbuds, talking shyly. Debra said, "Lou, Lou!" and she made an awkward twirl while he thought his heart would overflow.

Bursting into the large studio came three children, two girls and a young boy. They were focused on their roles: "I am the royal passenger, and you are the captain, and you are the pirate." Bare feet pattered on soft wooden boards. White gauze suggesting a sail appeared. A young couple, strained with worry, hurried up the stairs behind the children, but did not interrupt their play when they saw their boy transformed into a dashing and terrible pirate, his ship lost at sea. They all kept watch together for the dangerous sea king.

Two men stood near the edge of the room. One of them scrolled through sports news on his phone, glancing up occasionally to check on the girls, who needed nothing. Another man, in a creamy straw Panama, leaned against the wall, watching Lou and Debra and smiling at Fairchild and Andrew in the corner. He fell into a wistful reverie, but then the stairwell echoed with new footsteps and a dark-eyed ghost in a crisp linen shirt slipped in and went to the man leaning on the wall. "The goddess of summer called me," Hector said with a sweet, apologetic smile, "and I came."

HYL NORMAN WRITES FICTION AND NONFICTION, SOME OF WHICH HAS BEEN PUBLISHED. SHE HAS RECENTLY COMPLETED A PSYCHOLOGICAL MYSTERY FOR YOUNG ADULTS. A DELAWARE NATIVE NOW LIVING IN THE MIDWEST, SHE VISITS REHOBOTH BEACH WHENEVER SHE CAN, WHICH IS NOT AS OFTEN AS SHE'D LIKE.

EDITOR'S COMMENTS

This story caught my attention the moment it came in—always a good sign. The creative structure, lush writing, and clever confluence of story lines captured my interest and had me rereading it to see how the stories had come together. A heavier hand might have drawn straight lines to connect the characters, but this writer has used subtlety and suggestion to create a work that will have readers thinking about it afterward.

Haiku Kites

by Robert Hambling Davis

Every summer when I wasn't teaching, I helped my girlfriend Mandy with the charter boat business she'd inherited from her dad, along with his fifty-foot custom-built trawler *Cast Away*, which she moored at Indian River Marina. She'd been offshore fishing on that boat since she was five. My favorite picture of Mandy was a snapshot her dad had taken of her at that age, as she trolled astern with a boyish grin, brown ponytail, and eyes green as the riptide in the late-day sun. Now, twenty-eight years later, she captained *Cast Away*, her grin gone flirty, her ponytail swinging out the back of her ball cap, the one that said, "Faylene's Bait Farm: They'll Bite Hard on These Babies!"

As Mandy's first mate and all-round deckhand, I kept the boat shipshape, spelled her at the wheel, baited the hooks of screaming kids whose parents were too fish-crazed to help them, and removed stingrays from the hooks of those afraid of their catch. I wasn't a fisherman, had no interest in the sport, but was onboard because Mandy and I had been together six years and she'd come to expect me, especially at the height of the season. Besides, she was such a looker I was afraid of losing her if I wasn't around.

Be that as it may, I hadn't gone on the last four charters at the start of that summer. I'd spent too many of my vacation days out on the ocean, lurching about the deck, dizzy on Dramamine, never quite getting my sea legs. It was the end of the semester and I needed a break and time to prepare for Rehoboth's first haiku kite contest.

The unprecedented contest was my idea. I'd managed to convince the city's special events committee that the competitive flying of homemade kites that displayed original haiku would boost

Rehoboth's reputation as "The Nation's Summer Capital." The contest would be held on the beach by the boardwalk, and contestants would be scored on literary merit and kite design. I'd be one of five judges, the same number as in a poetry slam. To gear up for the contest, I'd been reading translations of Basho, Issa, Buson, and other classic Japanese masters, as well as modern American haiku by John Ashbery, Sonia Sanchez, Jack Kerouac, Diane di Prima, and African American novelist Richard Wright, who wrote over four thousand haiku in the last year and a half of his life, while slowly dying of complications from amoebic dysentery.

At Del Tech, I encouraged my freshman composition students to read haiku as an antidote to their wordiness and ambiguity. My reputation had spread through the school, and on the last day of finals someone posted an open note on my office door.

> *High on his perch,*
> *The lone crow rants*
> *At the baby peacocks.*

It was written with a sumi brush on rice paper, and unsigned.

That Friday night, when Mandy and I went out to dinner at Dogfish Head on Rehoboth Avenue, I showed her the haiku. Mandy read it over her fish and chips, then gave it back to me with a look of having tolerated a lame joke. She fisted her already squeezed lemon, extracting the last drops onto her fish, and scanned about for our server.

"Well, what do you think?" I asked.

"About what?"

"The haiku."

"You know I'm not into poetry."

"But you're a reader and must have an opinion," I said, and meant it, having applauded Billy Collins and Garrison Keillor for promoting poetry the average reader could understand—and what could be easier to understand than haiku? Three short lines expressing a clear, concise image, a word painting of the moment, to be recited in one breath. No wonder the form was popular.

Mandy waved her drained lemon at our server to get her attention, then scowled at me and said, "It's about vanity. One bird looking down on another, like that crow in the tree is better than a peacock on the ground. Well, I don't believe birds think that way, not even crows, who are supposed to be smart."

Seeing she was edgy and had a point, I agreed and launched into the literary hazards of anthropomorphism, the fallacy of attributing human characteristics to animals.

"Stop lecturing," she cut in. "You sound like that crow, if he could speak." Then, in a more caustic tone, she added, "It's a poem about you talking down to your students."

Before I could reply, our server was there. "Could you bring more lemon for my fish and tea?" Mandy asked her.

"Sure." She nodded at my empty bottle of 90 Minute IPA. "Want another?"

"Yes," I said, and she snagged the bottle and walked away.

"Those are high-proof beers—nine percent alcohol," Mandy said. "You've had two and don't need another." She dropped her throttled lemon wedge on the table. "You drink too much. You know that?"

"Let me celebrate. The semester's over—just need to grade a few more finals. Sorry I haven't been able to help you lately, but I'll be onboard soon. And those days when I'm not, I'll cook dinner in my backyard. Grilled flounder, sea bass, whatever you catch."

"You drink too much," she repeated.

Our server returned and set a dish of sliced lemon by Mandy's fish and iced tea. "Hope this is enough," she said. She set my bottle of ale by my glass. "Enjoy, and let me know if you need anything." She smiled at me, then turned and walked toward the bar.

"Quit staring at her," Mandy said.

"I'm not." I poured my ale. "I'm not staring at anything." I raised my glass as if toasting Mandy, and took a long drink. Then another. Damned if I'd let her bum me out.

She squeezed her lemon and held her tongue till we'd finished our high-tension dinner and I'd tipped a good thirty percent. Then she got up from the table and said, "Give me your keys. You're not driving."

I stood with a bellyful of crabmeat and pale ale and gave her the keys to my Prius. "Sorry, honey," I said, trying to make up. "I'm fine, really I am. It's just that I'm in a magnanimous mood with the semester over and seeing you again. Now, let's go back to my place and—"

"You remind me of my father," she cut in, louder than necessary. "Boozing to celebrate special occasions, till every day became a special occasion."

"Mandy, please, let's talk outside."

She pointed at the tip I'd left and raised her voice. "Is the extra for her service or her looks?"

"Her service," I said, taking a beat too long to say it. But I was embarrassed over the scene Mandy was making. "She was especially good, given how packed this place is."

"Is she one of your students?"

"No."

"She's one of your favorites, isn't she?"

Heads were turning. Diners lowered their forks and watched as Mandy lit into me. "She's the one who tacked that birdbrain poem on your door."

"She's not my student and never was," I said in a low voice. "Now let's go. We can talk outside."

Our server walked by with a tray of pitchers, saw the bills on the table, and smiled at me again. I gave her what I thought was a reserved, yet polite, smile.

"You can't hide your lying eyes," Mandy said, quoting the Eagles loud enough to be heard through the entire place. Then she turned and marched out.

She drove me home, gripping the wheel in both hands, her window open to let out "the beer fumes." She yapped about how I'd let my drinking get the best of me, like her dad, and look what it did to him. She accused me of shacking up with my students and that's why I hadn't been helping her.

"I'm not shacking up with anybody. You know I've been busy with finals," I said. "That, and the haiku kite contest. If you're not working next Saturday, I hope you come."

"Fat chance."

"It'll be like an upside-down fishing tournament, with contestants angling the sky with kites so poetically luring they'll catch the biggest fish in heaven, including the ones that always got away before." I concocted this metaphor on the spot, hoping she'd lighten up.

"Your artsy beach-day wingding has made you nutso." She goosed my Prius and glared at me, her ponytail flaring in the wind. "I'm casting off with a party of twenty at six in the morning and could use a hand."

"I've got to grade papers and—"

"If you're not too hungover."

She kept cutting me off. I was glad we didn't live together. She started crying as we passed the Lewes lighthouse sign. I told myself she wasn't angry with me, but with herself, and using me for her punching bag. It was that time of the year. She was touchy about my drinking because her dad had gone fishing alone on *Cast Away*, fallen overboard, and drowned. When the Coast Guard found his body, his blood alcohol content was .26 and Mandy, an only child of divorced parents and closer to her dad than her mom, blamed herself for not being with him that day. "If I had been onboard he'd still be alive," she'd told me several times.

She left a voicemail with her friend Barb to pick her up at my Lewes townhouse. When we arrived, Barb wasn't there and Mandy wasn't about to wait. She removed my house key from the chain. "Go in and don't come back out till tomorrow." She slapped the key in my hand, giving me the bum's rush into my own home.

I got out, in no mood to argue about the car. She drove off, squealing tires. I went in and drank the half bottle of Ginjo sake I had in the fridge, trying to forget the disastrous evening. The drunker I got, the more I wanted to know who'd written the crow-peacock haiku. One of my students with a satirical side? A team effort? Whoever it was, I wished they'd left me the poem earlier in the semester. I would've praised it in class to flush out the writer. Would I ever find out who wrote it?

Mandy didn't answer when I called at five the next morning. I took a taxi to the marina and boarded just before she cast off. She barely spoke to me. The sea was choppy, the sun hot. I hauled bait buckets of squid and smelts up and down the deck, hungover and stumbling about the wave-slapped boat. Around noon, Mandy flashed a come-on grin at a New York dilettante fly fisher on his first offshore trip. He winked at her and plastered his face with a hot-to-trot smile. No time to get to the head, I leaned over the rail and retched, dizzy and sweat-soaked.

I don't want to talk about the rest of that day.

During the week before the contest, I called Mandy and left voicemails. I told her to call me, then asked her to call me, then apologized for my behavior and any inconvenience I might have caused her. "Please call me, honey," I said. *"Please."*

She finally did and told me we were through. I pleaded with her to reconsider. She said she could no longer put up with my drinking, wished me the best, and hung up. I didn't dare return to *Cast Away,* afraid I'd see Big Apple with his arm around her.

I moped about my house, eating out of cans and forcing myself to grade the rest of the finals. I drank sake and read haiku, searching for a pain remedy. I found solace in Issa and Basho.

> *Life on earth*
> *Is as evanescent as dew—*
> *Why kill yourself?*
>
> *A snowy morning—*
> *By myself*
> *Chewing on dried salmon.*

But a day later I decided the haiku weren't a good match. I didn't want to kill myself, just get over Mandy. And while I loved Basho, I didn't want to eat his dried salmon.

The more I wallowed in the pain of getting dumped, the more I wondered who'd left the haiku on my office door. On my blog, *Sandcastle Butterfly,* I offered the poet a hundred dollars to meet me and write the text in "that unmistakable calligraphic script." I had one reply, from a joker who said I'd mistaken a poem for my lost dog. I could barely sleep, trying to solve this whodunit and trying to forget Mandy.

On a desperate whim, I got out my Rumi anthology, which I hadn't read in years, having shelved Sufi wisdom for Zen. I opened the book and feasted my eyes on this quote: "Don't grieve. Anything you lose comes round in another form." Hoping to lure the mystery haikuist, I plugged the contest on Facebook, Tumblr, and Twitter.

＊ ＊ ＊ ＊ ＊ ＊

When I arrived at the beach that Saturday morning, the sky was cloudless and the wind perfect for kite-flying, but my head still raged with the storm Mandy had put there. I was glad the stretch of sand from Maryland Avenue to Delaware Avenue was roped off and signed "Closed to Entry." I set up my placard on the boardwalk.

REHOBOTH'S FIRST HAIKU KITE CONTEST

9:00 TO 10:00 A.M.

UNLESS YOU ARE A CONTESTANT,

PLEASE STAY OFF THIS PART OF THE BEACH.

I set my folding table and five chairs at the edge of the boardwalk. The other judges arrived within minutes of one another. I'd chosen all four. Two had won state arts council grants for their poetry. Another taught writing workshops at the Osher Lifelong Learning Institute in Lewes. The fourth was a poet I'd met at an open-mic reading in Dover. He'd written over four hundred haiku and launched a YouTube channel of his readings. The judges brought binoculars, as I'd instructed. We sat at the table with our score cards and lists of the contestants' names and the titles and descriptions of their entries, as the thirty-two kite flyers chose their spots on the beach.

At nine o'clock I raised my bullhorn and said, "Contestants, you will be scored on kite design and literary merit, on a scale from 0.0 to 10.0. The three top scorers will receive cash prizes. Good luck and let your haiku fly!"

They launched their kites, speckling the blue sky with a motley array of colors. I didn't see Mandy in the crowd of spectators on the boardwalk. She didn't know what she was missing.

"A delta kite covered with pine needles and snow spray," read a description on the list. I looked through my binoculars at the kite's haiku.

Onto the pine,
Then onto the ground,
The snow falls twice.

"A round green multistring kite, with a watercolor of the friendly beetle," read another entry. I looked up at its haiku fluttering in the wind.

Jump, jump, ladybug!—
Ten thousand stories high I stand
Holding your cabbage.

Farther down the beach, another round kite flew this haiku:

Green tortilla
On a blue plate—
A lily pad for lunch.

What an assortment! The contest was diverse art in the service of beauty. I looked again at the boardwalk crowd, their faces beaming as they watched the show. The kites had revived their senses, raised their consciousness, enriched their lives. I basked in glory, silently commending myself.

Then three boys with boogie boards raced down the steps to the beach. No sooner had they reached the surf, screaming and kicking up sand, than others followed, invading my contest with their towels, chairs, cotton candy, and corn dogs. "Please stay off this part of the beach," I bellowed through the bullhorn. They ignored me. The other judges asked what they should do. "Score the kites," I answered. Reality doesn't exist to meet your expectations, I told myself, unconvincingly, as a steady migration of thoughtless jerks swarmed the beach. Why weren't the cops doing their job?

I took a deep breath, threw back my head, and let out a long sigh, trying to calm down. Then I saw a kite I hadn't noticed. It was black, shaped like a crow, its wings spread, the haiku in red calligraphy on its breast.

High on his perch,
The lone crow rants
At the baby peacocks.

It flew at least thirty feet above the others. I couldn't see the contestant for the crowd at the north end of the contest area. I checked the list. Sure enough, "Crow & Peacocks" was at the bottom, without a name or description, as if it were a last-minute entry. Why hadn't I seen it before?

"I need to stretch my legs," I told the other judges, and hurried up the boardwalk. When I reached Maryland Avenue, I still couldn't see the contestant. I went onto the beach and weaved my way through the crowd, looking up and down, between the kite and the obstacles in my way. I looked up a moment too long and bumped into someone.

"Watch where you're going, dude!" a bald guy with tattooed arms said, raising his fists.

"Sorry," I said, and stepped past him.

When I came to the bottom of that long kite string, I stopped and stared. Three plastic peacocks, with taut cords attached to the string and guy wires to the beach, floated two feet in the air, as if flying without spreading their wings. I stepped closer, looked again. The bottom ends of the cords were tied to the peacocks' necks. Was the crow their hangman?

After my initial shock, I looked around, hoping to spot the mystery contestant watching me, maybe laughing or wearing a roguish grin. No one fit the description. I flashed on J. D. Salinger and Thomas Pynchon guarding their privacy at all costs. Then, more apropos, I remembered stories of Zen poets sailing their unsigned haiku down rivers on small bamboo rafts. I would give this entry a 9.9 to boost the odds that it would win and force the contestant to come out of hiding and claim the prize.

I headed down the beach, walking along the surf. I hadn't gone far when I saw something overhead. It was the crow kite floating out to sea. The contestant had cut it loose. I could hear it cawing at me. I would never solve the mystery.

The joke's on you, I told myself. If you can't laugh at your own trip, it's time to stop taking it. The kite soared higher and higher. There seemed no limit to the altitude it could reach. I watched till it disappeared in the sky. Then I went back to the judges' table, turned over my score card, and wrote:

> *As my sorrow ebbs,*
> *The sun glimmers on the sea,*
> *And the sand warms my feet.*

The next day I sailed my haiku in a sake bottle down the Indian River, for someone to find and wonder who wrote it and why.

ROBERT HAMBLING DAVIS HAS PUBLISHED IN *THE SUN*, *ANTIETAM REVIEW*, *MEMOIR (AND)* (NOW *MEMOIR JOURNAL*), *PHILADELPHIA STORIES*, *SANTA MONICA REVIEW*, AND ELSEWHERE. HE'S BEEN NOMINATED FOR TWO PUSHCART PRIZES AND HAS RECEIVED THREE DELAWARE DIVISION OF THE ARTS GRANTS, TWO FOR FICTION AND ONE FOR CREATIVE NONFICTION. HE WAS A FICTION SEMIFINALIST IN THE WILLIAM FAULKNER CREATIVE WRITING CONTEST IN 2002 AND 2012, A CREATIVE NONFICTION FINALIST IN 2013, AND A FICTION FINALIST IN 2014. ROBERT HELPS DIRECT THE DELAWARE LITERARY CONNECTION, A NONPROFIT SERVING WRITERS IN DELAWARE AND SURROUNDING AREAS, AND HE COHOSTS *2ND SATURDAY POETS*, A MONTHLY READING SERIES IN WILMINGTON. HIS STORY "A VERY OLD WOMAN WITH ENORMOUS FINS" APPEARED IN *THE BOARDWALK*.

Face-to-Face (book)

by Judy Shandler

She was spreading her oversized Eddie Bauer beach towel over the sand she had first meticulously smoothed flat, all the while fuming. *What was I thinking?*

She carefully weighted each corner of the blanket with something heavy: two rubber beach clogs, placed diagonally across each other; a beach bag filled with sundries including (but not limited to) a book of Dangerously Difficult Sudoku and water-resistant sunblock; and a small cooler containing coconut water, organic plums, and PBJs on whole-grain bread. She had disciplined herself *not* to pack any cookies or pastries for the day.

Earlier that week, her phone had chimed just as she was reaching for her second key-lime-glazed donut (made with healthy soy-based shortening). She had a message on Facebook:

> Hey Sheila, here's a blast from the past! Remember me?
> Your Long Beach Island boyfriend, Hank Parson.

Flipping through a mental Rolodex of faces from the summer of '94 at the Jersey shore, she settled on a grinning seventeen-year-old boy with sun-bleached yellow hair. He was handsome, muscular, and very athletic—full of energy and mischief, but not exactly a deep thinker. In fact, the only question he ever asked was, "What's the score?" But they had fun that summer.

She remembered sitting beside him, not a care in the world, at a mere 105 pounds, hair pulled high in a ponytail, wearing a yellow two-piece that her mom had picked up on sale at Bonwit's. Now, twenty-something years later, she may have put on a few pounds (like, forty). And who goes in the ocean anymore, knowing people use it for a toilet? *Ugh. Disgusting.*

She read on (while finishing the second lime-glazed delicacy).

> I see you live in the Nation's Summer Capital! Looks like
> I'll be in Rehoboth this weekend. Love 2 spend the day
> catching up and riding the waves like we used 2 do.

Well, what the hell, she had nothing else going on for the weekend. The kids had just left for three weeks with Harold, and her calendar was wide open. At age thirty-eight and being divorced almost two years, she saw little chance of posting any exciting updates to her Facebook status—other than turning thirty-nine in December and being divorced almost three years. So she answered.

> Sure, sounds great!

They finalized the where and when; and only then, after the initial excitement of making weekend plans, did she pause to think, who the hell makes a date to meet someone *on the beach?* Wearing a *bathing suit?*

Apparently, the answer was: She did. *Damn.*

That's why, five days later, she was planted in a sand chair on Rehoboth Beach at Wilmington Avenue. No yellow two-piece for her these days; instead, she sported a skirted bathing suit with extra-firming tummy control, patterned in black and white for optical illusion. Not exactly a size 5. Plus, that swimsuit would remain forever hidden under her new short-sleeved cover-up, which was *not* coming off. She adjusted her wide-brim sun visor (also brand-new) and settled in. The flowing red scarf attached to her chair, per Facebook agreement, billowed in the ocean breeze as if waving hello.

A hunky guy sauntered by in a slick Speedo (with Speedo bumps, she smirked to herself). He casually checked her out and kept walking. *Screw you.*

She concluded he was too young to be Hank Parson anyway. Even factoring in a healthy lifestyle (or plastic surgery and body sculpting, for that matter), *he* couldn't be Hank.

She surveyed the parade of people around her—lovers, loners, families large and small; people in bikinis, people covered head to toe; fat people, skinny people; tan people, pale people; all kinds of people—they came to claim their patch of sand and sun, hauling coolers, umbrellas, and beach carts the size of small farm animals. She sat back to enjoy the show; because today, she was in the game, a player, ready to connect with a face from the past. Today she was someone *with a date.*

To her left, a pale-skinned man covered with freckles sat under a huge striped umbrella, reading, when suddenly three teens raced by kicking sand everywhere.

"Hey! Watch it!" he called to them, brushing sand from his face. He looked over and saw that her blanket, which had been set up so meticulously, was in ruins from the rambunctious interlopers. "Kids," he said, shaking his head.

"Yeah," she acknowledged, heaving herself from the low chair to fetch a whisk broom from her beach bag. (She had wanted to pack her battery-operated mini-DustBuster, but she knew a DustBuster at the beach would look just plain weird.)

"I'm a bit of a neat freak," she conceded, as she gave the whisk broom a quick workout. "With some OCD, I'll admit." Then she tugged tight—again—the corner of her Eddie Bauer blanket and smoothed it with her hand.

"Nothing wrong with neat," he replied.

She repositioned her rubber clog just so and stood to admire her handiwork. "It drove my ex nuts."

She noticed that everything he had with him fit in the perfect circle of dark shade cast by his huge striped umbrella. She checked out his hunter-green beach chair, probably Rio, she figured, and a matching green insulated bottle cozy holding his water. *Nice touch.* An older-model Wonder Wheeler was parked by the umbrella pole (the newer ones have wider flat rear wheels); and in his lap, a book. She read the title.

"Hey!" she called over, "check this out!" She pulled a copy of the same hardcover from her carry-all and held it up. "I'm about half through. You?"

He looked up. "Just started this morning," he answered. "Seems pretty good so far." He turned a page and continued reading.

"The author's a local, you know." She plunged her book back into the bag and pulled out her sunscreen. "According to *The Huffington Post,* you need to put on sunscreen *every single hour* for full protection," she announced, seemingly to no one. "People don't realize that. I put on my first coat before I got here."

With an audible sigh he closed his book. He looked over just as she flipped open the bottle. "You're using *that?*" he asked.

"Sure, it's got the highest SPF, 80. With water repellency."

He reached for the sunscreen beside him. "Maybe so, but I'll bet it doesn't contain any zinc or titanium. That's what my dermatologist recommends." He read from the label. "See? Zinc oxide, 3%; titanium dioxide, 5%."

It occurred to her that people were starving across the globe and didn't have running water or sewers, and here they were quibbling about the relative merits of one brand of sunblock over the other. But still, it *is* important to be an informed consumer. Her husband never understood that. "Yours only has 50 SPF. Mine has 80."

He held the bottle out to her. "Try it. Those two ingredients give the best protection against UVA *and* UVB, which I need."

She took his sunscreen and slathered generously. "Freckles, right?"

"My trademark."

She passed the bottle back and thanked him, making a mental note to research that zinc oxide and titanium business. *How in the world could she have missed that? And why hadn't her dermatologist mentioned it?* That would be something else to ask about.

"Hey," he said, offering his hand, "I'm Marcus."

She took it. "Sheila. Hi."

He stood up and folded his sunglasses, placing them exactly in the center on his green chair. Turning to her, he asked, "Hey, Sheila, want to get your feet wet?"

She demurred. "Nope, I kinda hate the water. Sorry." (That new cover-up was not coming off.)

With that, he headed to the surf, and she returned to her chair. As she briskly applied the hand sanitizer she had packed, she had an epiphany: *Maybe Hank Parson will be a no-show.* God, she hoped so. What the hell had she been thinking, anyway?

* * * * * *

Thirty minutes later, still no Hank. And no Marcus, either. Sheila adjusted her UV-protection sun visor and watched as a couple toddlers in sun bonnets dug their way to China. *Damn, it's hot.*

Marcus reappeared just as she pulled a chilled bottle of coconut water from her cooler. He nodded to her and then disappeared into his circle of shade. He soon emerged, toweling his head to dry his hair, standing near her in the sun.

"Want one?" she asked. "I brought two. The lady at the health-food store says coconut water is Mother Nature's most refreshing drink, packed with minerals and electrolytes."

"Thanks." He tossed the towel onto his chair. "It also has bioactive enzymes for metabolism and digestion." Then, looking embarrassed, he added, "I teach science."

"Well, Mr. Science, I brought sandwiches, too. PBJs on whole grain. I'm starving." Without asking, she pulled one out for him.

He took it and motioned toward his umbrella. "Hey, do you want to sit in the shade for a bit?"

Does a drowning man want a life raft? She grabbed her chair to join him, and the red signal scarf flapped joyously along.

She confessed she was not exactly a beach lover and it had been ages since she came and sat all day. "Turns out a healthy tan really isn't so healthy after all, you know," she lectured. "Besides, it's really not all that much fun to sit and bake in the heat like a corn muffin."

He disagreed. "You should have brought an umbrella, that's all. And use better sunscreen. Or go in the water once in a while."

She explained her views on the water—people (and fish) peeing, no telling what else is in there. Sorry, no can do.

"You're wrong there," he answered. "Last year, Delaware's beaches were rated top in the nation for beach water quality for the fourth consecutive year."

She conceded; he *was* the resident scientist, after all.

"And," she admitted, "I am enjoying all the people-watching. Especially now, sitting here. Hey, would you like a piece of fruit? I have a couple organic plums if you're interested." She scooted under the umbrella to get her cooler.

Suddenly, all around them, people stood and pointed to the water, where a pod of dolphins swam southward along the coast. The dolphins arched gracefully out of the ocean, glistening in the distance, gifts of silver and sparkling onyx amidst the emerald-hued waves, where they performed their aquatic ballet.

"Beautiful," Marcus whispered. And, as the dolphins disappeared into the distant sea, Sheila clapped at their departure.

He remarked that for a non–beach lover, she seemed to be enjoying herself. And, why had she come in the first place if she was predisposed to *not* liking the beach?

She rolled her eyes. "I was *supposed* to meet an old flame. Funny thing is, I had no interest in seeing him. Zero. But I *was* looking forward to splurging on a couple slices of gluten-free pizza on the way home." She laughed and shook her head.

"Maybe he's running late," Marcus answered. "I'm sure there's a reasonable explanation."

She shrugged. "Whatever."

When a trio of women covered in tattoos walked by, the conversation turned to body art and their mutual distaste for it. "Just check the Mayo Clinic site about tattoos," he commented. "Skin infections, blood-borne diseases, allergic reactions—all sorts of complications." He ticked each off with his fingers. "Crazy risky."

"I agree totally. I freaked when my husband got a tattoo. A sailboat, of all things. We never even owned a boat. I guess that should have been a clue."

The conversation moved naturally to their respective marital statuses. Both were divorced, both within the last few years, and both had children, although Marcus shared custody, whereas Sheila had full custody but with Harold getting most vacations.

Where they differed was metabolism. *Damn, isn't that always the way?* She pictured his freckles as little Pac-men gobbling all his calories, and fantasized about abducting a few of them.

"I follow a Mediterranean diet, pretty much," he told her. "And I avoid chemical additives and agricultural antibiotics as much as possible. And GMOs." He shuddered.

"Yeah, I stock up at the farmer's market. Lots of organics there."

"Have you tried the hydroponic lettuces and heirloom veggies?"

"Of course I have. I love salads." She felt her face instantly flame crimson, the unavoidable "tell" that followed her every lie. "Okay, okay—I like salads," she amended, "sort of." When he smiled broadly at her confession, she asked if he'd tried the sugar-free fruit pies and pastries at the market.

"Sweets aren't my weakness. I'm more a cheese man. And I have serious questions about those sugar substitutes."

Five feet away, Sheila's phone chimed in her bag.

"Scuse me a sec," she said, moving to her blanket. Stooping over her beach bag in the bright sun, and shading the screen with her cupped hand, she saw she'd gotten another Facebook message. It hardly took a rocket scientist to figure out who it was from.

Won't make it to RB 2day ☹*. Next week 4 sure?*

She tossed the phone back in her bag. *What a jerk.*

Both of them, really; what a perfect couple of jerks. What had she been thinking? That she was still seventeen and cute as a button? What had she been thinking!

She walked back to Marcus's shady circle but didn't return to her seat. She shrugged her shoulders. "That was the guy I'm supposed to meet. Not coming, as we should have surmised."

"Oh," he said. "Sorry."

"Yeah, it's official; I'm being stood up."

She looked around and sighed. "May as well get going, I guess." She picked up her chair and turned away, ducking under the umbrella.

"Hey," he said to her back, "if someone calls to cancel, that's not being stood up. That's just changing plans. Stuff happens, you know. It's a statistical absolute." When she didn't reply, he added louder, "No one is standing you up, Sheila."

She waved him off and slipped one foot into a rubber beach clog. She was overwhelmed with renewed feelings of being lesser than. *What had she been thinking?*

"Besides," he continued, "this is the best part of the day! You can feel how the temperature is starting to change."

She inched the other foot into the second clog. "Yeah, I suppose. Nice breeze." Her red signal fluttered in agreement.

She gathered her oversized Eddie Bauer beach towel and flapped it sharply in the ocean breeze, once, then twice. Marcus watched as she folded it, first in half lengthwise, then side to side, then in half again, smoothing it against her body and brushing sand at each fold. The corners lined up exactly. She tucked it under one arm.

He watched as she folded her chair with the red scarf still attached, and then reached for her cooler, no longer filled with organic plums, or coconut water, or PBJs on whole grain. The previously smoothed patch of sand, now disturbed by her movements, returned to its natural state. Like she'd never been there.

When she picked up the final piece of her beach paraphernalia— her beach bag, with the whisk broom—he bolted from his chair and decisively removed the bag from her hand. He set it down. "Um, I was just thinking…"

He took the cooler from her other hand and then took the chair she had tucked under her arm. Finally, he reached for her perfectly folded Eddie Bauer beach towel and carefully balanced it on top of the cooler (she would go nuts if it got sandy again).

"Hey, Sheila…" He cleared his throat. They were standing face-to-face, and she was beaming. "I was just thinking…how about we grab a couple slices of that gluten-free pizza?"

Judy Shandler writes a weekly column for *Delaware Coast Press* and has published articles in *Delaware Beach Life* magazine and *Coastal Delaware* newspaper. Judy's short story "There but for Fortune" was published in last year's Rehoboth Beach Reads collection, *The Boardwalk*. A member of the Rehoboth Beach Writers' Guild, she is currently working on a collection of linked stories, *Seagulls in the Parking Lot*. Holding an MA in creative writing, Judy teaches noncredit creative writing classes at Wilmington University's Rehoboth Beach site. She and husband Don are enjoying semiretirement in historic Milton, Delaware.

Judge's Comments

Face to Face(book) is exactly what I look for in a beach read: light enough to not weigh you down, but with a bit of substance where it's needed. The story reminds us to not dwell in the past when we could be looking at the future, and to see what's right in front of us instead of what's on our screen.

Second Wind

by Lisa M. Coruzzi

Brenda stood at the Rehoboth Avenue entrance to the beach, one hand holding a tote, the other shielding her eyes from the sun. She scanned the horizon for a direction to head, but by doing so, blocked the flow of the other beachgoers.

"Hello? Keep moving!" A large woman barged past dramatically, eyes rolling above a pouty mouth.

Brenda tripped forward and apologized sincerely, as befitted her British upbringing. Apparently, it was not customary to figure things out as you went along. Gerald had been an excellent planner; he'd have known exactly where they would end up, how they would get there, and what they would do once they settled. But Gerald had never been a beach person, and he wasn't here. Brenda was finally, after all these years, doing whatever the hell she wanted.

She continued toward an uncertain destination. The sand felt warmer than she imagined, the sun toasted her bare arms, and the ocean, with every crash, beckoned to her. Gerald had instilled in her an overdose of modesty, and Brenda became slightly flustered at the sight of so many bare-skinned bodies. There was nothing wrong with it, she knew. Still, Gerald's disapproval weighed in. He'd have pursed his lips in disgust.

The week before, Brenda had purchased a ladies' magazine at the grocery store, the kind with saucy article titles on the cover. She had made herself a cup of tea, gotten a plate of biscuits, and put her feet up in the living room to read. When she was done, she deliberately tossed the magazine on the coffee table. Brenda yearned to do so much—like relax with a glass of wine at a vineyard, drink beer from the bottle, and go to the beach.

She smiled, allowing comfort to take the place of control. She continued to weave around towels, chairs, and umbrellas, rather enjoying the carefree search for the perfect spot. A group of children ran past, long-legged, into the sea. Perhaps in a few hours she might take a stroll on the boardwalk and sample some chips from that Thrasher's place; they smelled heavenly. Brenda chuckled. Imagine eating and walking at the same time! Without a table napkin!

Farther ahead, teens played volleyball over a makeshift net. Beside them, a couple as brown as raisins reclined in chairs, soaking up the sun. Gerald really had been such a snob. He had refused to go anywhere crowded and made sure that the two of them kept the same circle of like-minded friends. During a dinner party at their house, one of Gerald's colleagues had asked, in a drunken haze, why she was still married to that stuffed shirt. The heat had risen in her cheeks, partly a reaction to the impudence of the question and partly because she'd wondered the same thing over the years. Leaving had always seemed much harder than staying, so she had stayed.

The thing was, Gerald was the only man she'd ever known in that way. They had met when Brenda was nineteen and he was twenty-one, when they both lived in a posh suburb of London. Her parents were old-fashioned and she was raised to accept, not to question. And so, one Sunday afternoon, Gerald was invited to supper. He arrived wearing a brown suit jacket with elbow pads and a tie. Brenda was quite taken with his industrious manner, and he wasn't so bad to look at—a bit thin-faced, but not unbearable. Their courtship moved swiftly; Gerald and Brenda were married within six months, and she truly felt that in time she would grow to love her new husband. They had never had children. In fact, Gerald had found the act distasteful, and after a couple of ungainly efforts, all sexual activity stopped. By the time he was offered tenure as a professor of economics in Delaware, Brenda was vacantly resigned to her life. But suddenly, Gerald was dead, and now she was intent on doing as much as she could in the time left to her.

She refocused on her spot, settled in with renewed confidence, and lifted her chin, only to be hit in the face by a ball. The stinging pain was immediate, and Brenda's head whipped back on impact, sending her hat away with the breeze. She cried out and collapsed backward. Her sarong opened to reveal ungraceful legs, and the tote bag spilled its contents across the sand. Shocked, Brenda felt for her nose; it didn't seem broken, but blood had begun to flow. As she sat up, the raisin-colored woman appeared.

"Oh, honey, I'm so sorry. Are you okay?" Brenda nodded, even though she felt far from okay. The woman turned her head to yell. "Philip Alan Pearce, I'm gonna knock you ten days into Sunday! Didn't I tell you to be careful? Didn't I? Now look what you've done!"

Philip Alan Pearce bounded to the woman's side. "I'm sorry, Mom." He bent over, squinting. "Uh...sorry, ma'am. I guess I hit a bit too hard."

"Ooh, you'll be sorry all right. Move your net farther up the beach." The woman gathered Brenda's belongings.

Brenda turned to look for her hat, which she needed to cover up what must surely be a terrible sight. Before she could spot it, a man with a big smile handed it back to her. His knees clicked as he crouched. "Let's have a look, then." He was unmistakably English.

"No, no, I'm fine, really."

"Ah, a fellow Brit! Well, let me put your mind at rest; I'm Doctor Douglas. Robert Douglas. From Surrey, originally."

Brenda didn't know why, but she giggled. From behind her hand, she replied. "Nice to meet you. I'm Brenda Price. From London, originally."

"Well, then," he carried on, "now that we've gotten the pleasantries out of the way, perhaps you'd let me examine your nose?"

Brenda was aware of people gawking. She glanced at the woman holding her belongings.

"Uh…I'm Angie Pearce…from right here in Rehoboth," said the woman, handing Brenda the tote bag. "Why don't you come back to our little tent? It might give you more privacy."

Brenda stood and, with the help of the doctor, moved toward Angie's patch on the beach.

"Here ya go." Angie pulled up a beach chair and disappeared inside the tent, which was a massive pop-up thing, open on two sides. She returned with a roll of paper towels. "Not as soft as tissue, but they'll get the job done."

"May I?" The doctor motioned to Brenda. Embarrassed, she removed her hand, knowing her face must be frightful to look at. The doctor showed no sign of disgust; he simply smiled while he gently cleaned away the blood.

Brenda kept her eyes ahead but focused peripherally on his face. He seemed to be around her age, with a neat salt-and-pepper beard and blue eyes. Quite pleasing to look at, she thought, and then winced when he applied pressure to her nose. Despite the view and the strange, comforting silence, her embarrassment faded to sadness. Perhaps Gerald had been right; staying within the confines of one's own home was the safest option. Certainly there, you didn't get bashed in the face with a volleyball. Dejection swelled over her eyelids and ran down her face.

"Now, now, what's the matter?" The doctor patted Brenda's hand. "Nothing's broken, the bleeding's stopped—you'll be right as rain in no time."

Brenda sniffed and winced again. She felt foolish; maybe she should have just started this phase of her life with that bottle of beer instead of a trip to the beach. She took a shaky breath. "Thank you for your help, Doctor…"

"Please, call me Robert."

"Robert. All right. And call me Brenda. Well, thank you for your help—and for saving this." She waved her hat toward him.

Robert continued smiling and offered a hand to help her up. He wasn't wearing a ring, which meant nothing, of course. Also, it seemed an improper thing to notice, but the absence of it gave Brenda a prickle of hope. For what, she wasn't quite sure. He placed his other hand on her waist as she found her balance. "May I escort you back to your spot?"

Brenda's glimmer of possibility faded as Gerald's presence loomed like a subconscious, sanctimonious schoolmaster. She wanted to just go home and lock the door behind her. But if she did, precious time would be wasted debating whether or not to answer the call in her heart for independence and freedom. But, what price freedom, replied the Gerald voice; she could get hurt, and hadn't that already happened? Why risk it again? Go home, Brenda, go home.

"Brenda?" Robert jolted her from the mental tussle.

"It's just that, well, my husband passed away some time ago and I'm trying to navigate the world by myself. Today was my first big excursion and I suppose he was right; it's safer to stick with what you know. So, thank you, Robert, but no. I think I'll just head on home."

Robert nodded. "I understand. My wife passed away a couple of years ago. It takes time to get used to things, doesn't it?"

Brenda, grateful for his empathy, nodded and smiled.

Angie approached. "Just checking—everything okay now?"

"Yes, I'm fine. Thank you for your help."

"Sure thing. Hey, listen, don't let one ball in the face stop you from coming around. This is a nice beach, and it's even more beautiful at sunset." Her face creased around a smile that stayed as she went to supervise her son.

Robert led her toward the water's edge and they strolled quietly together. She wasn't sure why he wanted to accompany her, but she liked that he did. Gradually, Brenda was soothed by the ebb and flow of the sea around her feet and by the sun warming her body. Sounds of delight and happiness filled the air. Seagulls patrolled for free food. Children yelped. All around, a constant chatter.

It occurred to Brenda that they had walked far beyond their destination. She laughed out loud—an effortless, genuine sound—and gestured back toward the beach entrance.

Robert's own laughter faded. "Brenda, I'm going to tell you something that might make you feel uncomfortable, but somehow I think it's okay." He paused. "I noticed you walking along the beach earlier—before you got hit by the ball. I wanted to approach you but really didn't know how. I'm a bit out of practice. You see, my wife was the only woman I've ever been with. But then, fate stepped in and, well," he smiled, "unfortunately for you, I found my chance."

Brenda's eyes widened in surprise.

Robert continued. "Anyway, I know you're just finding your feet, but I feel I must say—and I speak from experience—that taking risks and…and…doing the things you've always wanted to do, but never had the courage to, is one of the greatest gifts you can give yourself. Yes, you could get hurt, but if you feel hurt, you can also feel joy. And isn't it better to feel those things than feel nothing at all?"

Her chin wobbled and tears brimmed again.

"I'm sorry." Robert reached for her.

Brenda shook her head, sniffed, winced at the pain, and laughed in spite of it. "I'm not crying because I'm hurt, Robert, I'm crying because I know you're right. It's time to start living." She looked into Robert's eyes. They'd met half an hour ago but she knew that great things were at work. She paused, waiting for Gerald's disapproval, but he had been silenced.

She smiled. "Robert, are you hungry?"

He grinned. "Why, yes, I am a bit peckish."

Brenda grabbed his hand. "I know a place on the boardwalk; I hear they make great chips."

LISA CORUZZI WAS BORN IN THE UNITED STATES BUT RAISED IN ENGLAND, AND STUDIED DRAMATIC ARTS AT PLYMOUTH COLLEGE. SHE BEGAN WRITING AT AN EARLY AGE BUT SEGUED INTO THEATER AND ONLY RECENTLY STARTED TO WRITE AGAIN. LISA USED HER OWN EXPERIENCES FOR "SECOND WIND," HAVING RETURNED, BY HERSELF, TO THE STATES FIFTEEN YEARS AGO TO START LIFE ANEW.

Rehoboth Beach Reads

2015 REHOBOTH BEACH READS JUDGES

Austin S. Camacho

Austin is the author of five novels in the Hannibal Jones Mystery Series, four in the Stark and O'Brien adventure series, and the new detective novel, *Beyond Blue*. His short stories have been featured in four anthologies from Wolfmont Press, including *Dying in a Winter Wonderland* (an Independent Mystery Booksellers Association Top Ten Bestseller for 2008), and he is featured in the Edgar-nominated *African American Mystery Writers: A Historical and Thematic Study* by Frankie Y. Bailey. He is also the editorial director of Intrigue Publishing in Upper Marlboro, Maryland.

Alex Colevas

Alex Colevas has been a voracious reader since a young age, and has spent fourteen years working in the book industry. She is now the assistant manager of Browseabout Books in Rehoboth Beach; a large part of that job is reviewing books and deciding which ones the store will carry.

Dennis Lawson

Dennis Lawson is the Executive Director of the Newark Arts Alliance, a nonprofit art center and gallery located in Newark, Delaware. He received an Individual Artist Fellowship from the Delaware Division of the Arts as the 2014 Emerging Artist in Fiction. His stories were included in the first two Rehoboth Beach Reads anthologies, *The Beach House* and *The Boardwalk*. He has also published short fiction in the *Fox Chase Review* and, most recently, the crime anthology *Insidious Assassins*.

Laurel Marshfield

Laurel Marshfield is a professional writer, ghostwriter, developmental editor, and book coach who assists authors of nonfiction, fiction, memoir, and biography in preparing their book manuscripts for publication. She has helped more than four hundred authors shape, develop, and refine their book manuscripts—by offering manuscript evaluation, developmental editing, book coaching, ghostwriting, and co-authorship through her editorial services for authors business, Blue Horizon Communications.

Mary-Margaret Pauer

Mary-Margaret Pauer received her MFA in creative writing in 2010 from Stonecoast, at the University of Southern Maine. In 2011 she was awarded the Delaware Division of the Arts Emerging Fellow in Literature (Fiction) and in 2014, the Established Fellow in Literature (Fiction). Her short fiction work has received awards from the Delaware Press Association and the National Federation of Press Women. Her work has been published in *Southern Women's Review, The Broadkill Review, On the Rusk, Delaware Beach Life, Delaware Today, Avocet Quarterly, Avocet Weekly,* and *Wanderings,* and she is the author of two collections of short fiction. Ms. Pauer is on staff at New Rivers Press and reads for the American Fiction Prize. She has judged writing contests in Maine and Delaware and works with private writing clients from varied disciplines.

Judy Reveal

Judy Reveal is a freelance editor, book indexer, book reviewer, and published author. She has taught creative writing classes at Chesapeake College as well as at arts councils across the Delmarva Peninsula. She presents workshops at various organizations including the Bay To Ocean (BTO) Writers Conference, Harford County Library Writers Conference, Lewes Library Writers Conference, Dover Library, and is the coordinator for the 2016 BTO Conference. She writes book reviews for *New York Journal of Books,* and has indexed over 50 books during her career. Her most recent book, *The Four Elements of Fiction,* is nonfiction guidance for the newer writer. Her historical fiction, *The Brownstone,* finished as a quarterfinalist in the top 100 of the 2013 Amazon Breakthrough Novel Contest.

Also from Cat & Mouse Press

www.catandmousepress.com

A Playful Publisher

The Beach House

If you liked *Beach Days*, you'll love *The Beach House*. There is something for everyone here, from romance, history, and intrigue, to jilted brides, NASCAR drivers, outlaws, and even a ghost or two. The first book in the Rehoboth Beach Reads series.

Sandy Shorts

Bad men + bad dogs + bad luck = great beach reads. The characters in these stories ride the ferry, barhop in Dewey, stroll through Bethany, and run wild in Rehoboth. By Nancy Powichroski Sherman. Received first place awards from Delaware Press Association and National Federation of Press Women.

The Boardwalk

A fortune-telling machine with a mind of its own, professional killers hanging out by the hotel pool, granny run amok in Funland…what's happened to Rehoboth? Some very talented writers have created a book of great beach reads, that's what.
The second book in the Rehoboth Beach Reads series.

You Know You're in Rehoboth When

…the dogs are smaller than the martinis, you can't get ketchup with those fries, and happy hour starts at 9am. Whether you are a visitor or a local, you will recognize the unique charm of Rehoboth in this hilarious book.

A Rehoboth ABC

From swooping seagulls to frolicking dolphins, the sights and sounds of Rehoboth Beach are captured in this charming book.
Illustrated by Emory Au. Coming soon: *A Lewes ABC*.

A Rehoboth 1-2-3

Infants and toddlers will count their way to fun with this chunky board book, which features the beach activities young children love best. Illustrated by Patti Shreeve.

Resources for Writers

Cat & Mouse Press writing contests can be a great way for new and emerging writers to gain experience and perhaps even get published. Follow the Cat & Mouse Press Facebook page for updates.

When You Want a Book at the Beach

Come to Your Bookstore at the Beach

- Fiction
- Nonfiction
- Children's Books & Toys
- Local Authors
- Distinctive Gifts
- Signings/Readings

Browseabout Books
133 Rehoboth Avenue
Rehoboth Beach, DE 19971
www.browseaboutbooks.com